I0787985

# FLIGHT OF THE CORSAC FOX

## CORSAC FOX
### BOOK 1

## BLAZE WARD

KNOTTED ROAD PRESS

# ALSO BY BLAZE WARD

**The Jessica Keller Chronicles**

*Auberon*

*Queen of the Pirates*

*Last of the Immortals*

*Goddess of War*

*Flight of the Blackbird*

*The Red Admiral*

*St. Legier*

*Winterhome*

*Petron*

**CS-405**

*Queen Anne's Revenge*

*Packmule*

*Persephone*

**First Centurion Kosnett**

*Encounter at Vilahana*

*Consensus at Aditi*

*Hegemony at Dalou*

*Princes at Ewin*

*Empire at Gloran*

*Domain at Yaumgan*

**Additional Alexandria Station Stories**

*The Story Road*

*Siren*

*Two Bottles of Wine With A War God*


**The Science Officer Series Season One**

*The Science Officer*

*The Mind Field*

*The Gilded Cage*

*The Pleasure Dome*

*The Doomsday Vault*

*The Last Flagship*

*The Hammerfield Gambit*

*The Hammerfield Payoff*

*The Bryce Connection*


**The Science Officer Series Season Two**

*Alien Seas*

*Buried Among the Stars*

*Captain Navarre*


**Last Stand**

*Lost Dreams*

*Ghost Towns*

*Games People Play*

*Prophet and Loss*

*Dandelion*

*Emergency*

*Warchild*

*Moot*

*Doomsday Girl*

*Princess*

*The Coven*

*Preacher Man*

**Captain Daring**

*Revoked*

*Returned*

*Reborn*

**The Lazarus Alliance**

*Escape*

*Return*

*Rebellion*

*Revolution*

*Liberation*

*Retribution*

*Alliance*

**Shadow of the Dominion**

*Longshot Hypothesis*

*Hard Bargain*

*Outermost*

*Dominion-427*

*Phoenix*

*Princess Rualoh*

# CONTENTS

## AUDIT VESSEL 01794572158



## PRISON BARGE



## CORSAC FOX

# MARSHALL CASTILLON

# ONE

"ALL HANDS TO ACTION STATIONS," the call came over the speaker.

Ensign Ulysses Fortier—Uly—was already on duty, midship and midwatch, so all that was necessary was taking the time to reach into the equipment pack he had stashed in a drawer next to his watch station, pull out the emergency lifesuit, and quickly pull it on over his maroon and black uniform. Around him, the handful of enlisted crew he supervised were doing the same, though none of them were moving as quickly as he was.

Still, nobody was slacking. Hadn't while he'd been aboard this warship, but that was only twenty-three days at this point, and these folks were still trying to impress the new boss.

Overhead, the lights strobed three times and an alarm sounded before returning to normal. This watch space was already designated for Engineering and emergencies, so the starship's designers had assumed that folks in here would be ready for trouble as soon as something happened.

The stripes on his uniform's epaulets were Operations Blue, but the men and women around him wore Engineering Orange.

Uly wondered if they saw it as a punishment detail to be assigned to the new officer. Alternatively, Uly occasionally wondered if the commander, Captain Savatier, had assigned him the group with the worst attitudes.

He understood that most of this crew had served together for years at this point, while Uly had been transferred in at the same time that the Forward Cruiser *Marshall Castillon*, named for the famous Eva Castillon herself, had come into base and laid in supplies so that they could go out commerce raiding on their latest incursion against the *Combined Crowns of Danumash*.

Uly looked around and his engineers were all quickly getting into their suits, so he nodded and went back to monitoring things. With the call to action, he stopped being merely a lifeguard for the middle third of the ship's systems and became an active part of Damage Control operations. He and his crew would be the first line if something broke or another ship managed to get a wavebolt shot through the electroshield array.

"Sir, we should probably go ahead and monitor the relays at frame sixteen," Specialist Marlou called, nodding his head aft. "Any sort of hull flexing and something is likely to pop free."

"You know this ship better than I do, Marlou," Uly nodded back to the man. "You folks tell me where we need to be, so you can look good on the after-action reports, okay?"

That got pleased and perhaps surprised smiles out of the six of them. Again, him being the newcomer had upset the waters, and these folks hadn't settled back down.

Plus, Uly had gotten the impression that his previous ship, the Forward Cruiser *Vanguard Lesauvage*, had run things tighter that *Marshall Castillon*'s crew preferred. *Vanguard Lesauvage* had been put into drydock for a massive rebuild after a recent battle, which was why Uly had been transferred here.

He also suspected that the captain and senior officers aboard *Marshall Castillon* either knew who Uly was related to or had looked him up. There had always been an air of frosty formality around every interaction he'd had with other officers.

Maybe they thought he was some sort of spy for the Party? Granted, his father was an Assistant Deputy Secretary, an extremely high-ranking member of the Secretariat itself, though Uly didn't think the man would ever ascend beyond serving as a delegate to *Institutional Republic of Batyr*'s Annual Congress.

Father had mentioned more than once, quietly, about not wanting the headaches that came with becoming a part of the Presidium itself. Or the highest echelons of the Party Secretariat.

But Anselm Fortier was a name these officers might have recognized, and so remained skittish about his son, not that Uly could blame them.

He wasn't here to get anyone in trouble. Or to act as a spy for the Navy or the Secretariat.

No, he had gotten transferred to *Marshall Castillon* because *Vanguard Lesauvage* was going to be in drydock for a year being repaired, and Father had pulled a few strings to get Uly into a position where his career wasn't also stalled in the process.

Uly wasn't sure he wanted to ascend to the command ranks of Captain or even Fleet Captain, to say nothing of the flag ranks, from Echelon through Fleet Marshal. However, Father had understood that his son needed this transfer in order to keep those options open in twenty or thirty years.

A mere Ensign wasn't supposed to think about those things.

So Uly served aboard *Marshall Castillon* as the Forward Cruiser went commerce raiding against the *Combined Crowns of Danumash*, the so-called *Seven Kingdoms*, named from the original seven little entities that had later combined into a single monarchy, still intent on conquering known space.

Uly suspected that space was bigger than even *Danumash* suspected, but he was a lowly ensign, transferred abruptly to a different ship than the one he'd served aboard in the three years since he'd been commissioned, and nobody was going to listen to his opinions.

"All hands, stand by for abrupt maneuvering and combat operations," the speakers informed them.

Uly followed Marlou and the others aft and down a level for now, making sure he knew where everything was, because *Marshall Castillon* was an older ship than *Vanguard Lesauvage*. Different interior layout that had confused him more than once.

Marlou got to an oversized hatch and patted the bulkhead.

"Right here, sir," he said earnestly. "Got a pinch problem."

"Is it better or worse if you take the panel off now, Marlou?" Uly asked. "Does that panel hold things in place better than giving you an extra thirty seconds to get to the cabling behind it when something breaks?"

Sounds of surprise, quickly suppressed before he could look back and see who. Uly smiled anyway, assuming that the last officer over this crew had been some sort of rules lawyer. That would explain the team's behavior better.

Uly understood that sometimes you had to throw out the manual and do things on instinct.

"Probably better if we pop it, sir," Marlou nodded.

Uly nodded and stepped back.

"Two of you here, then," he ordered. "Marlou, pick who you want assisting. Two of you down a deck to frame eighteen and stand by. Two of you come back with me to monitor things at the station. You sort out the teams, because I don't know any of you well enough to do it accurately. Understood?"

Squawks of surprise, but again, good surprise. Relaxing a little around the new guy, maybe. Finally figuring out that Uly would trust their judgment to do things, especially as he had only three years in uniform and all of them had at least that, if not more.

"Ensign Fortier, report to Operations Space Eleven immediately," came the call over the speakers now. "Ensign Fortier, Operations Space Eleven for orders."

Uly suppressed the profanity and looked at his small crew with a nod.

"You folks are on your own until I get back," he said. "Keep things running and drag in any spare bodies you need if it breaks. Call the Chief Engineer or one of his people in that case and explain what happened, what you know, and what you need. Questions?"

Marlou was closest.

"No, sir," the man said.

"Good," Uly said. "Where the hell am I going?"

"Forward to frame four on second deck, sir," somebody said from behind him. "That one's just off the main bridge, opposite the captain's office in the main corridor."

Uly nodded, remembering it now. Twenty-three days had been a blur of activity, learning everything and trying not to embarrass himself in front of the crew. And not to make himself look like a fool with his other officers.

Why the hell did they need him up close to the bridge if combat was imminent?

# TWO

DIMKA SAVATIER, Captain of *Marshall Castillon*, studied the display and noted that the surprise had been nearly complete. Almost perfect, in that one *Danumash* freighter had taken an early hit that appeared to have completely crippled the ship.

The rest of the convoy and their escorts were maneuvering rapidly away, but freighters were slow and the smaller enemy escorts were badly outclassed by a Forward Cruiser, being mostly Interceptor-sized warships. They would break soon and flee, which left Dimka with a problem.

Or rather, an opportunity.

He'd left his First Officer in command next door for now and taken the Operations Space across the hall from his office. Better later if this looked like it was formal, rather than personal.

Dimka didn't like Ensign Fortier. And there wasn't a damned thing he could do about it. Not when the man's father was a dangerous Party operative who could ruin careers easily enough with a word whispered in the right ear.

Nobody in Dimka's family had ever joined The Industrial Protectors Party. The Navy was an apolitical organization. Or rather, all the politics were internal. The Party generally left them alone, even at his level. It was the flag officers who had to deal with interlopers asking stupid questions.

But Dimka knew that Fortier was a spy. An agitator sent to report on his ship.

Dimka Savatier wouldn't have it.

And *Danumash* had given him the perfect opportunity to rid himself of the annoying puppy.

The hatch chimed and Dimka pushed a button to open it.

Ensign Fortier stepped in and came to attention, breathing a little heavy as if he'd run here from midship. He probably had.

Always competing, that one. Always trying to make other officers look lazy and slack by comparison. Fortier had no understanding of how tightly aligned Dimka's crew was. How well he had trained them.

For now, he studied the young man.

One hundred and eighty-five centimeters, but only seventy kilograms. Tall and skinny, but he would grow into those shoulders in another decade and a half. Closely trimmed black hair that looked like it would curl if allowed to grow.

Long arms, long torso, narrow waist, long legs. Ethnically, Dimka placed him in the historical category called Turkic. Those dark eyes were staring at a spot on the wall above Dimka's head.

Better, the man was already in his lifesuit, with the helmet hooked to his hip and immediately ready for a breach, as suited his current responsibilities in Damage Control.

There was no way in hell Dimka was letting that dangerous spy on his bridge without a direct order he couldn't ignore.

"At ease, Ensign," Dimka ordered now, watching the man snap precisely into a new stance. Yes, too close to school, with all that marching and training to immediately obey orders.

Good.

"Lieutenant Dupuis is on medical report today with some

bug," Dimka informed the young spy. "One of the enemy ships has surrendered after taking damage, but the rest of the convoy is currently evading en route to fleeing entirely."

He paused there, but the young man remained silent. Just a slight nod of acknowledgment.

It was a shame that Dimka hadn't been able to shape the pup when he'd first come out of school. Then he might be able to trust him today.

Pity, really, as those connections could have been quite useful later.

"We expect the rest of the convoy to recharge their Variable Pulse Spatial Generators quickly enough and turn to escape us," Dimka continued. "*Danumash* tactical procedures, however, generally require a convoy such as this to remain coherent for at least three engagements, so when they spin up their warp bubbles, we will be able to track their pulse-wake and eventually overhaul them. From there, we can force them back out of warp. I must leave somebody behind to take charge of the damaged freighter, Fortier. That's you. As it is a small vessel, I will send one engineer and a small security team to accompany you. You will take command of the vessel and make for the nearest friendly port. Once there, you will make arrangements to return to base, at which point we should have returned with most of the convoy in tow and you can return to duty aboard *Marshall Castillon*. Questions?"

He could see ten thousand in Fortier's eyes, but most of them got discarded while Dimka watched. Then the realization that he was being functionally abandoned to his fate crept in. Again, discarded in an instant.

Smart kid. Too bad, really. He could have been something, had Dimka gotten to him first.

Two birds. One stone. Fortier would be out of his hair for a considerable amount of time, especially since that freighter had taken a hit through the bridge that might have decapitated the vessel.

When the puppy got back, six months might have elapsed. Perhaps a year. Maybe his damnable father would find a new assignment for the young hero, assuming he came back covered in glory, and Fortier could be transferred elsewhere.

Anywhere.

Or maybe Dimka would be lucky, and he'd never come back.

"No questions, sir," Fortier finally spoke. "Will we have a shuttle to board?"

"Negative, Fortier." Dimka smiled cruelly. "The ship is too small to have a bay, and I'll need them later with the larger ships. You and your team will jump across when *Marshall Castillon* maneuvers close enough, at which time I expect we'll go immediately to pulse-wake chase. Dismissed."

He watched the spy nod deeply, come to attention, and march out of the room like Dimka Savatier was the headmaster issuing discipline and rewards.

Not all that far off.

# THREE

ULY HAD GOTTEN A WRITTEN order printout, but it didn't add anything meaningful, other than to tell him that he would have Machinist Specialist Kolya Roux along, with Lead Trooper Dan Chastain in charge of Able Spacer Beranger and Crewman Travers.

Roux was a name he sort of knew, mostly because Uly's watches tended to be Engineering in scope, so he'd encountered the man once or twice. Dan Chastain wasn't a name Uly was familiar with, but he hoped that the Captain was at least giving him competent security forces, particularly if they were expected to board an enemy vessel and enforce discipline on a potentially restive crew.

Uly had stopped by his quarters and dug into his gear for a book reader that would keep him entertained for a couple of years, on the assumption that he might need it. Mostly, though, for the Lamellar vest he'd brought with him from *Vanguard Lesauvage*.

Modern combat at a personal level—say when boarding enemy ships or stations—could be swords or energy pistols, given the confines of fighting in narrow, pressurized corridors. Only planetside would you use a projectile weapon or rocketgun. Too easy to punch a hole in a bulkhead and kill everybody anywhere this side of a sealed bulkhead.

Depending on what you expected to face, you might wear Battershield armor, which was a ballistic cloth made up of layers of fine chainmail to protect against sharp edges and points. Alternatively, isomorph was an insulated cloth that offered protection against heat and energy weapons, being a type of superconductive weave.

Most of the time, people had to pick one or the other, because both were expensive, heavy, and somewhat rare.

Uly's father had given him the Lamellar vest as a graduation present. It covered his torso with isomorphic cloth that had Battershield plates a little bigger than his thumbnail attached all across the surface like fish scales.

Incredibly expensive. Extremely rare. Something that showed off his father's connections probably better than anything else, to have access to such equipment.

It wasn't that Uly was expecting trouble in boarding a ship that had already surrendered. Instead, he suspected that his prized vest might vanish if he left it behind, alone on this ship for six months or more. Someone was likely to steal it while he was elsewhere.

*Mine. Get your own.*

Quickly, he opened his lifesuit and strapped the vest on under it, sealing everything back up before heading aft to where Security was waiting for him. Time was short, but he didn't have to jog. Uly did it because he wanted a few extra moments to meet this crew before he led them into battle on an enemy ship.

Or whatever the hell was about to occur.

He entered the assault area and looked around.

"I'm looking for Lead Trooper Chastain," he said to the group of about twenty folks doing things.

Most of the faces turned toward him, but only one acknowledged the name.

He'd been expecting a man. DAN Chastain.

This was a woman.

She stepped out of the group and moved close.

Tall. Taller than him by a few centimeters. Athletic muscles to the point that she might have outweighed him. Dark skin. Black hair that showed even more curl than his.

"I'm Chastain," she announced sharply, looking a little down her nose at him.

She had a square face, with a broad, flattish nose, very thin lips, and her brown eyes were ever-so-slightly slanted.

He'd have called her Afro-Siberian, if he had to come up with an ethnic combination, weird as that might be.

Absolutely female, though. Attractive but not stunning. Hard but not brutal. Lead Trooper, so she could probably fold him into knots any time she wanted.

"I'm Ensign Uly Fortier." He nodded to her. "Captain ordered me to lead a team over. That's you and yours. Where's Roux?"

"Here."

Uly turned to note the man standing with an equipment pack slung outside his suit and a toolbelt filled with everything under the sun, near as Uly could tell.

Anglo—almost albino—white skin. Hair somewhere between bronze and ginger, with hints of orange. It should have been cut at least a week ago. Maybe two.

Roux had an oval face with a cleft chin, a narrow nose, large ears, and large lips. Gray eyes that looked like they'd been blue originally, with all the color washed out by time. One hundred and seventy-eight centimeters tall. Average build.

Machinist Specialist, so an E-7, while Chastain was a Lead

with an E-8 rating. She'd be his Second-in-Command effectively. For what it was worth.

"What are you rated for?" she asked, gesturing to the weapon holstered on her hip.

"Most things," he answered. "I prefer an Exoripper pistol and Shadowwhip sword, given the option."

"Need armor?" she asked.

Uly opened the suit to show her his Lamellar underneath, not really caring right now what they thought about Uly's father or his connections.

She nodded and turned to someone. Uly realized that there were several armorers here, with arms lockers on the deck. One of them started pulling out gear, and Chastain handed him a weapon's belt identical to hers.

Chastain, however, had a Heavy Exoripper pistol and was holding what looked like an Icemace, a telescoping baton that could be anywhere from sixty to two hundred centimeters long and delivered a cryogenic ice effect to stun muscles and minds. As well as a good whomp upside the head.

The Shadowwhip she handed to him was basically a slightly curved saber with both edge and point, as well as a stun charge that could overcome Battershield armor. Useful in boarding actions like this but was more an officer's symbol of rank than anything.

Chastain gestured him towards the airlock, where Roux joined them, as well as Beranger, who was short, squat, and strong, plus Travers, long-limbed and skinny like ancient legends of trolls. About as pretty to look at, too.

Uly pulled his helmet on and watched as Chastain fitted a spare airtank to his suit's backpack.

"Testing, channel three," he said.

"Good," Chastain nodded. The others echoed the sentiment.

"We're crossing with a free jump and thrusters," Uly

reminded them. "The vessel has been disabled, according to the captain. As soon as we're in their airlock, *Marshall Castillon* will go to warp, and we'll be on our own. Everybody had a potty break?"

That got chuckles.

"We're good, sir," Chastain said. "Not our first pigeon we've taken this way."

Uly nodded. So much he didn't know, but *Vanguard Lesauvage* hadn't been dedicated to commerce raiding like this ship and crew.

Still, he could learn quickly enough.

"Boarding party, stand by to depart," Captain Savatier's voice came over the line now.

Uly made sure everyone's lights were green, then gave the sign to the folks back in the main chamber to seal them in and evacuate the airlock for deep space.

Shortly, he would be on his own.

# FOUR

DAN WATCHED the new officer move with deliberation but not hesitation. She knew that the Captain was playing something of a practical joke on the man but wasn't sure what *she'd* done to get on Savatier's bad side this week. Maybe he'd assigned her to babysit the kid?

Fortier looked about twenty-four, so she had at least five years on him. And probably another five years of service since she'd enlisted as early as she could. The Navy was a way of life in her family with her father and both his parents as career enlisted.

Plus, she'd wanted out of the house to escape her more traditionalist mother and sisters, both of them now happily married and having kids. Yuck.

Nobody ever called her Sheridan. Just Dan. Sounded like a guy's name. Fortier had obviously been fooled from the initial surprise on his face.

At the same time, he hadn't bristled at her height or mass. Both greater than his. Lots of men did, even unconsciously. The darkness of her skin also marked her distinct from a lot of *Batyr* culture, but her homeworld of Aurtan was like that. She'd had to deal with a certain racism based on color her entire military career, which had been a bit of a shock after her youth back home.

But she was bigger and tougher than most folks, too. Travers didn't count because that boy didn't seem to have any pain receptors when he started pushing with those long limbs. Might tear shit, but that could be healed later.

Not a bad team. Smaller than she would have preferred, especially if Savatier was dumping them here.

Lowly Lead Troopers didn't question officers. Smart ones knew to ask experts.

Fortier earned about a zillion gold stars when he turned and studied the small group, nodding inside his unpolarized faceshield as he focused on her.

"Who should be leading the assault?" he asked, head tilted back just enough to be obvious that she was taller.

"We expecting shooting?" she countered.

He shrugged.

"Captain Savatier said that they had surrendered," Fortier replied. "Looks like a bridge hit forward, so they might be completely confused right now. Maybe resentful. I've never done this sort of thing. If you have, you know better than I do what to expect when we get there."

Dan nodded back. Sound thinking. A lot smarter than he looked. Usually, they had to make Lieutenant or even Senior Lieutenant before they got that wily.

"Beranger, you're on point," she decided.

Man was short enough that she could shoot over his shoulder or head if she had to. And Travers could reach over everybody if she needed more guns pouring fire into a corridor. Didn't matter what the new officer did at that point, as long as he stayed out of the way.

Fortier nodded and remained silent. Ceding her tactical control that easily? That would be a welcome surprise.

Dan was used to Lieutenant Dupuis, who had to have opinions on everything, right or not. And occasionally got a little handsy, but never so much that she might punch him in the face for it. He was one of Savatier's golden boys—The In-Crowd.

Dan wondered if the Captain had ordered the man to go on medical report so they could foist Fortier off on her, and then Dupuis would make a miracle recovery in about an hour.

That right there left a sour taste in her mouth.

"Airlock team, we are about to vent you to space," came the call over the headset. "Everyone polarize your helmets."

Dan checked her thruster backpack and unlimbered the controls in her right hand while she drew the Heavy Exoripper with her left. Safety on for now, but something of a security blanket, at least until they boarded and she had to decide whether or not to switch to the Icemace hooked to her backpack and out of the way.

She lined up behind Beranger and flexed her shoulders.

Deep in her soul, she knew she wasn't going to see the ship or the captain again for a while.

That also left a sour taste in her mouth. Maybe one of these *Danumash* punks would give her a reason to use unreasonable force shortly.

# FIVE

ULY HAD MAINTAINED his freejump qualifications for EVA assaults while on *Vanguard Lesauvage*. But those had been for training. He'd never attacked an enemy ship before.

Fortunately, Chastain and her people seemed perfectly at home, so he fell into her wake as they crossed the vacuum, though he didn't draw a weapon yet. He was the only officer here, so Uly figured he was supposed to be thinking strategically.

Let Chastain handle tactics. She obviously had a better feel for it than he did, at least here. Starship combat was what he'd been training for. Not petty piracy.

Still, they crossed quickly. The gap was only a few hundred meters and both ships had been at rest relative, so they were making good time.

"Boarding team, *Danumash* forces are responding on channel eleven," came the message from the ship.

"Understood," Uly replied. "Boarding team stay on channel three for now. Chastain, join me on eleven to talk to them."

Her helmet was polarized like his, so he could only read her body language. Still, Uly thought he detected a hint of surprise. A tiny flinch.

He supposed that most officers expected the enlisted grunts to do all the work and stay out of the way the rest of the time. To be merely hands without accompanying opinions.

In Uly's mind, Dan Chastain was his Second-in-Command now. Executive Officer. Acting Commander, if he were the new acting Captain of this long, damaged sausage in front of them.

"Enemy vessel, this is Ulysses Fortier from the *Batyr* Forward Cruiser *Marshall Castillon*," he announced after switching over and waiting three seconds. "We are approaching your airlock now. Reply on this channel."

"This is Quartermaster's Mate Midshipman Thorley Eldridge of the *Danumash* Freighter *King Hewitt II*," a voice replied hesitantly. "Senior surviving officer. What are your orders, sir?"

Senior surviving officer? A *Midshipman*?

*Batyr* didn't even use the rank outside of school when everybody was a Midshipman One to Four depending on your class.

No commissioned officers had survived? At all?

What a stupid way to run a ship, if all the officers had been forward. The ship truly had been decapitated in that case.

"Meet us at the airlock unarmed, Eldridge," Uly ordered. "The rest of the crew will maintain duty stations and continue with their repairs when we come aboard. I will take command, and you can brief me at that point."

"Thank you, sir," Eldridge replied. "Understood."

Chastain released her flight controls long enough to hold up three fingers. He joined her down on that channel.

"That's new," she said.

"Something went wrong over there," Uly agreed. "Don't know what, but I think they'll generally behave if that's the case, because I suspect that these are kids even younger than me, and less prepared, trying to figure out next steps."

"Sir, *Danumash* vessel like this probably has a civilian crew with naval officers seconded," Beranger spoke up suddenly for the first time since they got introduced back on the ship. "Freighters that get impressed into service usually are handled that way. Not the first one of these we've taken."

Uly nodded.

"Thank you, Beranger," Uly replied. "If so, we'll sort them as necessary. Will that include a civilian sailing master?"

"Sometimes," Beranger offered. "Happens when an owner decides to take transport contracts. Weird mix of civilian and military aboard when you do that. Civilians are usually easier to deal with, because they're just employees, ya know?"

"Got it," Uly said. "Again, you have a better hold on this concept than I do, so make sure you tell me things that I might not know, okay?"

Long pause.

"Yes, sir," Beranger said in a quieter voice, echoed a moment later by Travers.

"Headed in now, sir," Beranger announced as they got close.

The airlock was an open mouth on the side of the ship, but it had a monstrous bay door at the front end where you could probably drive a big ground transport up to handle cargo.

Medium-sized transport. What *Danumash* classified as a Shipper, between the smaller Couriers and bigger Dropships. *Marshall Castillon* had hammered them with what looked like a six-decimeter wavebolt. 6dm. Cruiser-scale firepower capable of reaching a considerable distance and hurting things.

Especially if you caught them by surprise. This ship, *King Hewitt II*, looked like someone had set the plasma torpedo to punch a hole in the electroshields, when nobody had thought to raise their shields in time, so the torpedo had instead bored a tunnel through the bow of the vessel from side to side.

He'd seen starlight through that gap on approach.

The airlock was a civilian thing. More a long, slender hallway between two rooms than the oversized assault chamber they'd left behind. Beranger and Chastain went in first, while he waited outside with Travers and Roux.

The hatch cycled and he watched.

"We are inside now," Chastain kept up a running commentary. "Pressure is coming up. Green lights, so the inner doors are opening. Welcoming party of four, in suits but they have not put helmets on yet. We are entering. Stand by or listen on eleven."

Uly switched up.

"I am Lead Trooper Chastain," she said, with a reverb in the background suggesting her external speakers were on. "Which of you is Eldridge?"

"Me, sir," came that voice. "Ma'am?"

"Lead Trooper, Midshipman," she said coldly. "Fortier will be along shortly."

"Understood, Lead Trooper," Eldridge replied.

Uly nodded to himself and motioned the others into the airlock with him. It would be a tight fit for three, but he wanted everybody inside now, because he knew that Captain Savatier was about to spin up a warp bubble and leave him behind to his fate.

Or perhaps, his destiny.

# SIX

DAN WATCHED the midshipman stand at a sloppy attention that spoke volumes about discipline on this ship.

Or rather, the lack thereof. Captain Savatier would have had that boy's ass running laps around the interior of the ship in a twenty-kilo pack until he straightened his shit up.

She had her Heavy Exoripper out and vaguely pointed at them, mostly to make a point rather than a threat.

Four of them, all in a tight cluster. Two teenage boys, from the looks, with two older ones, more like young adults. All wore the black jodhpurs and belted gray tunics of the *Danumash* Navy. Two Midshipmen, a Specialist, and an Able Spacer from the rank insignia on arms and collars. None were armed. That was good. Meant that they preferred surviving what was about to happen.

Every once in a while, a ship that had properly surrendered would suddenly swarm a boarding party and turn the tables. Depending on what happened at that point, folks might get mean. With *Marshall Castillon* gone, she and hers might be thrown in the brig. Or killed.

Captain Savatier would hunt such renegades down individually if that happened. If they broke their ransom in the process, *Danumash* High Command might do it as well.

There were rules in this game. Even a lowly Lead Trooper understood that, but she was frequently at the tip of the spear, as it were.

Regardless of whatever she'd done to piss off the Captain this week.

Behind her, Dan heard the airlock cycle and open. Fortier stepped into view, along with the other two, then walked past her to the other group.

Interestingly, he did it in such a way that he didn't step in front of either her or Beranger, in case they needed to shoot someone. Useful to know. He was sharper than he looked and moved quietly without trying to show off.

Dan found herself liking this new officer. He was a lot of things that Lt. Dupuis never even dreamed of being, which was probably why Savatier didn't like the ensign.

Fortier reached up and detached his helmet with a click and a pop, hanging it from his belt and running a gloved hand back through the curls.

"Eldridge?" Fortier asked.

The one in the middle perked up, nodding.

"Here, sir," Eldridge replied.

Dan studied the youngster. Tall, though not as tall as her. Bulky instead of muscular, like he carried a walrus layer of fat around the middle and in his face. Beady eyes and skin lighter than Fortier's. Almost as pale as Roux. Hair kept buzzed to maybe five millimeters length, though already showing signs on top where it would be badly receding by the time he hit thirty.

"I'm Ensign Ulysses Fortier, *Batyr* Navy, Eldridge," the boss spoke clearly. "I am formally taking command of this vessel under the recognized rules of warfare and your honorable surrender and ransom in combat. Do you have any questions?"

"Negative, sir," Eldridge replied. "I stand relieved of command, sir."

"This is Engineer Roux," Fortier continued. "Lead Trooper Chastain will be in charge of security, with Beranger and Travers assisting."

He turned to look around, and she saw the grim determination in Fortier's eyes. He had the same sour feeling about this that she did. Outside, *Marshall Castillon* was probably already in their warp bubble, racing at fast FTL after the rest of the convoy.

They were on their own.

"Helmets off and let's get to work," he announced.

Dan holstered her pistol and reached up, clearing her helmet and getting a smell of the life support systems over here.

Rich, with a strong undertone she couldn't place. Earthy and a little sour, like a dash of vinegar added to a sweet drink.

"Eldridge, as there are no commissioned officers aboard other than myself, I will be relying on your crew," Fortier said. "However, I am appointing Lead Trooper Chastain as my Second-in-Command, so any orders from her will have precedence."

All heads turned her direction. Eldridge's eyes got ugly.

"I ain't taking orders from no *washenzi*," the youngster muttered, just loud enough that she could hear it.

The other three with him got big, shocked eyes in that moment. Dan started to take a step forward to have words with the little punk but stopped cold when Fortier slugged the man in the jaw so hard the man went over backwards.

As Eldridge started to get up, Fortier stepped into the Midshipman with a kick hard enough that he might have cracked ribs.

Finally, Eldridge was flat on his back, with Fortier's Shadowwhip sword touching the front of his throat.

"One word, Eldridge," Fortier rasped harshly. "Any word."

The tableau held. Beranger and Travers were locked in on the three others with death only a trigger pull away. Dan blinked in shock.

Not at the reaction of a fine *Danumash* gentleman sailor. The *Combined Crowns* had a starkly hierarchical society. An aristocracy of racism, privilege, and wealth that was almost perfectly opposite everything *Batyr* stood for.

*Washenzi* meant uncivilized. Barbarian. In a *Danumash* mouth, connotations of being less than human.

Wasn't the first time Dan had heard that particular term thrown in her teeth. Usually, there was nothing she could do about it either, coming from a *Danumash* officer prisoner or maybe just a random vehicle on the street.

That was one of the reasons she enjoyed this job. That look in the eyes of a *Danumash* prisoner on some captured ship, when they looked at the color of her skin and realized that she was in charge.

First time one of her own officers had ever laid somebody out for it.

No, her shock was due to Fortier's reaction. Officers were supposed to be gentlemen and gentlewomen of their own class, even in a society dedicated to eliminating inherited wealth and power for an open meritocracy where the tall, black daughter of an enlisted man could walk down a street without being catcalled or sexually assaulted with impunity.

Most *Batyr* worlds were pretty good about that, though not all. And not all people, but they were exceptions. In *Danumash*, they were the rules.

And the rulers.

Eldridge had apparently never been in a position to be punched in the mouth for his casual racism. Dan wondered if he was the son of a baron. Those were almost a dime a dozen on some worlds. Or maybe a third or fourth son of a planetary count?

Eldridge quickly discovered humility as Dan watched, almost as shocked as the kid with broken ribs and a sore jaw. He shook his head side to side meekly, otherwise unmoving.

Fortier glanced back.

"You, other Midshipman," he snapped angrily. "What's your name?"

"Astronomer's Mate Sterling Huff, sir," the other officer trainee stammered nervously. Probably wondering if he was next. Fortier only had to lean forward slightly at this moment to kill Eldridge.

"Huff, you will escort this prisoner to the brig," Fortier ordered. "Beranger and Travers will accompany you. He is relieved of duty and will be brought up on charges of insubordination and dereliction of duty when I have a chance to hold a captain's mast. Am I clearly understood?"

Dan wondered if Huff was about to piss himself, but he nodded.

"Beranger, take charge," Fortier ordered, finally stepping back.

Eldridge only moved when Huff and Beranger started to lift him, doubling over in groaning pain.

"Permission to escort the prisoner to medical first, sir?" Beranger asked carefully, obviously unsure where the edges of Fortier's rage were right now.

"Granted," Fortier replied angrily. "Chain him to the bed if necessary."

Ouch.

Fortier slammed his sword home hard enough that everybody jumped a little, including her.

On balance, she might enjoy serving under this guy.

# SEVEN

ULY FOCUSED INWARDLY as hard as he could to control that hot flame at the base of his stomach. Beranger and Travers got the prisoner out of the room before Uly lost his temper again, which was good. He gestured Chastain closer and nodded a silent apology to her, before confronting the remaining crew members.

Both military, as Beranger had suggested that civilians would dress as they chose. These were in crisp uniforms.

"Identify yourself," he rasped, still sucking deep breaths in through his nose to cool his core temperature.

"Specialist Quintin Butcher," the taller of the two replied. "Assistant Bursar."

Banker, then. His appearance put Uly in mind of a loyal dog, which was rude, but still accurate, with bright blue eyes that were like two big windows looking out on the afternoon sky. Bone-white skin and short black hair, with an air of helpfulness and probity that you never expected from a ship's banker.

Doubly so a *Danumash* vessel, where the position was frequently sold to the highest bidder, who then made his profit from the crew's general needs, offering loans and selling sundries beyond the minimal basics the fleet provided.

"And you?" Uly turned to the shorter man.

This one had the look of an artist, with narrow, brown eyes. Luxurious, curly, yellow hair styled in a manner that reminded Uly of a sea urchin for reasons he couldn't have named. Like Uly, a little longer on top than perhaps regulations allowed, but shorter on the sides. The man was short and had a slender build. Oddly, his skin was deeply tanned but otherwise lighter, in a society where skin color was often a factor of social rank. He looked out with a smile, from under bushy eyebrows.

"Specialist Drew Roscoe, sir," Roscoe replied. "Trainee sailing master. I was assigned to secondary operations, minding the young gentlemen."

"All the officers were on the bridge when it was destroyed?" Uly asked.

"All the *naval command* officers, sir," Roscoe stressed carefully.

"Oh?" Uly leaned into the man now, sniffing a potential problem he would need to address.

"This vessel has a…unique cargo, sir," Roscoe said slowly.

Beside him, Butcher nodded rapidly in agreement. Must be good.

"Go on," Uly ordered.

*Marshall Castillon* was gone by now. Whatever weird shit was about to unfold was on his head as commanding officer.

For good or ill.

"Uhm, it might be best if I showed you directly, sir," Roscoe hemmed and hawed a little. "Let's just suggest that the bridge hit that took out the officers wasn't the worst thing, though I'm severely saddened that Hylda happened to be among them."

"Who?"

"Hylda Hobbs, sir," he nodded. "The Sailing Mistress and

owner of the vessel, banks and mortgages notwithstanding. She was the only one forward I'll miss."

Uly considered that. A female ship owner and sailing master was exceptionally rare in *Danumash.*

He nodded and Roscoe turned to depart, with Butcher in the man's wake. Uly glanced over at Chastain, but she seemed to have recovered her equilibrium and grinned at him for the briefest moment.

Still strangers, but he could work with that.

Roux just shrugged but understood that they needed to sort things out before he could go to work on repairs. Doubly so if he might be the senior surviving engineer aboard.

Through the hatch, they crossed a main corridor then continued down a smaller one. There had been a scent in the air Uly couldn't place. It got thicker as the next hatch opened and they stepped out onto the floor of the main cargo hold.

Uly had been expecting boxes and shipping containers. Instead, the space had been built up like offices. Even the overhead had been modified, because whoever had done the work had used steel with a different sheen that left a distinct seam in the ceiling where the front and rear thirds of the ship had been linked later to form a full second deck.

The first person Uly saw in the space was a civilian. Male, but his long, blond hair was in a braid that seemed to trail halfway down his back. The man looked serious, but only slightly, as if it was a mask over irrepressible joy. Certainly, the blue and bright yellow checks in his shirt and matching pants were not the attire of a dour man.

"Hey, Blair, there was a small problem with the *young gentlemen,*" Roscoe called, drawing the man to his feet and walking towards them from about fifteen meters. "Captain Fortier is in charge now and will have questions. I didn't tell him anything about the cargo."

A range of emotions passed across the other man's face in a heartbeat. Interesting.

In the distance, an older man and a middle-aged woman emerged from an office on the right, along with a younger male. Unlike this Blair person, those three wore *Danumash* naval uniforms in gray and black, with the two older ones being officers and the younger dressed as an enlisted man.

Uly decided that he liked Blair even more, based purely on his sartorial choices.

"Blair Mitchell," the man said as he stepped close and nodded. "Ship's Nurse. The others are xenobiologists, so I'm the only Human specialist around."

"I beg your pardon?" Uly found himself saying, sounding far stiffer and formal than he'd thought.

"The, uhm, cargo, Captain," Blair Mitchell replied carefully. "They're...well, let's not put too fine of a point on it. They're slaves, sir. Aliens, at that. The species is called Mazhin, but they speak Standard better than most of us do."

The two officers had stomped close enough to overhear. The male's face had gone red.

"What are you telling them, Mitchell?" the older man thundered as he continued to stomp closer.

Uly took a step and leveled a pointing finger at the man like a gun while the stranger was still ten meters away.

"You will remain silent," Uly ordered in a hard, angry voice. "Midshipman Eldridge is already in the hospital for insubordination. Your other choice is to join him there. *Am I clear?*"

The three *Danumash* naval personnel stumbled to a stop like they'd nearly flown into an asteroid field. Blair grinned, but those three couldn't see anything but the back of the man's head until they got closer.

"You were saying?" Uly turned back to Blair as Chastain stepped into view.

She had her Icemace in one hand. It clicked loudly in the sudden silence and extended to two meters long.

A woman not playing around.

Uly wasn't either, but he was five people against the entire crew. Hopefully, he could recruit some allies.

"Alien slaves, Captain," Blair grimaced. "Mostly Mechanicals with a couple of Technicals and a few Socials."

Uly kept his temper under control. More or less. One hand might be flexing into a fist and relaxing.

The *Institutional Republic of Batyr* didn't keep slaves. All men and women were created equal, and all species, with citizenship and meritocracy being the signature points of *Batyr* culture. That included the exceptionally rare aliens who wished to join.

*Danumash*, on the other hand, was an aristocracy. With slaves.

Intellectually, Uly knew that there were lots of alien species out there. Humanity had just grown up in a weird pocket that didn't have many close galactic neighbors. *Batyr* had even fewer, facing a hollow spot in the concentration of surrounding stars.

And *Danumash* kept alien slaves.

Uly promised himself that all the humans in charge would make it safely home. That he would not unleash hell on them for doing what their culture taught was right.

However evil it might be.

Something must have showed on his face, because Blair had stopped and gone a little whiter around the edges. Gulped, even. The other three looked poised to flee, rabbits discovering a hound on the trail.

Uly swallowed and took a deep breath.

"Mechanicals?" he asked in as calmly a tone as he could manage right now. "Technical? Social?"

"Right, sir," Blair nodded. "No Physicals."

"Explain it to me," Uly ordered, lost at the terminology.

"Oh, right," Blair nodded again. "Mechanicals build things. Artisans and repair folk for the most part, Captain. That sort of thing. The two Technicals, near as I can tell, are genius research scientists. Or were before we got hold of them. The Socials include a cook and a couple of females that are…"

His voice failed there. Trailed off like an abandoned road not quite reclaimed by nature. A gap in the forest you could follow if you were feeling adventurous.

Or angry.

Uly went ahead and inserted the word. *Prostitutes*, though he doubted that they got paid for it.

Standard didn't have a good term to encompass *sex slave*.

If Uly had his way, there would never be a need, outside of a history book.

And pigs might fly.

He took another breath to try to calm himself. Mostly so that the next words out of his mouth were polite instead of emotional.

Ulysses Fortier was the captain of this vessel until he got it home and could turn over command to someone else. That included the entire crew.

Even the ones he didn't like.

Uly nodded thanks to Blair and stepped past him, feeling the man turn in place and fall in on a flank like Roux on the other side.

He walked closer to the other three, though not close enough to punch anybody without taking several steps.

Best not dangle temptation out there.

Rabbits, facing a hunting hound.

"I am Ulysses Fortier," he introduced himself in a voice about as cold as deep space. About as friendly, too. "I am the captain of this ship until I am formally relieved. Is that clear?"

The three nodded.

The male in the center was about fifty. Gray and jowly.

Heavy around the middle. Had the look of a boffin about him in ways that were only obvious if you started listing little details. Soft hands. Paler skin than even most of *Danumash*. Sad eyes. Hint of breakfast fallen on his belly and wiped off but leaving a tiny grease stain behind.

The woman might be a well-preserved sixty but looked more like a ragged forty. Bags under her eyes told of sleep issues. Beyond slender down into gaunt, with an odd, greenish tint like jaundiced skin stretched over a skeleton. Hair already gray with bits of blondish brown in the tips remaining. Scared eyes unwilling to hold a lock with his before they fell.

The youngster on the right was naval enlisted. It was there in the set of his spine. The way the head was back and rigid. Not quite at attention but sliding that way.

Youngster? He was probably Uly's age, but Uly had just turned into a commanding officer in charge of a captured enemy vessel. Already he felt old.

The young man cringed a little but remained silent. The other two were officers, with the older man having rank tabs identifying him as an O-5, an Adjutant, while the woman was an O-4 or Senior Lieutenant. Uly's O-2 didn't matter comparatively. Both were medical staff, not command.

And Uly was in command until ordered otherwise.

Midshipman Eldridge had been correct that he had been the senior surviving command officer aboard.

Huff would replace him now.

Uly focused on the older male.

"Doctor…?" he inquired, reading the tabs on the shoulders.

"Farley Spence," the man said in a quiet, scholarly type of voice. "Doctor of Xenomedicine. I suppose I'm in charge of the cargo that way. Or at least their physical wellbeing, as I cannot speak to their social or intellectual needs."

"Why not?" Uly asked. It wasn't a friendly question, but it also wasn't a howling demand for justice.

Yet.

"We're keeping them alive, yes," Dr. Spence replied. "But would it have been better for them to die in battle rather than become our slaves? I cannot answer to that. I was only charged with keeping their bodies whole, so you would need to ask a philosopher or a priest."

Interesting concept. Might be a load of hokum. Might not.

And Captain Ulysses Fortier was now in command of a slave ship.

He turned to the woman and scowled at her.

"Doctor Jasmine Atwater," she nodded without making eye contact. "Like Farley, a xenomedical expert."

Uly nodded at her forehead and turned to the youngest one.

"Biomed Specialist Leith Masters, Captain," he said in a polite voice. "With Blair, I'm the one on the front lines dealing with colds and nutrition for the crew."

At least he called them crew, and not just *cargo*.

Uly made a note to interview all four of these people individually, as it felt like they were all hiding things from one another. Or trapped in the military cult of racial superiority that was the *Combined Crowns of Danumash*.

He turned to Blair.

"Which of your charges would be the best one for me to be introduced to first?" he asked, willing to let the civilian pick.

Just like storming an enemy ship, there was something to be said for letting a known expert provide an informed opinion.

Interestingly, Blair turned to Biomed Specialist Masters first.

"Piruz?" he asked.

To Uly, it sounded like a name.

Masters grinned.

"Yeah," he agreed. "Then probably Haydar."

Blair nodded. Something the little people had going to get around the two Doctors? The two officers?

All manner of currents under calm surface waters. He felt like he would need a scorecard to keep all of the names straight, but he would get there.

They were all the way in the water at the deep end of the pool.

"This way, please," Blair announced, turning and walking into the den of offices.

Uly followed, uncertain what he'd gotten himself into as the others followed.

# EIGHT

ULY LOOKED around as the group trailed him into an open space that almost felt like the commons of a dormitory.

Until most of the rooms turned out to be cells, with actual metal bars blocking the doors.

And...aliens.

Each cell had a single body in it. All of them were watching him. Some leaning directly on the bars. Others sitting in chairs or on their bunk deeper inside.

Alien...

Humanoid. Uly would start there.

Pale skin with a blue hue underneath, instead of the pink you got with Humans.

Larger eyes than a Human. Rounder, too. Vertically slitted pupils like a cat.

Instead of hair on their heads, they had...

Uly felt a moment of pure dread crawl through his entire being, taking him back to ancient horror stories.

Those were either tentacles emerging from their scalps or maybe snakes. He wasn't close enough to tell for certain, and walking by too fast to stop and stare at one, however rudely that would come across.

Blair was moving towards a specific cell. Uly followed.

The person inside felt male at first glance. Tall and thin, rather like Uly was, so they were about the same height. Roughly the same build, which suggested that the aliens were generally leaner than Humans.

Felt friendly though, even as he conveyed a reserve as Blair got close.

"Piruz, this is Captain Fortier," Blair said. "He's in charge with Captain Winter dead. Captain Fortier, allow me to introduce Piruz Kossari. His species is Mazhin as we are Human."

Uly nodded to the man, studying him. Blair was close enough that the two could have touched, but Uly stayed back out of reach.

Out of something…

Those tentacles moved restively. Up close, Uly didn't see eyes or poison-fanged mouths, but his imagination was good enough to add those details.

He wondered what his nightmares would be like for the next however long.

"Greetings." Uly forced his mouth to work. "I am Ulysses Fortier of the *Batyr* Navy. This vessel was captured in honorable combat, and I'm given to understand that all the officers died on the bridge. Either way, I am in command, with orders to get this ship to a friendly, *Batyr* port. We had been expecting…"

What? Or better yet, how to say it?

"A non-organic cargo, Captain?" the Mazhin gentleman asked with a knowing grin and a crisp eloquence that would have been perfect for reading the evening news.

And much of his body language appeared similar to Human. All the tentacles almost seemed to be sniffing the air to taste Uly's scent.

Scent. It was stronger here. Sharper. Was that the smell of Mazhin bodies he'd picked up earlier?

"Yes," Uly agreed with that assessment. "Non-organic. And I've already encountered personnel problems with one of the Midshipmen aboard. Eldridge is currently in medical, because I'm pretty sure I cracked a few of his ribs when I knocked him down then kicked him. From there, he's going into a cell rather like this one until I decide what to do with him."

Those eyes slatted open like vertical blinds, almost causing Uly to jump backwards.

"Eldridge?" the Mazhin asked carefully.

"Eldridge," Uly confirmed. "He called Lead Trooper Chastain here *washenzi*. Among our kind, that's a highly insulting term."

"Humans got the world from Mazhin originally," this gentleman, this Piruz Kossari, nodded. "It is just as insulting among our kind."

He turned to study Chastain, standing off and back where she could keep watch on things.

"Yes, I could see that," Kossari nodded then turned back to face Uly. "So, what will you do, Captain?"

"I need to repair this ship," Uly replied. "Originally, I had been expecting a mixed *Danumash* crew of military and civilian. What does it change when I add in newly freed Mazhin prisoners?"

Not slaves. They had stopped being slaves when Ulysses Fortier assumed command. As he would get the ship home to a friendly port, he would see the prisoners of his prisoners free as well.

Whatever that took.

The man—Man? Yes—studied Uly's face closer, pupils wide.

"*Batyr* does not keep slaves," Uly growled angrily to the unasked question.

"What would you ask of us?" Kossari asked.

"Your word of honor that you and your kin will help me repair this ship and get it to a *Batyr* base," Uly said. "From there, I'll have to figure out how to get you home, but that's later. Are you safe from the *Danumash* crew? Is that crew safe from you if I ordered all these cells opened right now?"

Spence made a strangled sound that got every head turned to look at him, but froze up again, eyes wide and face beet red.

"Yes, Doctor Spence?" Uly asked. "You wanted to offer an opinion?"

"Honorable surrender," he managed to squeak.

"Indeed honorable, Doctor," Uly nodded. "Which is why I am not immediately swapping all the Humans into these cells. Right now, I need bodies. Blair informs me that a large set of your prisoners have repair expertise. I'd like to use that, but not at the risk of having a riot or small war on my hands in the process. Do you plan on being a hindrance?"

Spence turned white. Probably finally understood what had happened to Eldridge.

"No," he whispered.

"Excellent choice," Uly nodded, turning back to Kossari's smile.

"Some of the crew might be troublesome," the alien man said. "Blair can point them out for you adequately if officers like Winter and Botterill are dead."

"Botterill?" Uly asked, turning to Roscoe now.

"Ship's Knight, sir," Roscoe nodded. "Master of Arms of ground combat, as opposed to Master of War. I do not think I would be wrong suggesting that he was an asshole that a great many people won't miss. Right up there with Butcher's old boss, Senior Lieutenant Beagle, the Ship's Bursar."

Uly had a flash of insight at the various lines of demarcation on this ship. Officers versus enlisted versus civilian. And now versus captors and former alien prisoners.

Messy. Complicated. And they might manage to cancel each other out entirely, without the officers around to cause trouble, and the Mazhin thrown in and promised their freedom later for working now.

Uly turned back to Piruz Kossari.

"I cannot make such a promise for this tribe myself, Captain," he said.

Uly nodded.

"Blair suggested that we talk to you first, and then someone named Haydar," Uly replied. "Is that the person to ask?"

"Indeed, Captain," Piruz nodded back. "The old one would be my first choice, though I understand that Blair thought you should speak with me first, as I have a better understanding of your kind."

"Why is that?" Uly asked, intrigued.

This man would likely be the interlocutor to talk to the other aliens, if that was the case.

"I'm the best versed in Human cultures, Captain," Piruz grinned. "And Kossari translates into your tongue as something like *horse thief*, which has connotations of a fast talking, used-camel salesman."

"I see," Uly said. "We shall talk more."

He turned to Roscoe and Blair.

"Haydar next?" Uly asked.

# NINE

HAYDAR RAMEZANI SMELLED the new Human approaching. This one used a differently scented soap than the *Danumash* crew on a daily basis. Also in the soaps to wash his uniform, as well as that of the tall, dark-skinned woman accompanying him. The short male accompanying also smelled of engines being repaired.

Haydar let his tentacles taste the air. The shits in charge of this ship only kept one flavor of soap, an overly floral stench that overpowered everything and didn't allow one the complicated *mélange* of laundry to express personal tastes and values.

As if you should wash everything with the same flavor, every single day.

In that, Haydar understood that Humans had almost no sense of smell. They were a sight-driven species. Predators, but a hunting kind. Nearly blind in the dark, where Haydar or one of the others would barely be slowed.

This Fortier smelled of violence. Human adrenaline amped up to excessive levels slowly evaporating from his pores. It was not fear. He and the tall female brought aggression. The fear smell came from the Humans Haydar already knew.

He let the faintest smile touch his lips at the consideration that the fools of this vessel, this *King Hewitt II*, had suffered a loss on warship combat that left them at the mercy of an unforgiving enemy.

*Paybacks could be an utter bitch, couldn't they?*

Blair Mitchell led the new Humans close, from where they had been engaging with Piruz down the cell block. Like Spence, the newcomers probably had no concept of how much communication the Mazhin could have without words. As they relied on sight, Humans also relied on sound.

Limited.

Captain Fortier smelled young. Younger than Blair. Perhaps the same as Butcher or Roscoe. Newly adult, but not for long. Growing into his size and wisdom, but with a long road ahead of him on both notes.

Fortier smelled healthier than most of the *Danumash* crew. That was good.

The tall, darkly skinned woman smelled like danger. He made eye contact with her and understood that she contained violence to be utilized as an art form. None of the Mazhin prisoners were her match. Perhaps no three of them in her current state.

Even Fortier was more dangerous than any of Haydar's local semi-clan.

"Haydar Ramezani, this is Captain Fortier of the *Batyr*," Blair Mitchell said formally. "The ship's new captain."

"Greetings in the name of the Convocation, Captain Fortier," Haydar nodded deeply.

He could say those words, as the others had generally elected him clan elder of the artificial cluster of strangers that *Danumash* had inflicted upon them. None of his cohorts was within a sixth generation as the Mazhin measures such things, not counting the twins who were almost a single person anyway. Haydar wasn't sure they could have done a better job at randomization had they relied on anything beyond specist ignorance.

*Danumash* had that in spades.

"The Convocation, sir?" Fortier asked, brow below his Human hair furrowed. "I am unfamiliar with such a usage."

Haydar smelled the honesty of the response. *Danumash* didn't understand that their lies smelled badly.

"The Mazhin, Captain." Haydar nodded and tried to smile without lecturing the young bull in front of him. "We gather as the recognized *Clan Lords in Congress Assembled*, where the Hall of Lords speaks and the Hall of Voices executes. As my comrades are not blood relations, they have taken it upon themselves to appoint me to speak for them."

"Clan Lords," Fortier asked. "Did I understand you correctly? And you are an unfortunate random conglomeration of folks instead of representing a single clan?"

"You did, Captain Fortier," Haydar said. "Also, Piruz mistranslates his name, which would traditionally mean *Dealer of Horses*, rather than horse thief. But he also likes to tell grand and exciting stories which sometimes only occasionally touch on the truth."

Fortier nodded with a quick grin, then pivoted slowly in place.

"I count ten Mazhin in immediate sight," the Human said when he turned full circle. "Is that correct? And complete?"

"It is," Haydar replied.

"Roscoe, what's the count on surviving human crew, civilian and military?" Fortier asked.

"Fourteen, sir," Roscoe said.

"How many Midshipmen?" Fortier asked, still standing

directly in front of Haydar, close enough to measure by smell but out of reach.

"Eldridge, Huff, and Wyndham were in secondary control," Roscoe said. "These four in Xeno Life Sciences. Engineering has Old Man Michaels in charge, with Toft, Tyson, and Simonson."

"So you, Butcher, and who's the remaining person?" Fortier asked.

"Able Spacer Delbert Blakeslee is manning secondary with Wyndham right now," Roscoe said. "Not much to do with everybody else gone and us not sure what happened next."

"I brought four more with me," Fortier said. "First thing first, we'll need to collect up all the weapons on this vessel, including personal ones stored in cabins. Then Huff and Wyndham need to make some decisions. I'd like to get all these prisoners engaged in repairing this ship so we can start to limp home. I doubt that my ship will come back this direction for a while with a full convoy to chase, but the escorts might decide to slip away, in which case I prefer to be elsewhere. Is that likely to become a problem?"

"No, sir, but I'd rather not have to answer for Eldridge's behavior or whoever might take exception to you punching him in the gob," Roscoe said. "If you get my drift?"

"I do," the captain nodded, then turned to stare at Haydar. "Shortly, I would like to see about unlocking these doors permanently, sir, but right at the moment, I need to sort out the rest of the Human crew. Would your people be willing to help me escape *Danumash*?"

"We absolutely would, Captain," Haydar decided, speaking now for this tiny Convocation of souls that had entrusted him with their lives. "And we can."

"I shall hold you to that," Fortier smiled fully, finally. "We're off the deep end now, and I have no idea how far down the bottom might be. Or what monsters might lurk in those dark, cold depths."

Then he turned to Roscoe and directed all the Humans to depart, taking his refreshing smell with him.

Others inquired on the faint breeze of life support, but Haydar had nothing to add to what they could already smell.

Change was coming. Would it truly be for the better?

# TEN

ULY FOLLOWED Roscoe and Butcher aft. Engineering on a vessel this size usually encompassed both decks, set behind solid bulkheads that could keep explosions contained and vented outwards.

The smell as they crossed the main frame hatch was oil and ozone. Something had a slow leak dripping somewhere. Probably small enough and hidden enough that nobody had ever decided to pull major components out and fix them.

Uly had gotten a lot of training on damage control procedures over the last two years.

"Hey, Marlowe," Roscoe yelled as they entered the busy space. "New captain for you to meet."

Interesting way to phrase it. Far less formal than Uly was used to.

But then, looking around at all the massive boxes and pipes and ducts everywhere, this was clearly a civilian vessel, rather than a purpose-built military hull. Those were designed to exacting tolerances, and everything had a prescribed place instantly recognizable at a glance.

This was vaguely organized chaos.

Three heads popped up from behind one of the generators where the second-floor deck was a maze of catwalks above large generators. A fourth person appeared from around the side below them. All male, but this was a *Danumash* vessel. That the sailing master and one of the doctors were female was already a high number for the *Combined Crowns*.

Uly came to rest and let the four come to him. More space over here to just talk instead of craning his head back to yell. The others joined him, and the engineering crew took that as their cue to climb down.

Three young and one older, all wiping hands on rags and jumpsuits already covered with grease, dirt, and possibly blood, depending.

The old one seemed in charge.

"Lead Engineer Michaels, this is Captain Fortier of the *Batyr* Navy," Roscoe introduced him. "He's met Piruz and Haydar, and he put Eldridge into medical with cracked ribs for mouthing off."

The stress on that last part suggested a man with a history of disciplinary issues. Even for *Danumash*, he must be exceptional at what he did, to have not been forcibly retired.

Michaels smiled and licked his lips before speaking. Lines on his face and neck suggested a man around fifty. Perhaps coming up on his thirtieth year of service and ready to qualify for an exceptional pension?

The man was thin, but Uly could see muscles inside his jumpsuit. Average height, but with long arms. Clean shaven but had a face that looked like it wanted four days of gray stubble to really complete it.

"Captain," Michaels finally said, nodding. "Kids and I are repairing the Spatial Generator. It took a hard surge when you blew up the front half of the ship. Life support is in good shape, but most of that got moved up with Haydar's folk on the rebuild."

He fell silent then, studying the new group.

"Lead Engineer?" Uly asked.

"Again," the man nodded with a wry grin. "Third time."

"Third?" Uly asked, shocked. He'd been promoted to Lead, then reduced in rank, only to claw his way back up twice?

"Yup," Michaels nodded.

Uly turned to Roscoe, certain that any story he got would leave out details, but Roscoe's would be more…something.

"How?" Uly asked.

"He's really good at what he does, sir," Roscoe said, head tilting back and forth as he spoke. "Just tends to have a problem dealing with dumbasses. And we got a lot of those. Had, excuse me. Way fewer now."

It was becoming obvious whose side Roscoe was on. Maybe the man would want to change uniforms when this was all done and was trying to make a good appearance now?

Still, Uly processed all Michaels had said and tried to fit it in. *Batyr* was about discipline. Egalitarianism. Openness.

*Danumash* was a strictly hierarchical structure where birth, then wealth, played the largest roles in your destiny.

Uly studied the man. The three with him were all young. Two of them were civilians that looked hardly older than Midshipman Huff.

"Michaels, I brought Machinist Specialist Kolya Roux with me," Uly said, turning to indicate the quietest member of the group so far. And in general. "E-7 to your current E-8. As this is now officially a *Batyr* vessel, will you have a problem if he's breveted to Chief Engineer? What you would call your Master of Machines? Will I have problems?"

Michaels turned to lock a hard stare in on Roux. Both were of a height. Even of a coloration, but Uly had never realized how much Roux looked more like a *Danumash* immigrant to *Batyr*, compared to the folks he had grown up around. Albino was not his coloration. Merely *Danumash* paleness.

Roux, for his part, took two steps forward, until the men were about arm's length apart, a silent battle of wills.

"Variable Pulse Spatial Generator is off-line," Michaels said abruptly. "Thoughts?"

"When was the last time you replaced your secondary fuse breakers?" Roux replied. "Better, how long ago were they inspected and maybe passed anyway because somebody didn't want to have to buy new ones? Or did your primary engine generator behind it blip under the load when we killed your shields then bled their shit all over the nearest machine?"

None of that made any sense to Uly, but all four of the *Danumash* folks nodded and relaxed.

Michaels turned back to Uly and something harsh had left his face.

"Him, I'd let work on my machines," Michaels announced sagely. Then thumbed back at the three youngsters. "These three usually can't find their asses with both hands, a map, and a flashlight."

"Hey," the oldest of the three barked.

"Usually," Michaels corrected himself with a laugh. "You're a blind squirrel with acorns when it happens."

Whatever that meant, the four shared a laugh and relaxed a whole additional notch.

"As long as the orders involve fixing shit and not stretching the budget so the officers earn a quarterly efficiency bonus, I'm good," Michaels announced.

That much, Uly understood. Money not spent on repairs and maintenance was poured back into a fund for the officers to share. Uly presumed that they expected to be transferred elsewhere before the various systems failures inevitably caught up with someone.

"Next questions, Lead," Uly said, causing everyone to pause and sober. Heads came to stillness watching him. "I also have access to another repair crew. What Roscoe called Mechanicals but are now classified as freed prisoners. Would you have a problem if I assigned some of them back here as well?"

The three youngsters were poised to run, just as the three doctors had before, uncertain what the response would be. Or how much trouble they were about to face.

Michaels rocked his head back and forth, biting his lip in concentration. He even looked around furtively, staring at Roscoe and Butcher. Roscoe nodded. Butcher paled.

"So, here's a thing, Captain," Michaels finally said in a quieter, conspiratorial voice. "Ship like this is old and worn. Shoulda been sent to the breaker a long time ago, but Hylda was all set to make her spot in the galaxy and become a gentlewoman one of these days. The kids here were never trained to fix shit this old. Most of it was being phased out when I was a pup. That's part of the reason I still got a job and the stripes, 'cause I could keep this heap limping along when likely nobody else could."

"Okay," Uly replied, mostly to prompt whatever that other shoe was that was about to drop.

"Ever' once in a while, I'd slip forward, usually in the evening when the Docs were all off having dinner or maybe retired fer the night and drinking alone in their cabins." Michaels nodded to himself, lost in some reverie. "Then Sadeq and I might talk about stuff. Mazhin tech's not that different. In fact, I'm pretty sure *Danumash* and maybe *Batyr* use third-hand or maybe fourth-hand Mazhin designs. Either bought, stolen, or built from old plans and wrecks. Sadeq's the best of that lot for ideas when I run dry."

Uly was shocked to his core. On the other hand, it made sense if the disciplinarians of this ship had preferred to keep their hierarchy in place. Michaels struck him as the kind of engineer that didn't give two figs about process and rules if he could make something work. Regardless of who he had to talk to or yell at.

Folks who thought like Eldridge would have a problem with that.

Uly noted that the three younger engineers were waiting with nervous faces for him to speak. To bring down the wrath of the gods on Michaels for making shit work with the help of aliens.

What a stupid, fucking way to run a navy.

"Michaels, as soon as I sort out the remaining two people, expect help back here," Uly said. "You and Roux organize work shifts and teams and let me know what you need. Priority is the ability to transition to warp, even for just a short period, so this vessel is not here if anybody else comes along looking for us, because the shot that killed the bridge took out the Neutron Omnipulsar in the process."

"Yup, knew that," the man said. "That was the power surge nobody was expecting. The generator was feeding it full tilt and didn't shut down fast enough."

Uly turned to Roux and smiled.

"Roux, you are now officially Chief Engineer, but I highly recommend you listen to your combined staff. Questions?"

"Not until the Lead and I talk turkey, sir," Roux nodded with a quick smile. "Then we'll know how far and how fast we can run."

"Excellent," Uly said. He turned to his guide. "Roscoe, let's go take a look up at my new home in Secondary Control."

# ELEVEN

DAN TRAILED the group as they made their way up a flight of stairs to a space over and a little forward from Engineering proper. Below and behind her, she could already hear Michaels and Roux going two hundred kilometers an hour in a technical jargon so esoteric as to be another language.

Voices were calm, though, so she didn't figure she needed to stay and babysit. Like Fortier, Michaels had surprised her with his willingness to work with aliens.

She'd spent too much time having to suffer that same sort of racist abuse in certain circles, unable to strike back. Might be part of the reason she'd eventually ended up in a job that let her officially crack heads together. Or whomp assholes with long sticks.

Butcher was being quiet. Roscoe was handling the tour guide duties. Fortier looked like a captain should, all formal and serious.

They were on their own. But it could have been much worse.

Fortier stopped Roscoe short of the hatch and whispered something in his ear before the latter opened it. Telling the man to remain casual apparently, because Roscoe didn't immediately call "Captain on the deck" when he entered.

Instead, they all simply walked in, and Dan got a look at the control space that was the new bridge, at least until somebody managed to repair the old one. Assuming that they could. If the ship was that old, probably not worth the effort and would instead be parted out in a shipyard somewhere.

Octagonal in shape, with three stations on each side and a hatch directly across that probably went to the head, since she'd seen no other spots during the tour. Cramped, with too many stations in one space. And presumably all the officers had been on the bridge.

One Midshipman and one Able Spacer here. The Mid wasn't touching anything on his console, hands back just watching screens. The Able Spacer was doing all the work.

"Gentlemen?" Fortier asked as they all stepped in.

The two looked over, panicked, and shot to their feet. Again, the Mid at perfect attention and the crew member actually doing the work slouched over in such a way that he had one eye on Fortier and one on the screens, eyes floating back and forth constantly.

Weird.

She studied the Middie. Younger than Huff or Eldridge. Maybe only fourteen, but *Danumash* parents liked to get their sons aboard ships young in order to accrue seniority points later when the important ones became flag officers. Time in space counted at that point.

Then Dan looked closer and understood why the youngster hadn't been touching anything. His insignia indicated that he was a security marine. Like her.

"Armsman Solomon Wyndham, sir," the youngster said, his voice cracking halfway, though he kept right on going. "Minding operations while Eldridge and Huff were meeting you, sir!"

Fortier stepped past Roscoe and Butcher, leaving her guarding the door, Dan supposed. He turned to the spacer and nodded.

"Able Spacer Delbert Blakeslee, sir," the other man said.

Dan compared the two final pieces of the puzzle. Wyndham stood short and bulky, with the promise of adding another thirty centimeters and maybe thirty kilos of muscle at some point. Just the sort of build you needed to be a Master of Arms.

Blakeslee was vaguely average, with faraway eyes and brown hair. And a refusal to keep eye contact with his captain as he monitored the ship.

Dan approved.

"Armsman?" Fortier asked Wyndham.

"Aye, sir."

"How old are you, Armsman?" Fortier pressed.

"Just turned fourteen, sir," Wyndham replied, eyes locked on a point just over Dan's shoulder.

"Wyndham, this is Lead Trooper Chastain." Fortier turned to gesture at her. "She will be Second-in-Command of the vessel. She will also brevet to Master of Arms, and you will report directly to her. Will that be a problem?"

Dan wondered why Fortier was setting the kid up like that. Eldridge had stuck his dick in a wasp's nest and gotten removed from the crew. Was Wyndham going down with him?

Was Huff doomed as well?

Wyndham turned his head just enough to make eye contact. Dan smiled, knowing that dark brown skin and kinky hair was anathema to large swaths of *Danumash*, unless someone had been ennobled as a Duke at some point in spite of their color.

Rare, but not impossible. Stupid, but not her culture.

Wyndham let his eyes trace her stance, down to her boots and back up to the Icemace in one hand. There was a hint of panic there, but he contained it well.

"Sir, no problem, sir!"

Fortier turned to look at Dan.

"Is that acceptable, Master of Arms?" the captain asked.

Dan had never been formally appointed to the position on any of the ships she'd helped capture. At the same time, *Marshall Castillon* had never abandoned them in the field, letting Captain Savatier immediately put aboard prize crew officers who were buddies of Dupuis to take charge.

Kolya Roux was acting Chief Engineer. Dan Sheridan could be acting Master of Arms. It would look good on her next enlistment contract. Maybe worth a little extra cash every month, at least in retirement one of these days.

"It is, sir," Dan nodded back.

Fortier nodded to himself at some unvoiced conversation.

"Blakeslee, sit down and keep flying the ship," he ordered.

Dan watched him move to the station, making Wyndham slide to one side so that he could sit. She gestured the youngster to come stand next to her. If nothing else, he would need continued training, plus she could get a sense of how well the former occupant had trained his troopers.

If Eldridge was a reflection of the dead Captain Winter, then Wyndham would teach her about this Botterill fellow.

"Butcher, as you are Ship's Bursar, and as the Quartermaster and original Banker are dead, I will expect you to brief me in six hours with the current state of supplies," Fortier announced. "Roscoe, as newly promoted sailing master, however trainee you might think you are, let's sit down with the astrogation computer and plot a path that gets us to a friendly port in less than a lifetime."

He paused there, eyes ten thousand light-years distant before they came back and locked on Dan.

"You track down Huff and the others," he ordered. "Have Huff give you a tour forward and figure out where everybody can bunk tonight, crew and visitors. Later, I'll have Roux and Michaels tell me how long until they can patch the hull and what we've lost."

She nodded. Second-in-Command stuff, rather than Lead Trooper, but he was treating her like the officer he didn't have, when he might not trust Huff or Wyndham.

Eldridge was a lost cause she wouldn't miss.

Dan nodded to Wyndham to follow her and reversed course.

They were on their own, but it could have been much worse.

How bad would it get before they got home?

# KING HEWITT II

# TWELVE

ULY WATCHED his screens closely but didn't interfere.

"Stand by for star drive," Roscoe called across the compact bridge.

Astronomer's Mate Huff was technically sailing, but he and Roscoe had both admitted under questioning that Huff's experience was entirely book-learned. Huff had at least spent a lot of time in simulators, but Roscoe had flown the ship itself. Or at least monitored things in the dead of night when the officers forward were asleep.

Or drunk, as Uly had come to understand after nearly a week with his new crew.

One-third of forward consumables had been dedicated to alcohol. Enough to float a small land vehicle if he wanted.

Uly drank at the low end of expected for social occasions. *Vanguard Lesauvage* hadn't been a boat dedicated to consumptions. *Marshall Castillon* had been. *King Hewitt II* seemed to be entirely lubricated with exotic and rare brands of booze. The expensive kind.

Maybe he could trade it with somebody when he got to a settlement. Better than money, he supposed.

"Engaging star drive now," Roscoe called, pushing a button.

They'd tried this a few times, but mostly to locate shorts and burnout spots that might not show on repair screens. This was the first time Uly had expected the bubble to actually hold coherence for longer than a second.

With the bridge space destroyed by a through-and-through shot, Michaels and Roux hadn't bothered doing more than welding repair plates in place to hold air in. As a result, Secondary Operations was the bridge. Crowded and badly organized, but Uly didn't have the time, resources, or personnel to rebuild the bridge into the space he would have preferred.

Not if he wanted to be home inside six months.

*Marshall Castillon* had ranged deep into *Danumash* territory for this raid. Not quite cutting directly across, but certainly looping around their stars clockwise on a map into regions Uly hardly knew at all.

Around them, *King Hewitt II* vanished inside a warp bubble, falling away from a high-density spot the systems generated directly aft into a warp-vacuum forward. At least mathematically.

Relative acceleration against the outer universe actually began to rack up acceptable numbers.

He'd lived the last week in quiet terror that one of those *Danumash* escorts would finally circle back to rescue this ship and find him.

Depending on who they were, they might reward him for throwing Eldridge in the brig, but Uly expected that it was more likely he would end up badly beaten while resisting arrest and put into medical himself.

Eldridge was still sullen, but his cracked ribs were mostly healed, and he was now confined to his cabin, except when he was escorted to the shower every morning and the head twice a day.

Beranger seemed to be looking forward to that duty. Sending Dan might have been rude.

Might be worth it, too.

"It's holding, Captain," Huff said, his voice a little loud with excitement.

But Sterling was also only fifteen and had never been put in charge of anything in his life. Captain Winter and his First Officer, Commander Pickering, hadn't trusted the kids with any responsibility.

Uly nodded and continued to watch readouts. He'd taken over the station that Eldridge had had previously, so he had Huff on one side and Roscoe across. Blakeslee normally monitored communications, but thankfully had had nothing to do but work this week.

Behind them, an unoccupied system began to trail off in the distance. The convoy had been using that as a waypoint to organize on their way to one of the seven capital worlds at Aessex. Uly had quietly begun to wonder if some spy somewhere had told *Batyr* where to hunt. Or if a disaffected traitor had done so.

Either way, *Marshall Castillon* had apparently known exactly where to lurk to surprise them.

At least there weren't any locals to bother the ship while they'd fixed what they could. Now, Uly just had to thread a needle to someplace at least neutral enough that they would trade with him, while they all found a way around the edge of *Danumash* space.

At least he had a lot of booze to trade with somebody.

"Hey, I'm starting to get a heat warning," Roscoe called.

Uly studied the gauge. Iffy, but they were also working with fragile equipment. And they'd managed a reasonable distance in the last few minutes.

Pulse-wake would still lead someone to them, but they'd have to look.

"Shut it down," he ordered. "We'll wait here and let Roux and Michaels sort it out."

"Shutting down," Roscoe replied, pressing a series of buttons.

"Engineering, this is the bridge," Uly said into an intercom. "This is far enough for me for today. Congratulations on the first success. Everyone knock off early and have some down time before dinner. The various problems will still be there tomorrow for you."

Around him, the others cheered quietly. Success was an intoxicating brew. Owning it because you'd put in the hard work was even better.

To date, Eldridge had been the only hard case among the crew, though Uly occasionally caught grimaces on faces that didn't think he was looking.

He couldn't fix *Danumash*, but as long as everyone else maintained military discipline, he didn't really care. *Batyr* and Mazhin crew outnumbered *Danumash* aboard, plus he was pretty certain that not all of the *Danumash* folks would join any attempted insurrection. At this point, they might even be hung by their own folks as pirates.

There were rules for this kind of warfare, after all. Honorable surrender was just that. Ransom for good behavior, and Eldridge was going to be brought up on formal charges of insubordination for refusing to accept a Black enlisted woman as his superior officer. Whether that one particular word also got him *Conduct Unbecoming An Officer* tacked on wasn't something Uly had decided yet.

Wouldn't until later. Maybe Eldridge would decide to get over himself before *King Hewitt II* got someplace important and Uly could just let it go without ending the kid's career.

Eldridge was, after all, a product of *Danumash* culture, so Uly's standards of personal conduct could not be applied. Military discipline was a different matter.

"Huff, Roscoe, let whoever is in charge of cooking know that they can move things up a little," Uly decided. "I'll take bridge watch for now while you stand down and nap or something."

"Thank you, sir," Huff said as they both rose. "I can take evening watch after dinner."

"You, Roscoe, and Blakeslee sort that out," Uly replied.

He watched the two depart with a spring in their steps that hadn't been there a week ago. But then, a week hadn't left Uly with any sort of high opinions of Captain Tevin Winter, Commander Addison Pickering, Adjutant Rigby Botterill, or Senior Lieutenant Driscoll Beagle. The other officers and midshipmen hadn't left as bad a taste in the mouths of the surviving crew, and everybody genuinely missed Hylda Hobbs and her civilian Quartermaster Hendrix Dodham.

Even Haydar and Piruz had nice things to say about those two.

Most of the rest of the Mazhin crew largely kept their distance from Uly, and he was fine with that. There was one other Technical besides Haydar, an acknowledged genius named Roshan Anyari who was nerdy and quiet most of the time. Five Mechanicals were largely dominated by Piruz as far as personality.

Two female Socials that were actually musicians more than anything, as apparently the Human officers refused to lower themselves to raping alien women. Which was good, because otherwise Uly might have taken a nastier approach to things around here.

Nasrin Monfared was young and beautiful, even by his skewed, Human standards, while Omid Adl was older, homelier, and fantastic playing an eight-stringed instrument like an acoustic guitar called a carggant.

Dinner tonight would no doubt be cooked by Vahid Siah, nicknamed *The Spatula* to distinguish him from his identical twin Azah Siah, *The Wrench*. Everyone had commented on how much better chow was when the Human sailors weren't taking turns cooking.

Morale was good. And getting better on a daily basis. Now, he just had to escape *Danumash* space.

The hatch opened and Dan entered, by herself.

Uly went to rise, but she gestured for him to remain seated, moving to the spot Huff had just vacated.

He watched her bring that console live and lock the hatch, sealing them in and isolating them, though Uly supposed that any of the repair crew could tap the audio circuits if they really wanted.

Dan wanted privacy.

Uly leaned back and watched the woman.

# THIRTEEN

DAN STUDIED ULY. He was no longer Captain Fortier, except when there were folks around. Uly, short for Ulysses, an ancient name lost in the mists of history. They could just be people when they were alone. She suspected that he needed that, because he was suddenly on his own and in charge far beyond anything he'd ever expected. That much he'd whispered at one point.

He watched her quietly. Uly did lots of things quietly, thinking and observing before moving. Before jumping in with an opinion and action, Eldridge notwithstanding.

And he treated her like his Second-in-Command.

"I've been looking at some maps," Dan began, uncertain as to the best way to start. The best approach to take.

She'd known the man for five days. Not long enough to truly take his measure.

However, if they'd finally gotten the ship working, she'd run out of time to stew.

Uly nodded at her warily.

But then, he'd only known her for five days, too. And all of them had been aboard an enemy vessel surrounded by potentially hostile mobs.

Dan licked her lips and considered her words carefully.

"*The Seven Kingdoms* are kind of like a pinwheel when viewed from overhead," she continued after a moment, watching his careful nod. "*Batyr* is more a pie slice that is kind of wedged in between two of *Danumash*'s fingers and overlapped on both flanks."

Again, the nod, eyes never leaving her as Uly waited for her to get to a point or ask a question.

How many officers had she ever known with that sort of patience?

"And we're at about ten o'clock, if this was a map," she said. "There might be a place where we could go, instead of trying to sail directly home or skirt the outer edge of *Danumash* systems trying to hide."

There. She'd said it. Admitted knowing things that maybe hadn't been generally spoken about anywhere but back on *Marshall Castillon*. Or whatever High Command officers sent the ship raiding.

Uly's face pulled into a question, eyes big, jaw drawn with his mouth closed, elongating everything.

"This was not our first mission deep behind enemy lines," Dan replied to his unasked question.

"No, I got that impression," he offered. "What I haven't figured out is if Savatier ever planned to come back for us, or if I'd go into the history books with folks like Bligh for stupidly impossible sailing feats if I managed to bring a ship and crew home."

Dan blinked. He'd figured that out?

If she'd thought he had any hope of actually doing it, she might have kept her mouth shut, but she had no interest in being marooned or shipwrecked somewhere. Especially not if the nearest folks were *Danumash* punks who kept slaves and maybe didn't extend their Humanity beyond paleness.

Plus, she was one of two Human females aboard. Plus the two Mazhin. And a lot of men.

She'd rather not have to beat them all up. Some of them, like Uly, weren't half bad as people.

"There are spaces beyond the *Danumash* worlds where *Marshall Castillon* has pulled into port with captured ships," Dan explained, wondering if she was setting herself up for a court-martial when she got home for telling Uly all this.

*When* she got home. Not if.

"Human?" he asked.

She shrugged.

"There are also some Human colonies out there," she replied. "If you go too far, you end up in Auga space. The Auga Empire is huge, but distant. In between, you'll find folks like Zuath, Ugotha, Emro, and Thogin. Big bubble of space, as I understand it, though, because the *Danumash* tend to be less than pleasant neighbors. At least if you're not Human."

"What about the Mazhin?" Uly asked. "Where are they from?"

Dan grimaced. Uly's eyes got big again.

"I'm not sure," she admitted. "I don't remember ever even hearing about a world where they were the dominant species. Maybe they are from the side of Auga space? Or beyond? I don't really know."

His scowl spoke volumes. But it was also the reason she was here. Dan doubted that any of the *Danumash* folks that had survived would know much. They were enlisted or kids.

And Uly wouldn't know because he'd never served with the raider squadrons. He was strictly a line officer kind of guy, fighting battles with other *Danumash* Middleweights and maybe Capital ships.

Not preying on Lightweights and civilian shipping.

"What might be the best world for us to aim at, then, assuming I can't convince Haydar or Piruz to give me some coordinates?" he asked.

There. That was why she was here. He had asked her for a professional opinion. And after five days Dan knew that he would listen and probably act on it.

He trusted her. Didn't have much choice, but Dan got the impression that he might do it anyway.

How many officers had she ever known like that?

Dan turned and brought up an astrogation map, spinning it around and centering things from what she was used to. Curiosity, rather than training, but she'd wanted to know where they'd gone to meet such strange folks when Savatier and Dupuis put her on a station where there were hardly any other Humans around.

"There are a handful of worlds in this region," Dan said, highlighting them on the map. "We can trade with some. Others might want cash or Imperial Guilders to do business, and I haven't asked Butcher what he has for funds on hand."

"That's your assignment," Uly smiled now. "Second-in-Command and all that. You get me some of those numbers so we can refine where we're going, okay?"

"I can do that," she nodded.

He was already following her lead without many questions. Assuming her expertise and building on it.

She could come to like working for this guy.

"Since you're sitting the watch, should I have Vahid send you up some food in a while?" Dan asked, rising.

"Please," he nodded. "I'm obviously going to be busy with astrogation."

She nodded back and headed for the hatch.

Maybe she could help, but he'd be doing all the heavy lifting getting them home.

# FOURTEEN

ULY FELT knots in his shoulders and back from sitting hunched over too long. Hours bent staring at the screen, focused as he dug for every tidbit that they might have in their systems.

Pitifully little, upon reflection. But that made sense, since *Danumash* wouldn't want to admit to even knowing aliens existed as anything but servants, serfs, and slaves to be taken.

He had five worlds Dan had marked. Knew their stars by color and age. Knew names assigned by…someone. Uly wasn't sure who. They existed in a *Danumash* astrogation database.

He'd go from there.

The hatch opening brought him back to the present tense.

"Here to relieve you, sir," Huff said, entering.

"Ready to be relieved, Sterling," Uly smiled as he rose.

The kid had the making of a good officer. Without Eldridge around, apparently berating Huff for not hating others enough, Sterling had a gift for stellar cartography, sciences, and sensors that was better than many of the officers Uly had served with. Men with a decade more experience included.

Still, if the computer didn't know, now was not the time to

spring it on Huff. Uly had something better in mind. He closed his console down as Huff took another station.

"We're currently at rest, sir?" Huff asked with a hint of surprise, checking things.

"We are," Uly replied. "I'd rather we not drift, even out here in the darkness between stars, so I brought us to a general stop relative with the star behind us. We'll hold that until the warp bubble can be sustained better, and it won't make any difference at that point."

"Understood, sir," Huff said brightly, smiling. "I'm planning to just let the optics systems plot everything nearby and update our records. Is that okay?"

"It is," Uly replied. Then he walked over and dialed in a slice of the heavens. "In fact, start here and work your way outward in a visual spiral, Huff. I'd like to know what's over there, in case we end up turning that direction from our current course. There are some things that have been brought to my attention in front of us that I might want to avoid."

"On it."

Uly smiled and retired. The kid was training as a stellar cartographer. Might as well put that to use, without telling him *why* they were likely to change course so radically.

At least until he had a chance to talk to some folks.

# FIFTEEN

HAYDAR HAD INSISTED on modifying his new door when they'd installed it. Captain Fortier had immediately ordered the crew to remove all the bars across the cells and replace them with actual hatches on hinges, the kind that had locks on the inside, but Haydar found that closing it isolated him too much, while leaving it open meant that folks wandering by might take that as an invitation to chat.

So he'd had them chop it in half horizontally like a farmhouse door, with double hinges.

The top half open meant he could smell and see things going on in the main space. The bottom half closed stopped folks from immediately walking in.

It was good. Or bad.

Captain Fortier was standing there, though it was late in the ship's day.

Haydar wasn't much involved in the physical labor of repairing a badly outdated ship. Leave that for the youngsters. Instead, he was called upon regularly to come up with improvements to the overall design that could either be implemented during repairs, or form the basis of later upgrades from what was in place now.

The new bridge that might come into existence at some point, for instance.

Except that Captain Fortier was present. Exuded a smell of discovery, tempered with both confusion and curiosity. A being who has just discovered something new and also how much more wasn't revealed beyond it, perhaps?

Haydar rose and moved to the half-hatch, pulling it open and gesturing the Human in. The Captain had made it clear that he would not cross these thresholds uninvited. Ever.

Weird. Was he even Human? Or had Haydar gotten too jaded by spending his time around *Danumash* for too long? There was something to that.

Fortier sat, but only when Haydar gestured. Treating this tiny room like Haydar's castle.

It wasn't much, but it spoke volumes about the man himself.

"Captain?" Haydar asked. "How may I be of assistance?"

"I'm looking for an astrogation expert," the Human replied, eyes gleaming with that sudden knowledge. "And had hoped that you or Roshan might be able to help. Failing that, if any of the others might have some snippet of knowledge."

"Go on," Haydar prompted, curious as to what this new captain was up to.

Captain Winter had only visited once, mostly to express some manner of species superiority over the Mazhin who were his prisoners. The rest of the time, Doctors Spence and Atwater had been left to their own devices.

Not bad, *per se*, but not freedom. Not a door that could be closed when Haydar didn't want company.

"I have been speaking with Dan Chastain," Fortier continued, eyes not focused on anything in the room. "She told me about several star systems that she was aware of, well off our current path and beyond the currently acknowledged borders that *Danumash* claimed."

Haydar perked up at that. He and his people had been captured by *Danumash* raids into the galactic interior. Back towards Auga Space, though that was an impossibly large area when considered on any sort of map.

All of the Human realms combined took up only a small portion of Imperial Sector Seventeen, when seen from the Auga capital at Tuskyo. Had the Auga been more committed explorers, they and Humans might have found one another ere now.

"Which systems?" Haydar asked.

"Ohstad, Heire, Iethert, Masym, and Gorge," Captain Fortier said. "None of them appear to be worlds with a large Mazhin population, according to Chastain, so I'm not entirely sure where I might travel to in order to get your people home."

Haydar smiled.

"We are largely not planetbound, Captain," he replied.

"Not planetbound?"

"The Convocation decided to leave planets behind many centuries ago," Haydar nodded. "Instead, we travel the stars, trading and mining. In that, I suppose you might consider us a more civilized Ononguli Confederation."

"Ononguli?" Fortier asked, revealing just how rural Humans really were.

"Imperial Sector Twenty-One." Haydar actually smiled. "Though that is a polite fiction as the Ononguli will put aside all tribal rivalries to fall on any Auga fleet that attempts to cross the border."

"How big is the galaxy?" Fortier pressed.

"Huge, in terms of stars," Haydar said. "Immense, in the number of species that inhabit it. Even the portions that the Mazhin Convocation has encountered or heard stories about."

"With any luck, most of that will not be relevant," the Human nodded. "I take it there is no specific place I could plan to drop you?"

"Not close, no," Haydar shook his head. "As to the five worlds you mention, I am not the person to ask, as none of those names mean anything to me. However, Nasrin might be able to help. In spite of what the *Danumash* fools thought, she was trained as an entertainer, expert in several musical instruments as well as storytelling, cooking, and a raft of other skills designed for the salon rather than the bedroom."

Haydar watched the Human process that. Human history had something vaguely equivalent, known in ancient times as a geisha, though such still had modern connotations of prostitution.

And there was a secondary scent underneath. Interest, but Haydar knew that Nasrin was as well-formed as any Human woman, at least from the neck down. Convergent evolution, because there were only so many ways to solve the design of an upright, tool-using sentient, Zuath notwithstanding.

The sailors had lusted after Nasrin, but none had been able to overcome their cultural aversion to her alienness. Fortier shrugged when the others might have grimaced.

"If you think she might," Fortier said, standing. "Would you care to join me?"

"Me, Captain?" Haydar asked, a bit surprised.

"I am a male officer, about to knock on the hatch of a female crew member late in the evening," Fortier grinned a little lopsided. "Even if it is only in my own head, having another Mazhin accompany me, and an elder at that, would make me feel better."

"As you wish." Haydar rose from his chair.

But then, the Humans did not understand that all of his mini-clan had been listening in on the conversation, both audio wavelengths as well as olfactory. Nasrin would know he was coming. And why.

Humans were too parochial some days.

He followed Fortier out and across to where the man rapped on Nasrin's hatch, closed for the evening, though he could hear her moving around inside. Having tea without caffeine in it, with a touch of orange essence and a bit of beet sugar.

Not Haydar's drink, but a pleasant experience.

He stood to one side like a proper chaperone, grinning at the image, as Nasrin opened the hatch.

Mazhin and Humans were generally about the same height, with the same degree of sexual dimorphism. Males were around one hundred and eighty centimeters, with females generally closer to one hundred and seventy. Lead Trooper Chastain was tall. And muscular in ways that no Mazhin would ever approach. Male or female.

Nasrin looked Fortier in the mouth as she opened the hatch, head tilting back as her tentacles sniffed the air for cues.

She had been paying enough attention to air currents that her face was neutral now, rather than piqued at the disturbance.

"Good evening," Fortier said. "I hope I am not intruding, but if I am, I can come back tomorrow. I had a few questions, and Haydar suggested that you might be the expert to consult."

Her eyes slid over to his, which was mostly for the Human's perception, as she had been reading things with him standing so close.

"What is it, Captain?" she asked in a musical voice, standing her ground at the threshold.

"I am looking for information on five worlds located generally northwest of central *Danumash* on a galactic projection map," Fortier said. "Ohstad, Heire, Iethert, Masym, and Gorge. Are these places you might know?"

"Gorge is a vacation world," she said immediately. "Known for the great rift valley that gave the world its name when settlers arrived. Iethert is mostly farming and primary goods for export.

Masym has the most industry of the three, but I am not knowledgeable of Ohstad or Heire."

She paused and looked at both of them now, eyes going back and forth as her tentacles tasted the air.

"Are you intending to divert your current path that direction?" she pressed.

"Dan Chastain suggested that those five worlds were both beyond the reach of *Danumash* and possibly the sort of places where we might find leads to get us to the Mazhin eventually," Fortier replied. "We will need resupply at some point, as well as better repairs than this crew will be able to undertake with the tools at hand. I'd like to be someplace where *Danumash* can't recapture everybody, if possible. Thank you for your assistance. It has been most helpful. Later, I might bother you with more questions."

He bowed to her, then to Haydar, before turning and heading forward to where his cabin was.

Nasrin turned to look at him with all manner of questions, but Haydar had no answers, save for the obvious one.

"Yes," he said after the captain had gotten out of Human earshot. "I believe that the Human is serious about getting us home. And yes, I have hinted at how complicated that might be. Tomorrow, we shall gather and decide if we wish to return to *Batyr* instead and eventually find a way to acquire our own ship for the flight."

"Should we tell *Batyr*?" she asked. "Perhaps invite them on such a voyage of discovery?"

Haydar laughed.

"I don't think we're really ready to tell them that much," he said. "At least not yet."

# SIXTEEN

ULY WAS at breakfast with Dan when Koyla Roux and Marlowe Michaels appeared. Uly supposed that he should count himself lucky that Piruz Kossari hadn't joined them, as that would be absolute confirmation of some manner of conspiracy. Put those three in a room and they would immediately be up to no good.

Both men grabbed mugs of coffee and joined Dan and him at the table as Uly started shoveling things into his mouth as quickly as he could chew and swallow.

It might be an emergency. And it might give him time to stop and consider something before answering.

"Roshan had a thought," Marlowe said first.

Roshan Anyari. Genius two steps beyond being merely brilliant in the manner of Haydar Ramezani.

It already sounded dangerous.

Uly nodded for the man to keep talking while he scooped up another mouthful.

"We gotta rebuild a couple of relays where a frame pinched, so he thinks that he can improve the power throughput if we go ahead and move a few parts around," Marlowe continued.

"Upside, I think he's right. Downside, we're adrift without a warp bubble for a few days while we do that, on top of the week we've already been frittering away fixing things."

"Should you expand the access space for cable while you have a frame open?" Uly asked.

Both men got confused looks.

"Just before this, my damage control team wanted to open up a wall panel prior to any damage, because they knew that any hull flex was going to pinch a cable enough to probably short things," Uly explained. "This is not a warship, so an extra couple of centimeters of gap won't hurt. You can spray some sealant foam in there against a breach."

"Oh, you know that's probably a pretty good idea, too, sir," Marlowe nodded. "I'll ask Roshan and Haydar what they think. You okay if we rip engineering apart?"

"What does it gain me, Marlowe?" Uly asked.

"Maybe a better top speed in the warp, sir," Kolya spoke up now, but he tended to be quiet. "Much better stability while in warp, and less of a pulse-wake behind us for someone else to track. Right now, we're pretty much strobing a light at anyone coming up behind us with sensors on. Long term, maintenance will be a lot easier, because we're moving a secondary generator that was an after-factory modification and putting it in a place where it's not blocking three other things we need to get into occasionally. That's part of what failed originally. Cleaning in there took too much effort, so they were haphazard about it."

"How long?" Uly asked.

"Half-day to tear it out." Marlowe ticked things off on his fingers as he spoke. "Half-day to weld it all back in again after we move it. Day or two to tune things, depending on how well Roshan's calculations bear out. He thinks we gain ten percent top speed in a warp bubble, based on some things he did somewhere else that I don't ask about."

Uly nodded at that. Marlowe Michaels didn't care for authority. He only respected expertise. Which was why he was a Lead again for the third time. Insubordinate, but in a friendly way, as opposed to Eldridge's overt racism and specism.

And the former prisoners had allowed that they were all generally military prisoners of one sort or another, rather than civilians taken in pirate raids or something. Even the two women had been sailors in their own ways. They all had secrets, and Uly hadn't pried.

"Have you asked Butcher about supplies?" he asked.

"Have, sir," Kolya smiled. "Smaller crew so our consumption rate has gone down, even after losses from damage. We've got more than two months at full rations, which we can stretch if we need to."

"As long as you two understand that there's more to this ship than engines," Uly nodded. "Go ahead then and let whoever has the bridge right now know that I've approved it. We can spend two more days here without a problem."

The two men yipped happily and popped up, departing already deep in conversation. Dan was studying him.

"Command is frequently best when you have to pull back on the chains of an enthusiastic crew," he said, quoting his old Captain, Elouan Deniau, "rather than kick them in the asses to get them to move. I'm pleasantly surprised that Marlowe, Koyla, and Roshan are working well together, but it helps that I'm not micromanaging them. That seems to be Marlowe's general issue."

"What happens after we fix the engines?" Dan asked, face serene.

"Iethert or Gorge, I think," Uly replied. "The other two are blank slates, but a farming world should have food, and hopefully, metals we can trade for. A tourist destination might be willing to pay top dollar for the amazing wine cellar that Winter brought with him. We'll need cash to really repair things, and I'd like to do it quietly since we don't even have a Neutron Omnipulsar, to say nothing of a wavebolt of any size."

"And the Mazhin?" she asked.

Uly leaned back and grabbed his coffee, food mostly gone.

"I have no good answers, Dan," he replied, watching the woman's face.

Sure, she was his Second-in-Command, but didn't have the training for something grand like that. As she'd told him more than once, she was just a grunt with a big stick. Useful for keeping everyone in line, but he was the one that was going to have to plan. Lead.

Get everyone home.

"At least this crew isn't squabbling," she offered.

His confusion must have been obvious, because she smiled.

"I have an older sister and a younger one," she said. "Jocelyn is four years older. Gillian is fourteen months younger. We argued and fought all the time when we were kids. That's part of the reason I enlisted, to get out on my own. That and to not have kids."

"Not?" Uly asked.

He wasn't opposed to children. Just hadn't been in a position to find a future wife. Or have one issued by the Navy, as the old joke went.

"Both of them have much more traditionalist views on family and such than me," she grinned, white teeth starkly bright against her dark skin. "Nieces and nephews running around all the time. I'm still out having fun."

That much he could understand.

"What about being stuck with me for however long?" he asked, mostly on a lark, but her face turned serious.

"Honestly?" she asked, coldly sober suddenly.

Uly nodded, watching her eyes more carefully than he had.

"I think Captain Savatier set you up," she replied. "Not sure why, but he could have sent more people over. Or stayed long enough to realize the value of this cargo. Instead, he swapped you for Dupuis and left us."

"We were supposed to fail out here?" Uly asked. "I didn't know the captain worth a damn, but I also feel like I've been aboard *King Hewitt II* as long as I'd been on *Marshall Castillon*. And it will be longer shortly."

"One newly assigned officer?" she asked now. "One engineer? Three troopers? Usually, a hull this size would have required three times as many boarders. So yeah, I think you were set up. I'm a little pissed at it because I feel like I'm collateral damage here. Why does Savatier hate you, Uly?"

He looked around the dining hall past her shoulder, but they were alone right now. Vahid was back in his kitchen, probably reading recipe books for inspiration.

"Savatier? I have no idea," he admitted. "On the other hand, he knows more about me than you do, Dan."

She got perfectly still.

"What should I know about Ensign Ulysses Fortier, then?" she asked in precise, clipped tones. "Who were you before this?"

"Just another punk officer back aboard *Vanguard Lesauvage*," Uly said. "I think Savatier didn't like my family."

"Oh?"

"My father is an Assistant Deputy Secretary of the Industrial Protectors Party, Dan," Uly said quietly, wondering how well Vahid might hear things back there.

Or whatever the right verb was with those tentacles. They seemed to understand things they couldn't see.

Dan blinked hard, which was like the lights in her eyes going out for a moment before they came back.

"You're a *princeling*?" she asked quietly, using the common slang term to describe such young men and women.

The kind that lived on their connections rather than their accomplishments.

"I went to school to join the Navy," he reminded her. "Got commissioned. Got assigned a Forward Cruiser. Maybe my father's connections got me transferred when *Vanguard Lesauvage* went into drydock for a year, but I've worked for what I have."

He paused to sip some coffee. And to dial his voice and emotions back down a level.

Dan was an ally. He was doomed if she turned her back on him right now.

She nodded, watching him.

"So maybe Savatier abandoned us here," he continued. "Maybe he wanted me gone from his ship. I got the impression during that last meeting that he was never coming back for us, even if the rest of the convoy got away from him."

"They weren't going to get away," Dan said calmly.

"Exactly," Uly agreed. "We are on our own, but he was expecting us to find a crappy old tin can with boxes of stuff that could be stolen and sold off. Now I have—we have—a problem."

"The Mazhin," she nodded.

"I will not see them ever in *Danumash* hands again," Uly promised. "Period. But right now, that means that either we turn left and try to run for home, but we've got no guns at all on this ship, or we strike out into the unknown and hope that we can find someone who can help."

"You don't think Command would help?" she asked.

"Unknown species, at least as far as I remember," Uly replied. "Do they turn around and capture them all to milk them for information? If we didn't know about them, likely they come from the far side of the *Combined Crowns* somewhere."

"Planning to sail out there to find them?" she asked with a

grin on her face. The grin fell slowly. "You're going to, aren't you?"

"Thinking about it," Uly admitted. "That was why I let Kolya and Marlowe play. Better to do those things now. We need to run to someplace where we can get intelligence on our options, as well as food and resupply. But if we're supposed to be filed *Missing, Presumed Lost* by Savatier, I don't have to immediately return home. Better, if we're gone long enough and return as heroes, we might not have to return to his ship. You might want to, but I'd rather not. Especially if he's left me to die, and every day that passes, I grow stronger in that conviction."

"Go rogue?" she asked. "Pirate maybe?"

"What kinds of missions does *Marshall Castillon* normally undertake?" he asked, smiling like a crocodile. "Privateering?"

"That's right," she nodded. "But we're a Forward Cruiser. This ship isn't even armed anymore."

"No, but I expect that we'll have to fix that if we plan to cross *Danumash*," Uly replied. "Or skirt clear around the edges of their space and hope we don't run into anybody else like Savatier."

"Can we pull it off?" she asked, maybe a little breathless.

He nodded. Unarmed freighter. Middle of nowhere. Mixed crew where he had ten *Danumash* sailors, four medical staff, ten aliens, and the five people he had brought aboard including himself.

Trying to sail directly home was asking for someone to intercept him and recapture the ship. Nothing he could do to stop them, either, as it would likely be a *Danumash* ship that showed up, this far from home.

"I have no choice right now but to try, Dan," Uly said.

# IRON WASP

# SEVENTEEN

IT HAD BEEN A GRUELING two weeks, but they'd managed the impossible. Uly turned to look at Huff, Roscoe, and Blakeslee as *King Hewitt II* closed on the Iethert planetary system.

Normally, the four of them rotated on watches, with Wyndham spending most of his time training under Dan while the engineers aft were watching things like mother hens with new chicks hatching.

At present, Uly hadn't asked if any of the Mazhin sailors knew how to fly the ship, as that might be a step too far for Uly's newly recruited sailors. Whispers had suggested a few Human folks were merely accepting *fait accompli* for now, but they might get agitated at that point.

Best not to push. Eldridge was still a prisoner. Uly had spoken with the young man a few times, but he'd pretty much burned those bridges by putting the kid in the hospital. Not that Uly would have done anything different if given a second try.

Thorley Eldridge was the second son of a baron. Unlikely to inherit, unless something happened to his older brother. Like so many, he'd gone into the Navy as a way to make his fame and fortune that he might earn his own barony someday.

And the man was deeply, viscerally committed to his racism. As a result, he could rot in his cabin and spend his time with no more access to the systems than he needed for his computer training and those certifications that would eventually serve him well under another captain.

Not Ulysses Fortier, though.

"Huff, what's our status?" Uly asked.

Huff was still a Midshipman, so an officer who should get used to being in charge. Even if Roscoe liked to talk occasionally about *minding the young gentlemen*. Keeping them from pushing a wrong button or giving a dangerous order.

You needed reliable enlisted crew who could go gently about it without giving offense. Though Eldridge had apparently been known to use his size and age to bully Huff and Wyndham, as well as three others who hadn't survived: Atkins, Delaney, and Leonardson.

"We're about fifty minutes from dropping out of warp, sir," Huff replied crisply. "I'm planning on coming out clear at the edge of their control zone because we don't know what to expect."

"Very good, Huff," Uly nodded.

Positive reinforcement for dotting I's and crossing T's went a long way to making such things automatic later. Some *Danumash* captain would inherit Huff when this was all done, and Uly would like that man to have nice things to say about him and Dan on that day.

"Hey, that's weird." Blakeslee suddenly sat up straight and started typing on his keyboard.

Uly had just turned when the whole ship shuddered like an earthquake had passed down the length of the hull from bow to stern. Everyone was buckled in, but he worried that Kolya or somebody in engineering might have been injured, bouncing off something hard or sharp.

"Shit," Blakeslee yelled. "We've just been bounced out of warp again."

Uly turned to his screens as the tiny warp bubble that had been encapsulating the ship popped, dropping them back into real space. Usually that happened when two ships got too close together, like when the *Batyr* cruiser had ambushed a *Danumash* convoy. But the systems around him were still fragile.

"What happened?" he demanded.

"Sir, we're being hailed," Blakeslee said, his face white when Uly turned to look.

Uly found the channel and brought the signal up.

"Don't try to run," the voice said. "Don't try to fight, though I can tell just looking at you that you've gotten the sharp end of something already. Don't make me kill you in the process of capturing your ship, and everything will be just fine."

Uly had to flip a few switches to find the video component. It wasn't where all his training had automatically put his finger.

Then he found it and he gasped. As did the other three.

The person speaking looked male. At least the shadow of stubble on his chin and jaw gave that impression.

Humanoid, but most definitely alien.

It was the eyes that spoke loudest. Black orbs instead of the white Uly expected. Glowing red irises.

A pair of twelve-centimeter grayish horns emerged from both sides of his forehead, straight up and curled slightly back, almost like a goat. Long ears pointed out sideways.

Lean and hungry looking.

Uly had connected the video link, so the man was seeing an image of him as well.

"What the hell are you?" the stranger asked, speaking in a strange accent that went hard on consonants.

"Human," Uly replied carefully. "And you?"

"Ononguli, boy," the man said. "You going to be a problem that makes me blow you up and salvage your ruins?"

Uly considered his options. All bad. Nothing he could shoot back with right now. Nothing at all he could do if the man decided to poke holes in his hull and vent everything to space.

"Not a problem here," Uly decided. "What are your terms?"

Instead of answering, the man threw his head back and laughed.

# EIGHTEEN

DAN WANTED to do this armed. To fight to the death keeping the Ononguli raiders from boarding the ship.

Or had, right up until she saw how big that other ship was. Lightweight, but *King Hewitt II* was an unarmed freighter.

*Iron Wasp*, as it called itself, was at the heavy end for a corvette or maybe a light destroyer. Enough to blow *King Hewitt II* into scrap without even noticing.

That meant that she was down at the airlock with Uly and Haydar.

Waiting.

Huff apparently had the bridge, with instructions not to do anything, with Blakeslee and Roscoe present to enforce that.

Not that *King Hewitt II* could do much of anything.

Something metal banged on the outer side of the inner airlock hatch, letting everyone inside know that it was about to open.

That raiders were about to board. Dan doubted that they would be as polite and professional as Uly had been. Not the way *Iron Wasp*'s captain had laughed.

Reversing the original situation, she and Uly both had their lifesuits on, with helmets hung from their hips. Haydar had a spare suit that was a close enough fit but had whispered how dreadfully claustrophobic he would find it if he had to put the helmet on.

Human helmets assumed hair. And not much of it because folks wearing suits constantly tended to keep it buzzed short.

Not an option with sensory tentacles.

The hatch beeped loudly and opened.

Dan was unarmed. Not even her Icemace.

Nothing.

Uly was at the point of the triangle, and they watched six figures emerge, wearing a form of space armor only a little short of a full powersuit.

Every one of them was armed, with barrels pointed this direction.

"Which one's Fortier?" the leader demanded, hard, ugly tones emerging from speakers on both sides of his...*horns*.

"Here," Uly said without moving.

"Shit, you're a Mazhin," the man said in a surprised tone, looking at Haydar.

Like maybe his captain hadn't mentioned the variety of crew?

"That is correct," Haydar replied serenely.

Haydar knew about Ononguli but hadn't had much time to say anything to them other than another race of space-based warriors. Somewhere on the far side of Auga, whoever *they* were.

Dan had learned more about alien life in the last month than in the previous decade. Just how small was Human space compared to everything else?

"Total crew twenty-four?" the lead raider demanded.

"Twenty-nine," Uly corrected him. "Ten Mazhin. Fourteen Humans from *Danumash*. Five Humans from *Batyr*."

"Don't matter none to me, boy," the man growled heavily. "Yer all my prisoners now. Back up against the far wall."

Dan led them. She could hear the airlock cycling to bring in more pirates.

They weren't a formal navy operating under recognizable rules of war. Not like *Batyr* and *Danumash*. These six were all Ononguli, but no two were wearing anything remotely similar, beyond identical footwear that the captain probably bought by the pallet load.

Their feet looked Human enough.

"Conductor says to round everybody up and get them here for transfer to the ship," the leader said as six more came through.

"My engineer thinks that some of the reactors might destabilize if nobody is monitoring them," Uly replied. "Do you have any engineers here to take over the machine room?"

"You weren't listening to me, punk," the man said, taking several steps closer. He looked a little shorter than Uly and a lot heavier. "Conductor said round everybody up!"

"Fine," Uly said. "If the ship blows up afterwards, won't be my fault. Through here."

Dan managed to keep her mouth from falling open as Uly turned and started through the corridor to the cargo hold. The raiders had all depolarized their face shields, and a few of them weren't so lucky.

Still, eight of them fell in following her, with Haydar in the middle.

Through the hatch, the other nine Mazhin crew were gathered in a group, with the four medical staff Humans close by but not that close. Blair and Leith were closest to Piruz, with Spence and Atwater somewhat ostracized.

"The rest of my Mazhin crew," Uly gestured, but kept walking.

Dan heard mutterings over speakers not muted as the raiders followed, but nobody said anything coherent. The Mazhin just watched, tentacles almost like arrows pointed at the Ononguli.

"Two of you lot stay here and guard them," the lead raider snapped as the group walked.

Uly was stretching his legs. Haydar kept up. Dan kept up.

Inside engineering, nobody was looking up. Dan saw backs, butts, and tops of heads as Kolya and Marlowe had their three busy.

"Orders from the pirates to abandon your stations and become prisoners," Uly yelled loudly once all six had come through. "Form up here."

From his tone, he wasn't about to brook any nonsense from Marlowe. That one actually opened his mouth to say something, then stopped when several people pointed guns at him.

Being cranky was one thing. Getting yourself killed stupidly was a whole different matter. Marlowe subsided and set down a long metal tool, grabbing a rag to wipe his hands as he climbed down, with the kid Kit Simonson walking beside him.

All five formed up in front of Uly at something close enough to attention to not provoke most folks.

Uly turned to the man in charge.

"All yours," he announced.

The commander of *Iron Wasp*, who apparently had the title of Conductor, had ordered them off the ship as prisoners. And he had enough guns.

Uly had ordered her, Beranger, and Travers to specifically behave for now, understanding that they needed to survive today in order to escape tomorrow.

Assuming that was possible.

"You," the raider called, pointing at Cleve Toft, the other civilian engineering trainee. "He says it will blow up if you folk leave it alone. Well?"

"Probably not for a couple of hours," Cleve replied. "I assume we'll be on your ship by then, so it won't matter to me. Any of you boys know about double-sleeved coolant systems?"

Mutterings answered. Cleve shrugged.

"Boom," he offered. "Probably only annihilate the ship, though. Assuming we're far enough away or have shields up when the reactor goes supercritical."

More mutterings. Line troopers. Zero machine experience beyond guns and armor.

Dan knew the type. Had *been* the type for the longest time. Stretching herself beyond the basics had earned her that eighth stripe as a Lead Trooper.

Long pause in silence. For Dan, that usually meant an officer somewhere had chimed in on a private circuit with her as Lead and was updating orders.

Some things were universal.

"New orders from the boss," the man in charge snarled. "You lot back to work keeping it from blowing up. Next batch boarding will have some machinists. You'll show them what they need to do. Am I clear?"

Dan found it terribly informative that all five Humans turned to Uly now. Four of them had only known him less than a month, but had accepted him as their captain.

Humans were pack creatures, but that was fast by any standards Dan knew.

That the Mazhin had turned to Uly almost as fast as the Humans was also telling.

Uly nodded.

"As you were, then," he told them.

The five immediately turned and raced back to what they'd been doing. Dan had no clues, but Marlowe and Kolya had also gotten half-drunk a few nights ago and tried to explain it to her.

All she'd gotten out of it was an understanding of just how

good both men were at what they did. And how well the three trainees stacked up against folks back on *Marshall Castillon*. Even nineteen-year-old Kit Simonson was probably the equivalent of an E-5 Able Spacer to hear him engage his elders on technical minutiae. While drunk.

Uly turned to the leader. Dan did the same.

"Your orders?" he asked politely, putting the man on the spot while ceding all authority.

"Conductor wants to meet you three," he said, turning to one of his flunkies. "Haul them to the *Wasp* and watch 'em."

The trooper nodded and waved a hand. Uly led. Haydar was in the middle. Dan followed.

Things were out of their hands.

# NINETEEN

ULY WOULD HAVE LIKED to lean back and howl insults and abuse at the heavens. Anything.

He could not.

Commanding Officer. Set an example for everyone. Calm, cool, professional.

From being a privateer, he'd turned into a victim of piracy.

How, he wasn't sure, but the physics were sound. Every ship generating a warp-bubble left a wake through space when they passed. Another ship detecting it could turn to give chase. If they were fast enough, they could overtake you.

Once they got close enough, both bubbles destabilized and collapsed. Just like soapy ones.

Then you were back in real space, facing a ship ten times your size and armed, while he was aboard a broken freighter with no teeth.

No chance.

And no clue what Ononguli pirates were like. Even Haydar had been uncertain of their reception, save that Ononguli tended to be rare in Sector Seventeen, which was the Auga designation that included all of Human space as about five percent in one distant corner.

Ononguli were from Sector Twenty-One. A LONG ways away from here.

And pirates. Not wearing matching uniforms like he and Dan. Or the *Danumash* crew.

The Mazhin wore clothing that might be mistaken for a uniform, but that was the acquisition of cheap pants, shirts, and tunics in various earth tones ranging from sand through mustard to creamed coffee.

The Ononguli were walking rainbows when you got enough of them together, with no coherence to dress.

And, Uly suspected, no military regulations on their behavior.

He walked past the Mazhin again, nodding and keeping a polite smile on his face, though he suspected that those tentacles read him better. They seemed to.

He knew that Spence and Atwater hadn't realized it yet, but they saw the Mazhin as slaves, not people.

Through to the main airlock lounge, more troopers were flooding through, so Uly felt like a salmon swimming upstream.

Ononguli were Human sized and Human-scaled, near as he could tell. Heavier than Mazhin but all about the same height.

Grouchy pirates who still wore smiles because they'd captured new prey, but maybe less thrilled at finding it held a lot of former prisoners and not a lot of cargo.

Uly wondered if Ononguli could consume Human alcohols safely. Not a thought he'd ever had, but the Mazhin had given him a much better appreciation of variables in biochemistry recently.

Vahid—aka *The Spatula*—claimed that he could cook for any species in space.

The goon in charge of them right now said something over a

private comm channel because a corridor suddenly opened, and the four of them were in the airlock corridor.

*Iron Wasp* had docked with a good soft seal, because both ends of the airlock were open, with more goons on guard over on the far side.

Uly followed his minder onto the deck of an alien ship.

Taller ceilings. That was his first impression. Taller hatchways, but roughly the same width.

Horns.

Goat-like, from what he'd seen. Ten to maybe sixteen centimeters tall from both edges of the forehead. The top of the head was about the same as his, but they had horns above that.

Useful consideration.

The lighting was also a little dimmer than he was expecting. And a little more golden than the pure white he'd had on the last three vessels where he'd served.

All Human ships.

The trooper led them out of the staging area and to the right, then up two decks. Stairs like he was used to, if maybe a little flatter and wider than *Batyr* ships were built.

Eventually, he stopped at a hatch with an armed goon on either side and nodded. One of them opened it.

"In," the pirate said without much emotion.

Inside, Uly found the man he'd first spoken with, standing on the far side of the open room with several more goons guarding him. Art on the walls suggested a conference room of some sort, but no tables or chairs. Unless they had been removed or collapsed into the deck or walls.

Uly came to parade rest and studied the man.

Roughly the same height as the others, plus horns. Broader and heavier, but Uly knew he was personally skinny by Human standards. This man could have been a professional athlete back home.

Uly nodded to the man as Dan and Haydar came to rest beside him.

"So, Mazhin, these are your Human allies?" the man asked.

"Rescuers," Haydar replied. "Another group of Humans had captured my folk and were transporting us when Fortier's ship captured ours. They went after the rest of the convoy and left Fortier with us."

"A whole convoy of Human and Mazhin ships?" the man was suddenly quite interested, leaning forward. All his goons were paying closer attention.

"Indeed," Haydar agreed. "But the escorts were a series of Interceptors such as yours, and Fortier's vessel was a Fast Striker."

Fast Striker? Uly hadn't heard the term used that way before. *Marshall Castillon* was a Forward Cruiser on detached privateer duty. Did Striker mean cruiser to them? And Interceptor covered smaller escorts?

Uly filed it away.

"You, human, Fortier," the man said. "We don't have Humans where I'm from or where I'm going. What value do you bring? The Mazhin are a known quantity."

The way he said it suggested that Uly had only rescued the Mazhin slaves from Human masters, and now the Ononguli were going to hold the chains.

But he had ordered his crew to survive. Uly suspected that not even *Danumash* knew about things this far from home, so this knowledge needed to get back to High Command.

Somehow.

"I have five engineers of various skill levels," Uly said. "They are currently keeping the reactors stable. Four dedicated medical staff with expertise in Mazhin biology as well as Human. Four security troopers including Chastain here. And six sailors, including two officer trainees. I am the only officer aboard."

"Were," the man said.

"Sir?" Uly asked, careful to sound helpful and confused instead of challenging.

There was nothing he could do here.

"You were an officer, Fortier," the man said. "Now, you are a prisoner, just like the rest. We'll find a market for your kind. Mazhin and medical staff that understand them will bring more value. I suppose a Human medical expert will also be useful, but we've got enough veterinarians around if something goes wrong. What other cargo do you have?"

"The bow is mostly still hollow space where the bridge and forward gun were destroyed," Uly replied. "Remaining cargo is mostly high-end foodstuffs and alcohol consumed for pleasure for the previous crew of officers that were killed when the ship came under attack. Can Ononguli drink alcohols safely?"

"We can," he said. "Food?"

"One of the Mazhin, a gentleman named Vahid Siah, is a trained chef," Uly replied. "He can probably tell you the value and safety for your crew. The rest is mostly personal gear and ship's stores. The Mazhin prisoners were the valuable cargo."

The Ononguli Conductor studied Uly for a long moment.

"Why were you headed to Iethert?" he asked.

"We were on the far side of *Danumash* space," Uly said. "They are my enemies. We were headed there to resupply so we could sail long-ways around *Danumash* space to get home."

"With no cargo?"

"The alcohols would have value to Human worlds," Uly shrugged. "High-end stuff if you have the palate for it, but I don't feel the need. Trading that for food and parts would have gotten us a goodly distance, then we'd have made do."

"Interesting, Fortier," the man nodded. "No longer your problem, though. You're my prisoner."

"I don't even know your name, Conductor," Uly replied.

"You've never heard of the *Iron Wasp*?" he asked, incredulous.

Uly shook his head.

"Conductor Adrian Sobol," he said, executing a mock bow. "At your service. Now, take them away and dump them in with the other prisoners."

# TWENTY

HAYDAR WASN'T SURPRISED to find himself locked in an austere barracks chamber. Unpainted walls and floors. Triple bunks and empty foot lockers. Nothing else.

*Out of the frying pan and into the fire* was a phrase he'd picked up from Doctor Spence originally. It seemed to fit here.

He was surprised, however, at how few others were present. The Ononguli ship must have just started a raiding mission. Or gotten lost, considering where they found themselves today. Or had the pickings been so poor in Auga Space that they'd ended up this far from home trying to break even?

Haydar counted alien faces. Three of the gigantic Emro, all of whom appeared to be of the Moss School rather than the Sabre. Artists then, rather than warriors. The survivors of some previous incident? Too soon to tell.

Four Thogin, all of them shorter than the Humans and keeping warily to themselves. Haydar didn't know the humanoid species well enough to identify them by class or vocation by scent alone from here. He might have to actually break down and talk to them at some point. Or wait for Captain Fortier to do it. That Human would.

Add in ten Mazhin and nineteen Humans and the room was still sparsely inhabited.

Haydar did find it amusing that his Mazhin mini-clan didn't immediately laager up in a small species group in one corner of the room, as both the Thogin and Emro had done. Instead, they had taken up triple stacked bunks with most of the engineers together, Human and Mazhin, then he and Roshan, then Nasrin and Omid, then the remaining Human sailors with Fortier next to Omid on the bottom and Chastain on the bottom of the far edge, closest to the Emro.

Was the Convocation growing? Or had it added a second Clan with Fortier?

Interesting. And out of character for his kind, but Haydar was unfamiliar with any historical precedent for this type of social interaction. Anything might be possible once you broke down all cultural structures.

At least the Emro weren't Sabre. That would have been a potential problem, given that they would have greatly underestimated someone like Lead Trooper Chastain. Or foolishly assumed single combat by champions, as was their wont, when the Humans were more likely to swarm as an entire hive. Two and a quarter meters tall wasn't enough advantage against that many Human hands.

The Ononguli named Ruvim Boyko had been the leader of the first group to board *King Hewitt II*. He appeared now at the doorway, having removed his field armor but still armed.

And he had several troopers with him as he entered the room and stomped over to this end of the long chamber.

"Conductor wants to talk to the medical Humans and the Mazhin cook," he announced in a loud, angry voice.

Vahid stirred, though identifying him from his twin by sight alone might be impossible for most species. Other than the fact that Azad was bunking over with Piruz and Marlowe.

Blair Mitchell slid off his bunk, as did Doctor Atwater. Doctor Spence was slower to move, and Leith Masters seemed frozen in place. But that was common, as the Human tended to be rather inhibited when Spence and Atwater were around. The outcome of such verbal abuse suffered when the two were under the influence of various narcotics and soporifics as they ingested regularly to function.

"I said move it!" Boyko snapped, grabbing one of the bunks and rattling it.

"Hey, screw you, wog!" Eldridge snapped as he was dumped onto the floor with a thump.

"WHAT?" Boyko roared.

"You heard me!" Eldridge replied just as harshly, jumping angrily to his feet.

"Wait a minute!" Fortier said.

Haydar had never liked the cub but wasn't surprised when Fortier jumped up and tried to intervene.

Nor was he surprised when Boyko punched Fortier in the face first and drove him backwards over a bunk. Guns came up before the four security troopers, including Wyndham, could move.

Then Eldridge threw a punch.

Mazhin were not generally a violent species by nature. That required work on somebody else's part. As a result, he had not followed things well, other than Eldridge had apparently been stewing for a while over his treatment by Fortier.

He knocked Boyko on his ass, as Humans would have phrased it.

Boyko came up with a knife in his hand, driving it into Eldridge's stomach, then lifting the fool entirely off the ground.

Hopefully, the blow was as instantly lethal as it appeared, and

Midshipman Thorley Eldridge didn't suffer long. Because he was dead, and Haydar had no doubts that medical assistance would be denied to repair him.

The room had fallen silent. Boyko stood over the body with a bloody knife, breath rasping. Guns were up and shooters appeared ready to kill everyone in the room.

Captain Fortier staggered to his feet, but he was on the far side of the stack of bunks now. Probably for the best, as it served to keep him out of Boyko's reach.

"Anybody else feeling frisky?" Boyko snarled at the room in general.

Haydar moved enough to draw Boyko's eyes towards him, even as he turned to look to his left.

"Leith, Doctor Spence, I suggest you should rise now," Haydar said, smelling the jolt of fear that had frozen both Humans.

Chastain and her three underlings—did Wyndham count now? Probably—were coiled for battle, but Fortier was the one that had Haydar concerned.

No Human he had ever met had given off a smell like that, so Haydar had no emotional context into which to place it.

Looking at the man's eyes, however, Haydar could tentatively classify it as *xenocidal*. Not just enough to kill Boyko one of these days. No, Captain Fortier looked like a man happily willing to eliminate the Ononguli as a species from the anger etched into his face.

Rather an impossible task, but Haydar also wasn't willing to place wagers against the man right now.

Not with that look in his eyes.

And he hadn't liked Eldridge one bit before the snotty fool had gotten himself killed.

The tableau held, though. Leith Masters began to move. That

broke the stasis holding Doctor Spence as well. Both rose and joined the others.

"Get that and haul it to the infirmary," Boyko prodded Eldridge's lifeless corpse with a toe. "Just in case. And bring a bucket and a mop to clean up the blood."

His eyes never left Fortier's as he backed away, which at least meant that Boyko understood who the most dangerous person in the room was.

Around him, Haydar smelled a new scent from his kin. He hesitated to identify it but would not argue. In a way, it was a relief, because he'd never liked the responsibility.

The others had just formally decided to elect Ulysses Fortier as the new Speaker for their Convocation.

Haydar found himself agreeing with the assessment.

Humans had been welcomed into the greater galactic society.

May their various gods have mercy on their souls.

# TWENTY-ONE

ULY SAT on the bunk and methodically clenched and unclenched his fists. Haydar sat on one side of him. Dan on the other. Around him, his crew — all of his crew — watched, save for Marlowe, who was busy mopping. And refused to allow anyone else to help.

From the stories Uly had heard, Marlowe hadn't liked the boy any more than anybody else, but Eldridge didn't deserve to die.

Assuming there'd been a way to keep his mouth shut.

Water under the bridge now.

Still, he'd been Uly's responsibility, even as a prisoner and an asshole.

"You okay?" Dan asked in a quiet voice.

Uly turned to look at her.

"Pissed beyond all measure," he replied honestly. "Not many people I hate in this galaxy. That one will hang from a yardarm in low gravity before I'm done."

Haydar had the look of a man lost, but Uly figured somebody else could explain it to him.

"Later," Dan assured him. "All of us are in on that. What do we do now?"

Uly watched the two groups in the back corners of the long room.

Three green giants on one side. Assuming Human standards, one male and two female, but only because those two appeared to have breasts.

Across from them, four petite Humanoids that Uly would have classified as elves from some fantasy video game. Tall, pointed ears. Big eyes. Fine hair. Slight builds.

Tiny, if the bunks were the same scale. As much smaller than Humans as the green ones were bigger.

He turned to Haydar and nodded to the far end of the room.

"The larger ones are called Emro," Haydar nodded back. "Moss School, rather than Sabre, I think. Artists and scholars, rather than warriors."

Whatever that meant. Except that Dan seemed to recognize them as well and had mentioned the species as someone he might find out there when they went looking.

"The smaller are Thogin," Dan said, confirming that she knew more than he did.

Still, Dan had made it clear that she took orders from him. That he was in charge, as the only officer.

Even the two remaining Midshipmen were only *trainees* until they received their commissions.

"Prisoners like us?" he asked both of his…friends. Yes, friends, weird as that was.

"One would presume," Haydar nodded.

"How does the Convocation handle aliens?" Uly asked.

He wasn't prepared for the way all the man's tentacles came forward. Or those of other folks nearby.

Center of attention had never been so *visceral* before.

"We have taken a vote, Captain," Haydar began, but Uly interrupted him.

"Not Captain anymore," he corrected. "That was when we were aboard *King Hewitt II*. Now, I'm just Uly."

"Uly, then," Haydar said, tentacles still nearly torpid. "As I was saying, we have taken a vote, and my clan have decided to elect you as the Speaker for our Convocation, Uly. Assuming that we will remain prisoners together for some time yet."

That was an even bigger surprise than Boyko killing Eldridge, though Uly supposed something like that was bound to happen eventually with a person who couldn't keep his racism inside.

"What does that mean?" Uly asked.

"You remain our captain, Uly," Haydar said simply. "Until such time as we are separated again."

*Oh…*

Uly wasn't sure what to make of that. He had a different problem today, though.

"Those folks down there," he nodded again. "Are they likely to share a common language with Humans?"

"They are," Haydar said. "Standard is just that, spread across a considerable distance of stars and civilizations. Accents will vary, but the words are generally the same."

Uly wondered what that meant, when *Batyr* hardly knew any aliens. *Danumash* apparently knew them but didn't like them one bit.

Eldridge's behavior was the rule among the upper classes with his racism and specism, not the exception.

"How bad do I look?" he asked Dan.

"Half a raccoon," she chuckled. "I could punch you in the other eye to even things up if you'd like."

"Maybe another time," he said with a grin. "At least they know where I got it."

"Hopefully, they'll appreciate it as well," she said.

He rose now and began walking slowly towards the far end of the room. Dan and Haydar joined him, but everyone else remained where they were. Less threatening.

He aimed towards the Emro first, so it didn't look like he was trying to loom over the smaller Thogin.

Two females and one male. Probably. Assuming Human standards on absolutely no evidence at all.

Talking to the strangers was his responsibility. As Haydar had said, Uly was in command of three crews.

He stopped at a respectable distance and nodded his head to them, wondering if Human body language translated. The Mazhin might have learned from *Danumash*, after all.

"I am Ulysses Fortier," he introduced himself. "Human. Leader of this group of Humans and Mazhin and formerly captain of the ship that the Ononguli just took."

He paused there, watching.

Up close, they were even bigger than he'd initially guessed. All three were standing by the time he arrived. The smaller woman looked to be two and a quarter meters tall and maybe weighed double what Uly did. Broad shoulders that tapered down to a broad waist and wider hips.

Take a normal woman and stretch her sideways twice then vertically once.

And dip her in green paint.

The small female also gave off the impression of great age. Hopefully, wisdom as well, as she had a look of serenity about her, while the male and the bigger, younger female both looked awkward and nervous as they watched him.

"I am Suka Kuri," the eldest replied, looking down on him from her immense height with what he took to be a wry smile. "Exemplar of Arts of the Moss School."

"I am not familiar with Emro culture," Uly replied, gesturing.

"My friend Haydar Ramezani informs me that you would likely be friendly. This is Dan Chastain, my Second-in-Command."

"Hiko Seiichai, Seeker of the Arts," she indicated the male, standing with his hands behind his back and slowly rocking back and forth. "Yanouk Miyoshi, Student of the Arts."

The titles had no meaning to Uly beyond the words themselves, but they were obviously titles. Ranks, he supposed, from the relative ages of the three.

He nodded to all three of them.

"I am unfamiliar with the Ononguli as well," Uly continued. "What might you be able to tell me?"

"They are lost, Captain Fortier," the young woman said. Yanouk. Pretty, in a heavy, green kind of way. He supposed. Not a set of standards he'd ever expected to need.

"Lost?" Uly asked.

"Driven beyond Auga zones might be a better way to describe it," Suka explained. "They were on a raid deep into Auga territory for glory, and apparently something went wrong."

"That is a thing I can appreciate," Uly murmured.

"Oh?" the old woman asked.

"It is a long story," Uly nodded. "Perhaps it would be best if I only told it once?"

He turned to watch the four Thogin watching him. They gave the impression of birds alighted on a wire, though from here he couldn't tell if they were sparrows or hawks.

Uly took three steps that direction and stopped.

"Would you care to join us for a bit?" he asked the four.

Two Humans and a Mazhin were no threat to three Emro, regardless of age, though training would perhaps factor in, if they were primarily artisans.

He might look intimidating to four Thogin, though, all of them around a meter and a half tall, with the tallest being maybe one hundred and seventy centimeters tall. Still half a head shorter than Uly.

Plus, all four had slender builds like him. Skinny and muscular, instead of big and bulky like the Emro behind him.

The four sparrows considered his offer. Uly watched them all form into a compact circle from which whispers emerged. And an occasional head that popped up to look. Perhaps to make sure he wasn't sneaking up on them.

Smaller Humanoids probably had to have that as a survival mechanism.

Closer up, all had pale skin more reminiscent of *Danumash* than *Batyr*. Pinkish like a Human. Fine hair. Bright eyes in a variety of colors.

"What did you say you were?" the oldest asked now. His voice was surprisingly deep for such a slender body. Blond hair almost white, but not faded with age. Emerald eyes that seemed to glow.

"They are Humans," Haydar called across the space. "From a quiet, distant corner of Sector Seventeen. Most of them have hardly left their own zones to even know most other kinds even exist, let alone know them."

"Are they safe?" the Thogin asked.

"They can be terrible warriors when pressed," Haydar replied. "And skilled artisans. This group set out to be explorers, not expecting Ononguli."

"Nobody expects Ononguli." The man laughed. The other three joined him. "Best we expect is that they find some agricultural colony to sell us to, rather than sending us to the mines."

Uly waited patiently as the group came to a consensus.

"Okay, Human named Ulysses Fortier," he said as they took a bold step this direction. "Tell us your story."

# TWENTY-TWO

DAN STOOD off to one side as Uly finished his tale. The four Thogin introduced themselves as Ethir, Waltin, Ralphye, and Hobse once they'd decided to join the group. They remained skittish around the three Emro. And the Humans.

Dan wasn't worried about the green folk. None of them moved with any sort of dance or close combat training that she could detect. The Thogin were small and fast. She had the impression that they could move like rabbits when they wanted.

"You mean that you didn't even like the one that was killed?" Ethir asked when Uly was done speaking.

"That is correct," Uly nodded. "He would have been even more racist and specist against your two groups, though I suppose that Suka's size would have tempered his behavior."

That got the old woman to laugh uproariously, slapping her thigh with delight. Exemplar of Arts, as the woman had explained, was the highest rank a scholar could achieve, granted by acclaim only, when most only rose as far as Adepts. A living legend among her kind, so Dan was suitably impressed.

"Why did you put up with him?" Ethir asked when folks settled again.

"He was part of the crew I inherited," Uly said soberly. "I didn't have to like him. I was responsible for him. I am responsible for his death and will avenge it. The rules our kind fight under are well understood and honored."

"Good luck extending that to the Ononguli," Ethir laughed sourly. "They only know power. If you have more, they bend the knee. If not, you do."

"We'll see about that," Uly said, causing many heads to snap around suddenly in surprise.

He smiled.

"They don't know Humans at all, I suspect," Uly continued with a terrible smile that warmed Dan's soul.

That was a promise of heads on stakes as a warning to future generations. Dan's kind of thing, though she had to stop and remind herself that she wasn't just part of a Human crew now. From the way the Emro and Thogin were acting, Dan suspected that Uly was building out an even larger crew without realizing it.

He could be quite charming when he needed to, but utterly compelling when he locked in on something and got to work. She'd seen that. Found it quite impressive for an officer.

Looking back all of a single month at *Marshall Castillon*, she could see why Captain Savatier didn't like Uly. He would have eventually made all the other officers on the ship look slack by comparison.

And while Dan wouldn't have minded remaining with the big ship, this had certainly been an adventure, though the thought of being sold into slavery filled her with a rage almost as terrible as Uly's smile promised.

A sound at the far end of the room was the hatch opening.

That one Ononguli punk didn't enter the space. Just shoved

Blair and then Spence in so hard that they stumbled and fell. The other three were prodded in at gun point, then the door closed again.

Uly was already moving. Dan was in his wake. Interestingly, Haydar was as well.

The rest of the crew had sprung into action and gotten there first, but nobody appeared injured.

Uly centered on Blair, so Dan joined him.

"Status?" Uly asked.

"They asked us a lot of questions," Blair said. "Mostly generic medical stuff. A lot like my boards to get certified initially, so I assume the guy across the table was a doctor of some sort. Then we got deep into treating Mazhin and Human ailments and illnesses. I got the impression that those folks were thrilled to have competent med staff, to deal with new aliens they didn't know."

Dan studied Spence and Atwater. Both showed signs of shock. Masters was his usual, quiet self, but she'd come to understand that part of that was being around the two doctors. When you got him alone, Leith turned into a normal person.

Dan turned to the crew hovering nearby.

"Marlowe, see Doctors Spence and Atwater to bed so they can relax," she ordered, mostly to give them something to do. "Blair and Leith, we have some folks for you to meet. If the ship is short of med staff, you might be called upon."

Dan turned and brought them back down and introduced them to Suka and her charges, plus Ethir and his cousins. She thought they were all cousins, though it was hard to trace when they started rattling off those connections.

Uly and Haydar had come as well. Vahid had joined.

"How's their cook?" Uly was asking.

"Probably burns water," Vahid laughed. "If I wasn't a prisoner who they feared might poison them over dinner, I got the impression that they might have hired me on the spot. I bet they're tired of canned stew about now."

Dan shared a laugh with the others. There was Navy cooking, then there was the art that *The Spatula* brought when he was in the kitchen.

"Suka, Ethir, this is Leith Masters," Uly introduced them as the group formed again. "And Blair Mitchell. Both are trained medical staff with xenobiology experience. If you get hurt or sick, they would be the ones likely to get you taken care of."

Both groups studied the newcomers closely.

Dan stood back and listened as the two got introduced to everyone and started asking medical questions. Baselining potential clients against future need. Possibly adding two more species to the collection the Uly had already formed, considering the way the former crew of *King Hewitt II* had taken to him.

Food interrupted the conversation. A section of wall slid up, revealing several tables in a small alcove. The three Emro moved immediately.

"They are on a timer," Yanouk explained as she gestured everyone into motion.

The Thogin moved faster, in spite of shorter legs. Something about churning to stay ahead of the tall folk.

The Humans were standing close, but not in the way. She and Uly got there with Suka.

Heated troughs of what smelled like canned stew, just as Vahid had described it. Cheap protein and fluid to keep prisoners healthy enough. Smells suggested someone had raided *King Hewitt II* for supplies that could feed the Humans.

Not enough for the group to eat their fill, but Dan supposed that you wanted those same prisoners weak and hungry. Just not so much so that they were too sick to work.

Or to bring a good value when you went to sell them.

For a moment, everything turned red in front of her. Maybe

she growled, because Uly turned and everybody else stepped back. Including the Emro who outweighed her considerably.

"You okay?" he asked.

"Later," she managed to reply through gritted teeth. "We're on the clock here."

"Agreed," he said, raising his voice. "Emro and Thogin first. Then crew. Everybody take a small bowl first time to make sure it stretches far enough. We'll come back for seconds once everybody goes through the line once."

The two other groups looked surprised but didn't argue. Probably expected the Humans to issue orders, since they were the single biggest species group. And the vast majority when you threw in the Mazhin allies.

Folks queued up and got quickly through the line. The Emro had taken larger bowls, but that was to be expected. Dan went last to make sure everyone ate, sending Uly through first over his objections.

He needed to be sharpest of the group if they were going to find a way out of this mess.

There was so much to learn here, in spite of being prisoners locked in a barracks. Or maybe because of it. At least there were others they could ask.

Nobody knew what to expect next.

# TWENTY-THREE

ULY WAITED until everyone was settled. Personal gear had been taken before, leaving everyone with the clothes on their backs and not much else. Somehow, he wasn't surprised when Marlowe produced a pack of playing cards from somewhere and started to teach Suka poker.

He nodded to Dan to join him and moved to the open corner of the room. It was closest to the one outside hatch, but farthest from the small bathroom Ethir had shown everyone. Better, it was as far away as he could get from the crew to talk to Dan.

Even Haydar has just glanced up when he walked up to get her, nodding to himself.

One of these days, Uly needed to take the man aside and learn more about those sensory tentacles, but it hadn't been important enough prior to this, and he assumed that guards were monitoring the room, so now wasn't the time, if the Ononguli didn't already know.

He moved to a bottom bunk and sat, patting the space beside him for her.

Sheridan Chastain moved like a tiger who woke up on the wrong side of the palace this morning, all grumps and growls.

"Talk to me," he more or less ordered. "Up until dinner you were holding it together well enough. Then something happened and I thought there would be dead bodies. What happened?"

"I got angry," she managed in a quiet voice.

"Yeah, gathered that," Uly said simply with a quick smile.

He was the only commissioned officer here. The person in charge, as it were, even if Dan had several more years in uniform than he did. He was the one making decisions, and that had extended to include the Mazhin as well, apparently.

"The Mazhin were slaves when we met them," Dan growled, back to that prowling tiger mode.

Uly nodded. Right up until he was in charge of *King Hewitt II*.

"They worked their asses off to help us escape *Danumash*," Dan continued. "Now they're back in the same situation, and we're with them."

"For now," Uly interjected. "Only for now."

"You have a plan?" She perked right up.

"I have a mission," he corrected. "Get us all home safe. Nothing in the last twenty-four hours has changed that. If that means Emro and Thogin as well, then that's just too bad for the Ononguli."

"They're pirates, Uly," Dan said, almost pleading with him now.

"And according to Haydar and the others, they must be a long ways from home," he nodded. "Maybe a little desperate that they've been unsuccessful so far in whatever it was they were doing. Small ships captured that netted Ethir and his cousins, as well as Suka and her two students. Nothing big. Then they grabbed us and all they got were bodies that need to be fed and cared for."

"And that's when I lost it," she nodded. "Not enough food to keep everybody full and healthy. Rations will be cut back to just enough to keep us alive, since they have medics that can treat things."

"Yeah, but I worry more about diseases that can jump hosts," Uly offered.

"We should be pretty good there," Dan said, sitting more upright as he watched.

"Why?"

"Convergent evolution tends to recreate big structures like the basic Humanoid shape, but we're all still based on different chemistry," she replied. "At least that was how it was explained to me at the time. Our DNA is based on four letters out of potentially dozens, so we can get things that hop back and forth to chickens or something, but an Emro disease will have a hard time even surviving in a Human host. Again, doctors and officers on *Marshall Castillon* told us grunts that. Biggest risk now is us trying to eat Ononguli food. Some of their stuff might have trace elements that are dangerous at some level."

Uly nodded. Sounded perfectly plausible, and that was as good as he figured he was going to get right now.

"Do me a huge favor?" he asked her as they watched each other think.

"You're an officer, Uly," she said, cocking her head. "You can order me to do things."

"Sure, but I need this to be on you, rather than something I demanded," Uly said. "These people are killers. Eldridge didn't deserve that, even if he was a spoiled brat. Boyko will kill any of us that give him a reason and not give it a second thought."

"Agreed."

"I need you to stay alive," Uly commanded, staring into her eyes and studying her soul as he spoke. "I need you reminding me that you know far more about these sorts of situations than I do. That you have constructive ideas I should listen to. That you are my Second-in-Command here, regardless of how weird things have gotten or might get later. I'm not sure I can do this without you, okay?"

Her eyes got big for a moment and then she grinned.

"I doubt that very much," she said. "You got us this far on your own."

"Never on my own," he replied sharply. "You were there from the start. As were many of the others. It's been a team effort, and it will remain so."

"You really think we can get out of this?"

"These assholes control my body, Dan," he said. "Not my mind. At some point, somebody will make a mistake. Don't know when, where, or how, but we'll be in a position to escape. Maybe exact a little revenge for Eldridge and everything else, but I'm not about to sacrifice any or all of us just to put a beam in Boyko's brain. We need to see everyone home. That includes abject cowardice rather than staying to fight, even a battle we might win. Paste that on your heads-up-display. Survival first. If we're alive, we haven't lost. Can't lose, because one of those dumbasses will stop paying attention at some point. Nature of the beast. Plus, as you noted, these are pirates, rather than dedicated sailors. Their discipline can't possibly be as good as ours. Wait for your chance. Take it. Exploit it ruthlessly. And leave me behind if you can get everyone else home. Am I understood?"

"No," she stated flatly. "I'm not leaving you here either. We all go home or none of us."

"Dan, the Fleet Marshals and Party Secretaries need to know what's going on out here."

"They already do, Uly," her voice dropped. "Forward Cruisers and Privateers are a whole different segment of the fleet, and we don't talk much to the folks back home. I've never met an Ononguli before yesterday, but I'd heard of them. Mazhin were new for me, but I understand now that they are galactic nomads, so they might not live on any of the worlds we know."

"And the Auga?" Uly asked.

"Big, bad, evil overlords," she grinned. "Way the hell over there, commanding an empire with thousands of planets across a dozen enormous sectors. All of Human explored space, if I remember an old briefing, covers less than ten percent of one Auga Imperial Sector, and *Batyr* is on the far edge of one, with *Danumash* closer but not by much."

"Should we go there at some point?" Uly asked.

"Everyone is supposed to be afraid of them, Uly," Dan replied. "They plan to conquer all of known space eventually, but aren't in a hurry. Sometimes, as the stories go, whole star nations will voluntarily join to gain access to advanced tech and trade, but they've never come our direction very far."

"And the Ononguli are from beyond that?" he asked.

"Somewhere, but I've never seen a map with any accuracy," she shook her head.

"Which means that our pirates are a long ways from home," Uly nodded. "Maybe they'll consider this the best luck they'll get and start sailing home. Maybe they'll decide that they can go after Human shipping and steal things. The point is, they will make mistakes at some point. Don't fall for a trick, but be ready to exploit it and escape. All of us escape. If we can steal a ship or even take over this one, we're in a better position."

"Uly, this ship has a crew of hundreds," she said. "Heavy frigate or light destroyer. There are only two dozen of us. How would you take it over?"

He shrugged this time.

"Don't know," he said. "Don't need to. Need you alive and thinking. Planning. Need the others watching. We've already recruited the Mazhin folks. Maybe we add Emro and Thogin as well. Maybe we build an entire army."

"We?"

"We," he assured her. "I can't do this without you, Dan. Remember that."

She nodded and kind of sat there processing.

Uly put a friendly hand on her shoulder and rose, leaving her there to return to the rest of the team.

Haydar watched him approach with a smile in his eyes and maybe the set of his tentacles. Uly had spent enough time around the man to start picking up body language.

Tentacle language. Something.

"That, Captain," Haydar murmured as Uly took a spot next to him, "was why we elected you Speaker of this Convocation."

He started to say more when the outer hatch opened and a group of armed killers entered, Boyko in the lead. They stomped over and Boyko pointed an ugly finger at Haydar.

"You. Mazhin," he growled. "You in charge of that lot?"

Haydar started to deny it, but Uly interrupted.

"He is Speaker for the Mazhin, yes," Uly said, turning to look at Haydar and hoping that the man's senses were that good.

*Lie. Survive. Just as Dan must, you must as well.*

Haydar nodded discreetly and turned to Boyko.

"I am," he said.

"Conductor wants to talk to you," Boyko growled. "Just you. Move along."

Uly watched them go and hoped that everything he'd just told Dan had been evident to Haydar.

He needed everyone, but those two most of all.

# TWENTY-FOUR

HAYDAR DID NOT BELIEVE that he rated seven armed gunmen to escort him through the unfamiliar confines of an Ononguli warship. Nor was he particularly honored to be so treated. He was a scientist. A researcher. A nerd.

Not a killer like Uly or Dan.

The Ononguli Boyko led him to an office and entered with one other guard, the remainder peeling off to do whatever pirates did when they were off screen in a vid. Not Haydar's entertainment genre of choice.

Conductor Sobol sat behind a desk waiting. Like the rest of the pirates, he wore a variety of colors and patterns in various shades of gray, all washed in the same load of laundry with an unscented soap and no vinegar.

Ononguli were generally the same mass as Humans, so much broader and heavier than Mazhin though about the same size. Uly looked like Mazhin below the neck, with only the skin color difference to tell them apart.

"Sit," Sobol ordered, pointing at a chair as Haydar stood patiently.

He complied.

Boyko and a second guard watched.

"Tell me about Humans," Sobol ordered.

Haydar considered his potential responses. He had been following the emotional turmoil of Dan Chastain, watching it calm as Uly spoke. And he understood that Uly would not be dissuaded from his belief that he could win.

"Stubborn," Haydar replied in a vague manner that obscured as much as it explained. "Somewhat primitive still, having only extended out into the galaxy in the last few centuries."

"Where is their homeworld?" Sobol demanded.

"I don't know," Haydar replied honestly. "The group you took originally represented two political entities. One is called *Batyr*, and it is the further of the two. The nearer is called *Danumash*. Both originate in the distant swamps of Sector Seventeen, in places not particularly well surveyed previously. How did you come to be on this side of Auga?"

Sobol scowled at the man, grinding his teeth. Then chose to ignore the question.

"What values do the Humans bring?" he pressed.

"Several are mechanics of skill," Haydar replied. "Competent enough to work with my folk repairing the damaged ship. The medical staff you have interviewed already. They were hired to maintain the Mazhin prisoners. The remainder are sailors of various skills, mostly trainees because the shot that damaged the ship went directly through the bridge and killed everyone there in an instant."

Haydar noted the twitch that passed through Sobol as well as the unnamed crew member. Boyko seemed immune to fear.

Haydar began to sniff at the killer. Perhaps he was one of those folks who were mentally broken enough to kill without conscience, but still whole enough to function otherwise? Such would drift into this kind of role if they could.

"Fortier captured the ship?" Sobol demanded.

"He took possession for his own crew, but the man is a low-ranking officer who was not well-favored by his own Conductor," Haydar replied.

It wasn't a lie. It simply left out important parts that Sobol wasn't informed enough to ask.

Mazhin found it almost impossible to lie, since sensory tentacles could detect almost any falsehood. At the same time, he had spent enough years in a *Danumash* prison to learn.

A Mazhin's reputation for probity helped since strangers would not expect it.

"A peon?" Sobol asked, relaxing some.

"Roughly," Haydar agreed. "His ship had ambushed the convoy that my ship was part of. In damaging my ship so severely, their Conductor had to leave a small crew behind while he went after more interesting prey."

"How big was Fortier's ship?" Sobol demanded, quite interested now. All three foes were leaning in.

"I never saw it," Haydar said. "From the bits I have overheard, it should have been a large, fast Striker. The convoy's escorts would have been smaller Interceptors like *Iron Wasp*. *King Hewitt II* would be classified under Imperial standards as a large Seeker, since it normally ran with such a small crew when only configured for cargo duties."

"A Striker?" Sobol confirmed, disappointed.

But then, a vessel of that size was as much more dangerous than *Iron Wasp* as this ship was over *King Hewitt II*.

"They called it a Forward Cruiser," Haydar nodded. "It was configured for privateering missions deep in enemy space. A pirate, if you will, but flying a military flag and operating as part of such."

Sobol muttered a profanity under his breath.

"Is it worth raiding Human worlds?" he demanded.

Again, a reputation for honesty was a two-edged blade. Haydar had been a prisoner and slave of *Danumash* for four years. And a friend and companion to *Batyr* for a month. Now, one of the Ononguli tribes was engaged in one of those raids that the history books might record if he was successful.

Assuming it worked.

"They might be," Haydar offered. "But they are also even more militant than Auga, maintaining vast fleets of warships for their private species war. I doubt that *Iron Wasp* is heavy enough to engage with some of their so-called cruisers and win. Perhaps even survive."

Because if Sobol tried and failed, it would be against a *Danumash* world, and Haydar and his people would be right back where they started a month ago.

"Why were you headed to Iethert?" Sobol changed directions.

"Fortier needed foodstuffs and repair supplies," Haydar replied with a clean conscience. "Away from *Danumash* worlds. If I understood correctly, his plan was to then skirt *Danumash*'s border counterclockwise to get to his own worlds."

Haydar could see Conductor Sobol doing the cartography in his head. Did he wish to go even farther from home? Against a foe potentially more dangerous kilogram for kilogram than the Auga? The Empire was vast and powerful, but did not maintain the same militancy Haydar had seen from Uly and Dan or even the dead officers of *King Hewitt II*.

Auga would simply send a fleet to bombard your world if you provoked them sufficiently. They didn't chase down pirates all that often.

"Is there anything out there worth taking?" Sobol mused.

Haydar took that as an opportunity to respond.

"Beyond *Batyr*, as I understand it, there is not much," he

commented. "Fortier has mentioned that there are few other star-faring nations as you get to the edges of the galactic disk. Presumably, his kind haven't yet crossed over to the next arm to investigate more fully."

Haydar wasn't particularly interested in doing so himself, as that would get him even farther from home and potential allies.

"Sector Forty-Eight?" Sobol queried.

Haydar had to stop and calculate that. The Auga had created their empire in Sector One, then mapped the next ring out and conquered it before extending the map to include most of this half of the galaxy. Many of those sectors were only theoretical, though, as nobody Haydar knew had gone there to look. Even Seventeen wasn't close to the Imperial Core.

"Possibly," Haydar replied. "Without a map in front of me, it might also be Forty-Seven or Thirty-One."

"Are the Humans worth the effort?" Sobol demanded now.

"Hard working. Stubborn. Educated." Haydar nodded. "Far more advanced than some of the species you might encounter. You should be able to get good value for them in many places."

He had to maintain openness in his stance. Uly would not appreciate it if his crew was sold off as workers to mines or latifundia, but Sobol might decide to cut his losses and kill them all instead.

That would never do.

Haydar had found a family. He would rather they survive, as Uly had instructed Dan, that they might escape later and somehow return home.

Sobol grunted and nodded to Boyko.

"Back to the barracks with him then."

Haydar rose and nodded politely. Sins of omission were not necessarily lies if Conductor Sobol didn't ask *his captured prisoner* the right questions in the first place.

He would return to Uly and the others and provide his Speaker the extra tools that man needed to escape and get them all home safely.

Somehow.

# TWENTY-FIVE

DAN and her three had moved several stacks of bunk beds by detaching them from the floor and sliding them close enough together to almost form a large single bed, though nobody was sleeping there for now. She wanted the space to practice. Specifically, the form of Tai Chi that the Navy had taught her.

After a month, Wyndham had learned the basics, but Dan was still refining her own understanding of the movements ten years later. She supposed that she qualified as enough of an expert by now, though her teacher had been doing it for thirty years before Dan had come along.

Stance. Breathing. Motion so slow that learning stillness was the hardest part. The form had eighty-two patterns and could be done in as fast as about five minutes.

Today, Dan was leading Wyndham, Beranger, and Travers at a rate that would take at least eighteen minutes to complete. Slow. Smooth.

Then they would break out and each spot the other for points, with her working with the youngster. He didn't have the grace of the other two men, given his awkward age and still growing, but his bulk suggested that he would be a big, dangerous man when he was Uly's age.

And he had joined her pack, having lost his own. She would make him into one of them, even though he might return to the *Danumash* fleet at some point.

Whoever got him as a Knight wouldn't be able to fault her for the time spent.

About three-quarters of the way through the form, Nasrin Monfared drifted closer, watching Dan specifically, though her tentacles seemed to take in all four of them at once in that way they did.

Dan concentrated on placing each pattern correctly and flowing smoothly into the next. None of the Mazhin had spent time around Dan and the security folks while on *King Hewitt II*, but everyone had also been busy with some tasks.

Nasrin and Omid had largely kept to themselves during the days, other than to help Vahid cook for the combined crews. In the evenings, they had sung, performed on musical instruments, and told stories to entertain.

And been quite good at it.

Dan finished the form and came to rest. Travers was on today, with Beranger a little off in his timing, and Wyndham still occasionally forgetting the next pattern and having to catch up. Or losing his balance on turns or steps.

Dan stared at the woman. Not hostile. Inquisitive. And she'd come to understand how much non-verbal communication the Mazhin engaged in.

"Dance?" Nasrin asked, tentacles swirling even slower than Dan had been moving.

"Of a sort," Dan nodded, standing now.

Nasrin was a little tall for a Human woman. Or Mazhin. Dan still had a half a head in height and ten kilos of weight on the woman.

"Of a sort." Nasrin smiled and nodded. "We have something similar, but we begin from a different emotional position."

"Oh?" Dan asked, watching the woman.

Nasrin took a step that brought her feet together and rested, flexing her knees side to side and wiggling her hips and hands. Similar to what Dan did to make sure everything was loose.

"You assume someone is going to grab you by one or both wrists," Nasrin stated in a scholarly tone. "Thus, you open by lifting both arms rigid to force your attacker to let go or lose their balance. This speaks to me of an argument in a crowded courtyard."

Dan considered the opening motions of the form. The way she had been taught, each of the first several patterns introduced a circular motion, in X, Y, or Z axis, to prepare a student by giving them tools to build upon later in the form.

And yes, you leaned forward and lifted both arms rigid before settling. It would drive someone back from grabbing your wrists or just being up in your face.

Dan nodded at the woman.

"We assume that the argument has already progressed to violence." Nasrin grinned. "Humans, as I understand you, are mostly right-handed, but you are not?"

"That is correct," Dan agreed. "The numbers are traditionally about ten percent, but because left-handedness is often associated with artistic ability, some fields of labor are over-represented."

"Mazhin are right-handed as well," Nasrin nodded back. "Thus, the first punch is often a right hand at shoulder height, striking for the face. At least with someone not trained in formal close combat skills."

Dan watched her shift her left foot out and settle. Right hand came across her stomach like a flat bar, almost but not quite touching the left elbow as the left arm went out about the level of the woman's breast.

Nasrin's upper body twisted, pulling her right shoulder and hip back as her right elbow came up and both hands turned over.

Exactly how you would grab an arm coming at your face.

Nasrin pivoted on her left foot by drawing the right back and across until she came to rest facing ninety degrees to her right from the initial stance. If she held a fist, your own inertia would be pulling you past her.

Right hand went down to her waist, while Nasrin's left hand came across to the right shoulder. Then she took a step forward, leading with a good shoulder bump that she'd anchored by holding your right hand in place.

An effective opening against a sudden fist. Withdraw and defend. Knock your opponent off balance or to the ground with minimal violence or effort.

The next move brought to mind a second attacker. Perhaps a friend a bit slow on the uptake. Head turns left and left arm sweeps out at shoulder level to block or clear a hand, followed by the right hand sweeping, trailing by ninety degrees, to grapple or grip.

Nasrin's feet pivoted again, the left coming all the way around to reverse her to her original left. Again, a sudden throw that would clear a foe or knock him down.

Dan liked it already, and no punches had been thrown.

Until now.

Nasrin, facing left, released the second foe and assumed someone directly behind her, turning to drive her left elbow back into someone's stomach as they tried to wrap arms around her from behind. Nasrin was now facing backwards from her start, so she had already engaged all four walls with only four economical movements.

Nasrin proceeded to turn again ninety degrees with the other elbow, then a reach to grab and pull someone off-balance and shove them away again.

Dan watched, rapt. There were only so many ways for a Humanoid to move while upright. All Human martial arts understood this and merely rearranged patterns or motion, giving them different names and emphasizing various elements.

This Mazhin form did not strike to kill much. Most of the motions seemed to be stepping out of the way of an attack and causing the attacker to stagger past, often with a jolt from the side that would leave them on the ground afterwards.

No follow-ups, though. Nothing indicating a kick to someone down.

In that, Dan recognized a similar art to her own, where the first option was always to knock someone down long enough that you could run away. Or throw them in front of a moving vehicle or an unmoving wall to let it do all the work.

Nasrin continued for a time before finally returning to her exact starting point, facing as she had. Dan was impressed, because her own form worked on forty-five-degree facings, the Combat Compass Rose someone had called it once. Nasrin's form worked on thirty-degree increments, so she had twelve directions she might turn and engage at a given motion.

"Dance," Nasrin grinned when she was done.

Dan shared it, feeling like an evil imp when she did.

"Dance," she agreed. "Assuming we have a few days, I would like to trade you forms. I can only imagine Beranger or Wyndham here adding all that motion to their strength."

"I have wondered the same," Nasrin said, stepping closer.

The five of them ended up in something of a huddle.

Dan wasn't surprised that the others had taken to watching the display. Nasrin moved with an amazing grace and the presence of a professional entertainer. Dan was surprised when both Uly and the Emro woman Yanouk walked over, though the rest of the room merely watched with interest.

"Dance?" Yanouk asked, deeply confused.

Nasrin turned to the student and bowed deeply, which surprised Dan.

"Dance as the Sabre school might understand it," Nasrin said, rising again. "Rather than the Moss."

"Oh," Yanouk exclaimed, seeing the play on words finally.

The Dance of Death. Of Mayhem.

"But the Moss could learn such a thing?" Yanouk asked innocently.

"Are we being observed?" Dan asked sharply in a quiet voice.

Suka stood and moved closer now as everyone fell silent, watching.

"I do not believe they maintain constant visual surveillance," the older woman said to the group. "Nor do they go back to review video, if they even bothered to record it. Instead, there are audio channels listening for signs of distress if someone cares. Hiko grew sick from food poisoning at one point, and I had to bang on the hatch to get someone's attention to provide him medical assistance. I think that we are largely a livestock cargo that needs to be fed occasionally. Or were when we were seven. I cannot speak to what Sobol might do now that we are so much larger."

Dan turned to Uly. Ralphye, the tallest of the Thogin at almost exactly the same height as Nasrin, had joined them, so all four species were present, with everyone else watching in rapt silence.

"Small group classes only," Uly said now.

Dan could see the man diving deep into tactical and strategic concerns.

"Nasrin, if you would teach Dan and Beranger first, they can start teaching the form to others while you watch from a distance and offer commentary. I don't want them to suddenly open that hatch and discover a small army drilling on a parade group floor. They might draw the right conclusions and be a bit upset."

Dan joined the others laughing. Uly might be young, but he had been trained to command, and had a natural charm for it. Plus, he'd been raised in a political family, so he understood the structures of power as well. The Mazhin had understood that and hitched their wagon to his. Suka and the Thogin seemed to be coming around to that same position as well.

"Nasrin, does Omid know the form well enough to teach it?" Uly continued. "Or any others on your team?"

"They do not, Speaker," Nasrin replied. "Some have certainly watched me practice, but none have expressed an interest in learning. Even I am not a warrior. This is an ancient form of dance that students are taught for performance's sake. I understand the combat elements of the dance but have never used them that way. Not like Dan has with her forms."

"You could," Dan spoke up. "The purpose of the form is to make certain motions automatic when trouble erupts. Humans, at least, often freeze at that moment, and must be trained to leap suddenly to violence. Or to react without thinking in this case, because someone does a thing, and your muscles know where to step in that moment. If three goons came at you with rape in their eyes, I imagine you'd have all of them on the ground before the first one rolled over to stand back up."

Mazhin blushed in the skin as well as the tentacles. Their blue tint underneath became more pronounced, and their tentacles retracted into squishy blue worms for a moment.

Nasrin blushed almost to the tips of her fingers and her eyes fell.

"Perhaps," she whispered. "I have been watching you move and it has awakened better understandings in how I have practiced my dance."

Uly nodded.

"Dan, you and Nasrin work together," he said. "Beranger and Travers, you work with Wyndham. Yanouk, did you wish to learn? Ralphye?"

Both nodded.

"Gender split then, to keep the guards off center," Uly nodded. "Yanouk, you join Nasrin for such training and practice. Ralphye, you are with the men, with Dan shifting back and forth to train as she learns the new form. Questions?"

There were none, so the larger group broke up. Dan caught Uly's hand before he took more than a step and held him close as the others stepped enough away to pretend to give them privacy. In an open room with no noise.

"Are you planning to start an army?" she asked quietly.

"Planning?" he grinned. "I've got one. I need you and Nasrin to make it deadlier when I finally need it."

Dan grinned back. She knew she had good street smarts, but not that much formal education.

That sort of thing was for officers, not tip-of-the-spear grunts. At the same time, he understood the nuts and bolts of violence in ways that she hadn't gotten to work with before.

Just how bad a person had Dupuis really been? Unfair comparison, she supposed, because he'd never done anything to really impress her. Uly seemed to do it daily.

"You got it," she said, sounding like a Second-in-Command now.

Uly nodded and she let him go.

For now.

Instead, she turned to Nasrin.

"Let's find someplace comfortable and talk about the philosophy of violence," Dan grinned at the woman.

# TWENTY-SIX

ADRIAN SOBOL HADN'T GOTTEN where he was by being stupid. Ruthless and smart had opened a path to make him Conductor of his own ship.

His own destiny.

At the same time, he was stumped, though still smart enough to call in his First Officer, Bakhtiyar Kobolle, the two of them in his office with the door shut and Boyko keeping people out.

*Iron Wasp* was deep in warp, trying to skirt some of the softer spots on the map, avoiding Imperial patrols to get home.

Humans had him confused, and Adrian didn't like that one bit.

"Have you confirmed that they really come in that many colors?" he asked his First Officer.

"Have," Kobolle nodded. "The four medics tell us that this isn't even all the options, either. We could have something about like Fortier's skin, but with a more red tint underneath. Additionally, a brown that folds over into almost a hammered gold. I've never seen anyone with skin as dark as that one woman if the species wasn't already all that color, and usually those are paler, with fur that's black. What are you thinking of doing with them?"

"Dunno," Adrian grunted. "The Mazhin think that some of them would be good mechanics, so we can find a buyer there, as long as they don't mind weird-looking serfs. The others seem to be strong backs and sailors, but there's no way in hell I'd hire them myself. You've seen how some of them look at us."

"Indeed," Kobolle nodded. "That dark-skinned woman looks good enough to give Boyko a challenge for toughness. Mining colony somewhere, or were you thinking of selling them as warriors someone else could try to break and employ as mercenaries?"

"Fortier and Chastain, the black woman, are too dangerous," Adrian said. "I'd have to find a buyer I didn't know, because I wouldn't want to burn a contact."

"Like we know anybody around here?" Kobolle laughed. "How the hell did we end up this far from the homestead?"

"Greed," Adrian reminded him. "All the places to raid closer are too well armed and prepared for us. Even the Auga have gone all porcupine these days because the Confederation is at something of a high point for ships and crew. But that's also too many of us raiding others. We tried something new. I'm not sure I would claim it as the smartest thing I've ever done, other than we can sell Humans as rare and exotic, so I figure we're good for at least a fifty percent markup on regular prices. Plus, the Mazhin are already a group, so somebody who knows the species will want to pick them up in bulk."

"Should we go back later and try for more Humans?" Kobolle asked.

"If we hadn't been gone for so long I might have tried a few smaller worlds farther out, but the crew's been out for nearly a year now and they're getting a little restive. Not having any really major scores hasn't helped their humor, though the appalling stash of flavored ethyl alcohol for drinking that we took off the Human ship is valuable. How can any species consume poisons like that?"

"The doctors said that they have the innards to process it better than we do, as long as the content is low by volume and overall mass," Kobolle nodded. "Weird species, though. I've also gotten notes about the consumption of other chemicals for hallucinogenic or other effects."

"That reminds me," Adrian said. "Did the woman doctor survive?"

"Touch and go still," Kobolle shrugged. "Apparently, she had been consuming various narcotics under the table without the others aware. Getting locked up without access to her stash put her into a hard detox that's been frightening to watch."

"Bad?"

"Screaming so bad we initially had to let the other doctor medicate her," Kobolle said. "Until he went into some sort of alcohol withdrawal himself and had to be put in the bed next to her. The other two seem to be handling it fine, but the doctors are both chained down in such a way that they can't scratch. The woman drew blood anywhere she could reach. Something about bugs crawling under her skin."

"BUGS?" Adrian demanded sharply.

"Not really," Kobolle chuckled. "But we had one hell of a mess on our hands until the one medic explained that they were all in her head, as a result of neural damage causing phantom pain. Had the whole unit isolated and fumigated anyway, just in case."

"Is she even worth keeping alive?" Adrian asked.

"We've got a tremendous amount of medical data on the species now," Kobolle shrugged. "Healthy and not. That will be worth extra to whoever ends up buying them. Probably you'll want to split the medics up and sell the humans off in four groups, so each has an expert on hand. We nearly killed her accidentally twice and intentionally once."

"But she's stable?"

"Stable enough," Kobolle replied. "Mostly incoherent, but that's the drugs the one medic is keeping her on while the body heals and rewires itself. Even he isn't sure her brain will survive, but he thinks the extra ten days in a coma is actually better for her than letting her wake up. Since the others agreed on that note, I'm willing to let them be. Plus, our own medics are getting a crash course in Human for next time. Assuming you don't want to keep one of the Humans long term and offer them a crew slot?"

"Not the doctors, if they both have personality issues they're addressing with consumption," Adrian decided. "How are the other two?"

"The Nurse, Mitchell I think they call him, is a civilian," Kobolle said. "Trained to a higher level than the other one, and a Human specialist. The other one is better trained across Human AND Mazhin, for what it's worth. I don't know which would be a better fit, but Mitchell is more relaxed about almost everything, so he might adapt better."

Adrian kept his grumbles to himself. On the one hand, four groups, each with a medic, meant better resale value later. On the other, if he went hunting Human worlds, having an expert on staff would keep his investments alive better later.

Was he ever coming back to this side of Auga? Sector Seventeen had been one shitshow after another. Having Humans as exotic animals for sale might break them even, however that would require a little luck when he went to deal.

Or should he hit somebody on the way home, instead of just running as hard and fast as he could and hoping nobody noticed him slip by?

Fortier had been after supplies at Iethert. That had proven to be his undoing, when an Ononguli raider happened to be close enough to his path to suddenly detect a pulse-wake appearing.

*Iron Wasp* was fast. Fast enough to turn and give chase. Fast enough to catch him.

Was there somebody else out there fast enough to catch Adrian Sobol?

Not if he didn't stop running.

"How are we doing on food?" Adrian asked.

"Human stuff is weirdly spiced, but doesn't appear poisonous, as near as we've been able to tell." Kobolle shrugged. "Bland as hell. We got a lot from their ship, but we've been reserving that for them. Partly to keep them healthier. Partly because our folks might riot if we started feeding them such boring crap."

"Remind them that the alternative might be half-rations before we get home," Adrian snapped.

A restless crew was the last thing he needed right now because they would start causing trouble with each other, lacking anybody else to pick on. And he didn't dare let them mingle with the Humans because that was his profit on this voyage right now.

"Half-rations might be a good enough reason to stop and sell some workers," Kobolle said. "Or trade the exotic, weird shit we stripped off their ship before we destroyed it."

"How soon until discipline starts to be a problem?" Adrian asked.

"Already is," Kobolle grimaced. "We only have about fifteen percent females in the crew, so every woman has as many boyfriends as she wants. Several more in the prison barracks or medical that they can't touch has them on edge. Especially Humans, who have all that exoticness thrown in on top of it. Six won't make a big difference with a crew this size, but folks are grumbling."

Adrian nodded. About what he'd feared.

You had to be desperate to want to deal with an unfriendly Emro woman. The Mazhin were at least predictable, as well as being smaller than Ononguli. That left two Humans, one of whom might be insane in the infirmary right now, and the other who looked like she might be able to take Boyko one-on-one with knives.

"Take a few hours and look at the corridor of systems in front of us," Adrian ordered. "Find me options to raid or trade. Some battle will keep these lowlifes engaged happily for long enough to get them home. Trade means we can throw weird shit in front of them as a shiny distraction. Again, long enough to get home."

"Understood, Conductor," Kobolle said, rising. "Not sure what's there, since we're staying down in the fens and marshes here, as it were, and not up on the Imperial Highways, but I'm with you. They're getting stale in the wrong ways and need some excitement."

Adrian nodded and the man departed, leaving him alone to glower in his office.

Excitement was the last thing he wanted right now.

# TWENTY-SEVEN

ULY STOOD off to one side and noted the crew arrangements. Three weeks had passed, based initially on meals served twice a day, then by a handful of bookslabs that had been delivered to keep folks entertained. Human ones taken off *King Hewitt II*, loaded with a lot of books to read, but more importantly they had large libraries of videos to watch and the ability to project a movie onto a nearby surface.

Having nothing to do all day would have made people grumpy. Even the pirates had been willing to provide distractions to their livestock. Or however they rated these folks.

The Conductor had made one mistake, though. He'd left them mostly alone during this time, save for the medical staff, which meant that Uly had more than a dozen martial arts students of four species studying and teaching each other. Even Suka Kuri had taken it upon herself to learn a new thing, at an age when many of her peers were happy to just express a single art and keep it alive for future students.

For Uly, the weirdest part had to be watching Nasrin, Dan,

and Yanouk practice. Just the three of them. Dan was tall for a woman, and still looked tiny next to Yanouk. All three moved like dancers, though. Professionally in Nasrin's case, combat in Dan's, and youth and flexibility for Yanouk, who was roughly equivalent to late teens for Human development.

All the men would pause and watch. Grace and power caused the crew to fall silent and appreciative, but the sound of a hatch opening and everyone suddenly found something else to do, talking, walking, or just turning away.

The three women turned inward like a sewing circle in the blink of an eye.

Uly rose as Leith Masters entered and gestured the man closer.

"How is she?" he asked, meaning Jasmine Atwater, who had been removed barely a week into captivity.

"Medically induced coma, but Spence thinks that it is almost time to bring her out," Leith replied warily.

"You don't agree?" Uly asked.

Getting Leith away from Spence and Atwater had been like night and day. Even then, it had taken some time before the stories had come out. Leith had been subject to vast emotional and intellectual abuse by the two doctors, because Blair was a civilian and could quit if he wanted to.

Specialist Leith Masters didn't have that option.

"She was skin and bones before this, sir," Leith replied. "Hardly any muscle left, but I have been working on some of the Ononguli to build me a device that I could attach to start working her muscles in the coma. If they bring her out, I'm not sure right now that she'll be able to even feed herself for a while. I had no idea the variety or dosages of shit she was taking at night. I mean, I knew she was up to something, but she had her own stash hidden somewhere, so my inventory count was never off. I am amazed she was able to walk and talk, with all that in her once I did a full bloodscan. Also amazed she balanced it well enough that her heart didn't explode."

"And Spence?" Uly asked.

"DTs, sir," Leith shrugged. "Nothing but an alcoholic having to go without. That was a few days in his case, plus a lot of screaming and rage until one of the other nurses slapped him a few times. He's mostly back. Really haunted, but this might be enough to keep him on the straight and narrow."

"Should you be the one making medical decisions instead?" Uly pressed.

"Honestly, Blair's better," Leith shook his head. "He's a nurse. I'm just a trained monkey. Only edge I have is knowing Atwater and Spence a lot longer than Blair."

"You two put your heads together and decide, then override Spence if you have to," Uly ordered the man. "He's not in charge anymore, so either the Ononguli Surgeon of this boat will make that decision, or I can overrule Spence. Keep that in mind."

"Seriously, sir?" Leith asked. "He's a doctor and an Adjutant. I'm just a Specialist."

"If we were back on *King Hewitt II*, I'd be your commanding officer," Uly reminded him. "Here, we're all prisoners of the Ononguli, so Spence has no authority at all, except where he wants to browbeat you. You don't have to allow that anymore, Leith."

"I'm *Danumash* Navy, sir," Leith reminded him. "He could bring me up on all sorts of charges if he wanted to when we got home, like you were going to do with Eldridge."

"Leith, I've always got a bunk open for you if you decide you'd rather quit *Danumash* than put up with that shit," Uly said quietly. "You and Blair can sail with me anytime, any ship, anyplace. Spence and Atwater can go back to their labs and their slaves. Am I clear?"

"Seriously, sir?"

"Absolutely," Uly said. "Those two haven't earned my respect like the rest of you have. Hard won, because I've watched you bust your ass to keep people alive and healthy, well above and beyond. That's rare, Specialist. Don't let anyone tell you otherwise. I'd put you in for commendations if we were home."

"Thank you, sir," Leith said, relief and amazement evident in his face and voice.

"Good, now go crash and take a nap," Uly said. "Dinner should be soon, and I'll make sure you're first in line. You're almost as skin and bones as Atwater must be. I need you healthy, too, sailor."

"Understood, sir."

Uly watched the man rise and make his way over to a quiet corner. That was another change during their time in residency. At first, the three Emro and four Thogin had each had a corner, with his folks over here.

Now, those seven had all moved closer, creating a zone on the outskirts where folks could nap, far away from conversations and movies at the other end of the room. It wouldn't be quiet, but quiet enough.

And he seemed to have expanded his crew by seven more.

Uly had no idea what that meant though.

A quiver passed through the hull and caused everyone to stop and look up.

"Marlowe, what was that?" he called over the silence.

"We're taking fire, sir," the Lead Engineer said. "That was a 4dm wavebolt set to detonate on shield impact rather than piercing mode."

"All hands, secure yourselves against battle damage!" Uly called as the hull vibrated a second time, this one hard enough to make people stumble.

They didn't have suits if there was a breach somewhere, but folks could at least be holding onto one of the bunks if the ship lost gravity. Hopefully, they were close enough to the center of the ship.

What the hell was happening now?

AUDIT VESSEL
01794572158

# TWENTY-EIGHT

ADRIAN WAS in his office when the alert sounded. Twelve hurried steps put him at the center of his bridge. Even that felt like it was too long.

"What's happening?" he demanded angrily as the hull began to rattle.

"Auga Audit Vessel slipped up behind us and flipped us out of warp, Conductor," Kobolle called from his station. "Shields are up and we're charging everything."

"Get the Omnipulsars working first," Adrian snapped. "If they're that close, we don't have long. Navigator, all engines full ahead on whatever heading you're on right now. Get us space to maneuver and fight. Astrogation, if we can get clear, plot a random course so we can try to lose him in warp."

Adrian threw himself into his seat and buckled the straps, even as a larger jolt rippled sideways through the fabric of the ship.

"Pulsar Gunners and Wavebolt Cannoneers, do not wait for orders to fire," Adrian overrode the noise around him with a yell.

"Let loose everything you have and add to it as weapons and generators come on line. I need time!"

Adrian typed quickly, bringing up his local screen and locating a good cannon scan of the enemy vessel.

Audit Vessel 01794572158. Sector Seventeen, with a leading zero because the Auga were planning that far ahead. Adrian remembered from somewhere that the entire galaxy might run less than three hundred Imperial Sectors, once they got around to mapping it properly.

Nobody was entirely sure what the back half of the disk looked like, except by scientific extrapolation.

Maybe he should run that far and never come back? Assuming he could escape this mess today.

Audit Vessels were anti-piracy patrol. Nobody out there built fleets to argue with the Auga.

No, he corrected himself. Apparently, Humans might, but Adrian didn't know what their ships were like.

This Audit Vessel was a large, fast Striker. Supposedly, the ship Fortier had come off of was similar, designed for speed and distance, rather than slugging it out at short range.

*Iron Wasp* was an Interceptor, a whole size category down.

He was doomed if he couldn't get to warp.

"Scanners, is he going for kill shots?" Adrian demanded as the ship rattled again.

"Negative, sir," the answer floated back. "They're set for fists, rather than shivs. He's trying to batter all our shields down."

Adrian smothered the curse unspoken. They wanted prisoners. Probably to hang as pirates.

Rightfully so in this case.

Still, it gave him options. *Iron Wasp*'s bow had gotten slewed askew by the bubble around it popping, so the engines were driving them down and starboard from his previous flight path.

Engines had a lot of mass to push against from a dead stop, but the Audit Vessel was even larger and would have to come about to chase him.

All *Iron Wasp* had to do was blink away and then start a random spiral. The Audit Vessel could still chase, but they'd either have to slow down to trace his line or overshoot it and backtrack.

If Adrian got a big enough head start, the wake might even fade sufficiently to let him escape.

On his screen, that Auga beast fired a salvo of large wavebolts.

*Iron Wasp* had two Neutron Omnipulsars, bow and stern, in such a way that they overlapped on the flanks. Those would not be enough for the six incoming.

On each corner, the four 1-decimeter defensive mounts rippled fire. Incoming looked like four and six DM bolts. Given time, the Omnipulsar could degrade it with a stream of coherent neutrons, but they were too close.

Instead, three of the four defensive bolts impacted, neutralizing incoming shots. Two others got hashed some, but not enough.

That last one scored a hard hit aft.

There was no sound, but Adrian felt something rupture aft, an earthquake transmitted through the ship's very bones.

"Kobolle?" he yelled.

"We just lost half our generators," the man replied.

"Shut down life support for now," Adrian ordered. "Everyone into suits instead. Kill forward shields and live with the risk. All power to rear shields and Omnipulsars. Fire all the wavebolts defensively against incoming bolts. If we don't get clear, we're all dead meat, people!"

"What about the prisoners?" Kobolle called. "They got no suits back there."

"They are the least of my worries," Adrian decided. "If they survive, they survive. If not, we're trying to escape with our own lives."

Outside, that Audit Vessel unleashed another salvo of torpedoes.

# TWENTY-NINE

ULY HAD MOVED to sit next to Kolya and Marlowe. They understood hulls and kept up a lively, running commentary between them as new sounds intruded from all directions. The life support blowers had stopped running some time ago, but none of the vents had slammed shut, so hopefully there was enough oxygen for everyone. At least for a while.

If Uly had the geometry correct, this room was a bit aft of midship and down a deck from the main corridor. Lower decks steerage on a passenger ship, comparatively.

"Interesting," Kolya mused, his head cocked and eyes distant. "Are those twin sixes, Marlowe?"

"Your guess is better than mine," the man replied. "Been listening to chickens with their heads cut off aft, trying to do the impossible."

"Kolya?" Uly asked, aware that the rest of the room had all moved close and were hanging raptly to everything they had to say.

"Listening to the ship fire, sir," Kolya replied. "One decimeter defensive turrets. Four of them, if I count echoes right. Two forward and two aft. A pair of Neutron Omnipulsars, again fore and aft. Those deeper thumps are the main guns. Feels like they put a pair of 6dm tubes in a single station. Way more firepower than a ship this size would have back home, where we'd normally have a single Four forward and maybe a second one aft, like old-time sailing ships on water with iron turrets."

"Pirate raider," Uly reminded him. "I presume the need to overawe their victims, as well as fight off the cops when someone finds them."

"Aye, sir," Kolya nodded. "We're almost in Heavy Destroyer or Light Cruiser land for firepower, depending. Nice wolf of a warship, but they ran into a bear today. Can't tell if the other guy is toying with them or not that good, because he's sequencing his fire for the most part. Slow load times, so this ship has a chance to reload, aim, and fire defensively."

"They aren't trying to destroy this ship," Uly decided, speaking aloud. "Cops, probably, come to capture them most likely. We're a single ship, and everyone agrees that they were far from home."

Uly turned to Haydar and Roshan, his resident geniuses. Neither had served in a formal navy of any sort, from what Uly had learned, but both were smarter than anybody he knew.

"Sneaking home and stumbled across somebody's path?" Uly asked.

Roshan nodded.

"Given our galactic coordinates when *King Hewitt II* was first captured, and then when we were captured the second time, I can place a cone of uncertainty on a flight path home with some degree of solid calculation."

Uly had to translate that while Haydar grinned.

"Did they try to go around Auga or through?" Uly finally asked, turning to include all his sailors and new crew.

The last week had uncovered all manner of interesting secondary skills in the people looking back at him right now.

"Given the intrusion of an enemy warship, I would presume that they attempted to cut directly across, Captain," Roshan replied.

The hull pinged weirdly right then.

Sadeq Akhtar, probably the best mechanic of a crew including both Kolya and Marlowe in it, stood up.

"Okay, they're done," he said simply, turning to Marlowe for confirmation.

Uly did the same.

"Engine hit of some sort," Marlowe nodded. "Probably cooling systems. You lose those in battle, and you have to shut things down so you don't explode. You sure, Sadeq?"

"Previous ones were generators or hull spaces," the Mazhin said soberly. "Something is no longer generating hull vibrations. I place it up two decks and aft."

Uly watched the man hold out an arm and point at a spot above the horizon.

Marlowe and Kolya stood and bracketed the man, sighting down his arm, then nodding.

"Likely." Kolya turned to Uly. "I expect that this pirate just ran into something too big to resist. Rather like us. Twice, for some of these folks."

Uly nodded and suppressed his grimace.

There were times he wanted to scream and rail against the injustice of it all, just like Dan. However, he was in command here, by those original orders to board *King Hewitt II* and return it to base. From tidbits that had been shared with Blair and Leith, *King Hewitt II* had been efficiently stripped, then the hull abandoned in space and used for target practice.

That ship was never coming home.

He still had the crew, however. Plus survivors of two others that had been captured in the Emro and Thogin sitting nearby and watching him for cues.

"Assume they've been taken until someone says otherwise," Uly ordered.

"Do we set up ambushes?" Dan asked.

Uly considered it. Bare-handed against armor and guns?

"You and Nasrin move to a spot where someone coming in can't immediately see you, in case they're dumb enough to just walk in and open fire at me," Uly called. "I'll be out here in the open to draw attention and possibly fire. Whoever can run the fastest, set yourselves in that corner opposite Dan so you can assist her and Nasrin if they need it or pick up weapons dropped by people they hurt. The rest of you be prepared to take cover. Suka Kuri, as an Exemplar of the Arts, I would appreciate it if you were to move to the restroom and hide, so you are not at risk if someone opens fire in here."

The old Emro woman studied his face for a long moment. He'd come to understand that she literally rated among the Moss School as a Living Legend, something less than one in ten million students ever achieved.

She smiled.

"No," she said distinctly. "In fact, I believe the Human phrase I've learned that would be most appropriate here would be 'Screw you, Uly.' I will stand with you. All of you."

Quiet, nervous titters filled the silence.

But she was right. He could not issue orders to her. That was the nature of being an Exemplar. She had no masters in the universe save herself. And he'd told her to stop calling him Captain for that reason. So, she had.

He'd brought this entirely on himself.

At the same time, Uly couldn't think of a better commitment of intent on her part. He turned to Yanouk instead.

Big woman. Cute, if you liked them green with black hair and the ability to bench press electric motorcycles.

"You will protect her," he ordered simply.

Yanouk nodded. Such was implied in becoming a Student of the Arts. And Hiko, while even bigger, wasn't nearly as fast or graceful. He did have one hell of a singing voice. Was apparently utterly brilliant at oil painting. Two left feet as a dancer.

"Move it people!" he yelled. "Look casual in case anyone is watching after this but prepare for violence at the drop of a hat."

Uly stood and moved to a spot on his right, where someone holding a carbine in both hands would naturally turn to their left when entering to aim it at him.

Presenting their blind side to the two dangerous women in that corner.

Hopefully, it would be enough.

# THIRTY

ADRIAN SLAMMED a fist into his arm rest, but it was no more forgiving than the rest of the day had been. Hopefully, he hadn't just broken any bones in his hand to top it all off.

"Status?" he yelled.

"We're just lost engine power," Kobolle replied, stating the obvious. "Generators are shutting down to vent heat into space. If we keep fighting, likely something overloads and detonates shortly."

All of Adrian's boards had gone red at the same time Kobolle's had.

"Shut it down!" Adrian ordered. "Contact that ship and tell them we'll surrender. I'd rather live to fight another day than have us all die meaningless deaths in the middle of nowhere."

Most of his crew would be shipped to a reeducation camp once they were identified. He and a handful of the officers in charge were likely facing death sentences, though he might get lucky and find a judge willing to commute that to life in prison.

The Confederation was forever swapping home hostages for captured warriors, so maybe he'd have a chance to see his home stars again in a decade. Adrian couldn't think of anything he'd done lately to piss off the Auga badly enough to hang for immediately.

Shit, he'd long-sailed around large chunks of the Empire expressly to see what was on the far side, rather than attacking any of their ships. How the hell was he supposed to know Sector Seventeen was going to be such an unlucky place for everyone?

Maybe he could trade that information for leniency? Something. He hadn't killed anybody but the one prisoner who'd provoked Boyko at the start, so a judge might look on that with favor.

Or not.

Entirely out of his hands.

He opened a comm.

"Medical."

"How are the two Humans?" he asked. "Ask one of the other two."

"Stand by, Conductor."

Adrian waited. One last salvo of wavebolts didn't slam into the shields now, so maybe the Commander over there had disabled those shots. Without engines and generators, they would have probably impacted on steel, killing everybody aboard the ship pretty rapidly.

"Conductor, the Human Blair says that the female can be moved, but care should be exercised when doing so, as she is still fragile."

"Understood," Adrian replied, grimacing again. "Put Blair in charge of her care. We're fucked here and the Auga will be taking everyone shortly. The Human will know better what she needs when they move us."

"Yes, sir."

Adrian looked around his bridge crew, most of whom wouldn't meet his eyes. Shock. Broken in a few cases. The

Ononguli Confederation had never been big enough to threaten Auga, but sufficient to keep them out of Sector Twenty-One. Sector Seventeen had proven his undoing.

All of their undoing.

He turned to Kobolle as that one held a conversation on head-phones and a microphone.

Their eyes locked.

"We're done," Kobolle said simply. "They're moving in to launch boarding shuttles shortly."

"Stand the crew down," Adrian ordered, even though every fiber of his being reacted negatively.

Survive today. Get most of his people where they might get home. Hope his bad luck turned eventually.

Nothing more he could do.

How had that one Mazhin prisoner phrased it?

*Out of the frying pan and into the fire.*

# THIRTY-ONE

DAN SAT with one foot carefully braced against a bunk leg, giving her an extra grip if and when she needed to drive off and attack a shooter at the door. Nasrin wasn't a killer but could move quickly.

Hopefully, her training would be enough to carry her forward when it happened.

There would be no time for thought. Only action.

"Attention to the crew of this vessel," a new voice emerged from speakers. "The Auga Empire has taken control. Crew members not currently assigned to repair operations will move to forward airlocks for processing. Prisoners captured will be processed as well once the crew is removed. That is all."

Dan turned and looked at Uly. He shrugged, then nodded.

They had developed enough of a physical shorthand for her to know that it might not be an issue shortly. At the same time, someone like Boyko might decide to go out in a blaze of glory.

She rose and slipped along the wall until she was right beside the door. If it was Boyko, he would go for Uly. Dan would have about one second to tackle him.

Or break his neck.

"What is the plan?" Nasrin whispered.

"Cover my flank," Dan said, pointing to the spot against the wall beside her.

Dan found the metal cold on her butt, but that helped with the adrenaline pulsing madly through her blood. Instead of fidgeting, she turned to measure the exact width of the door, then placed everything in her memory and closed her eyes to meditate.

Turn, step, lunge, punch. Assume Boyko. The longer that door remained closed, the more likely someone else would open it.

What they would do with all the prisoners remained to be seen, but at least whoever it was understood that there were prisoners to be accounted for.

Dan bided her time.

# THIRTY-TWO

ULY HAD WATCHED DAN SHIFT, understanding that she was preparing for the one-percent solution.

His job was the ninety-nine others. The voice had identified his crew as prisoners. Said that they would be processed after the pirates.

Uly had not heard the word *freed* at any point.

He turned to Haydar.

"Assuming Auga, what should I know?" he asked.

That had been one species that hadn't come up in any detail, but *Iron Wasp* had been sailing uninterrupted for weeks, so chances were good that they were deep in Auga space, or had tried to slip around an edge, like Uly had planned to do with *Danumash*.

"Physically short and broad," Haydar replied in a conversational voice. "Muscular and outwardly beautiful, as they mastered genetic engineering early and settled on those traits. They are reputed to have some sort of mental powers, originating in their third eye."

"Third?" Uly asked, surprised.

"Two hunting eyes like we have," Haydar nodded. "With a larger eye in the center of their forehead. They are the largest political entity, but have no official presence in Sector Seventeen, as far as I was aware. However, we may have crossed into another Sector by now."

Uly nodded. Imperial Sectors were huge. All of Human-surveyed space didn't take up much of Sector Seventeen. Not even a quarter of it. The Auga Empire spanned several such sectors.

Thankfully, none of them were close.

"They come," Piruz announced, eyes and tentacles focused on the door.

Had he been listening to their footsteps on the deck? The ship was silent, save that the life support blowers had restarted. Per Sadeq, they were running those on batteries right now.

Again, senses beyond Human. At least he could learn from them.

He had a full crew.

Uly drew a breath and rose. Someone opening the door would see him first.

He was also prepared to throw himself down and to one side after drawing eyes and fire.

Bold and stupid were different sides of the same coin, but he didn't feel like being suicidal today.

The hatch opened. A shadow in the hallway, but the figure didn't enter.

It was built like an Emro, but no taller than a Thogin.

"Prisoners, you will line up in the middle of the chamber for processing!"

Uly nodded to Dan and she relaxed.

That wasn't Boyko, so they were down to the ninety-nine. Hopefully, a new cage and not an execution.

She and Nasrin began walking towards him. The figure in the door did not react, but hadn't Haydar said that they had some manner of mental powers? That Third Eye, though he could only see a silhouette from here?

Had those powers told him that two warriors lurked in ambush? Uly didn't think that a Mazhin would have been surprised either, because their tentacles would smell someone that close.

He walked to the open space where the women studied dance and came to rest with his right arm out straight.

"Form on me," he ordered. "Three rows."

The sailors moved fastest. The Mazhin were next, with Suka Kuri, Hiro, and Yanouk in the back row next to Kolya and Marlowe.

Only when all Uly's people were arrayed did the figure in the door deign to enter, accompanied by half a dozen others.

The other six were armed, but the first one had nothing but an air of ultimate authority about him.

Uly assumed a him, as he had a neatly trimmed brown beard. Four of the six did as well, with the two having the appearance of breasts. Convergent Evolutionary Design in action?

And indeed, as broad and muscular as Emro, but only one hundred and fifty centimeters tall.

Handsome, though. But for his height, the man in front could have easily been a vid star. Middle-aged and rugged in that way that made women swoon, with two thin lines of white in his beard and hints coming in at his temples.

The two women were equally stunning. Built solid with shoulders wider than his, barely tapered waists, strong thighs. Gorgeous faces.

At some point, they must have either all had dark brown hair a little lighter than Uly's or settled on that design when they standardized their species.

The leader moved into the room and came to rest in front of Uly's crew like a Fleet Marshall reviewing a graduating class. His three eyes focused on Haydar, immediately to Uly's right. Dan and Nasrin were arrayed the same way in the second row.

"Mazhin, how did you come to be here?" the being commanded.

Uly listened to an abridged version of Haydar's history, plus those of his fellows, that filled in a few extra details from before *Danumash*. Then time under *Danumash*. Then the Rescue. Then the Pirates. Then the Auga.

It sounded quite impressive, when Haydar spelled it out that way.

"You," the Auga turned to Uly now. "Human. You claim the two Human crews as well as the Mazhin?"

"Until I can get everyone home, sir," Uly nodded.

"And the Emro," Suka Kuri spoke up from the back. "We are part of his crew."

"Same with us," Ethir called from the far end of the second row.

"Interesting," the man purred. "Irrelevant at present, but I will make a note in the files when you are processed. The medical staff includes two Humans and two Human patients. Also yours?"

"They were my doctors previously," Haydar spoke up. "All four have joined with Fortier."

"The one medic claims that the female patient cannot be moved," the Auga said simply. "Is that correct?"

"Did you speak with the one with golden hair, or the darker-toned one, sir?" Uly asked.

"The darker."

"That is Biomedical Specialist Leith Masters, sir," Uly said. "I asked him to take charge of medical treatments for Doctor

Atwater until she was better. If this ship is to be evacuated, is there a way to exercise extreme care in moving her?"

"She was your prisoner originally, was she not?" the man asked.

"She was," Uly nodded. "And my responsibility as her commanding officer."

"I will make a note, Human," he said. "You will immediately follow this crew member to your new barracks on my ship. We will transport you to a place where you may make your statements before a judge, once the records of this vessel have been processed and understood. At that point, your fate will be determined."

The man made a motion and one of the Auga men accompanying him stepped up and gestured.

Uly turned and automatically started to march. Then broke his rhythm and just walked, listening as the crew behind him did the same.

He'd only traversed these corridors once, heading to his prison. Now, they turned and headed forward, down hallways eerily empty of bodies, save for occasional armed Auga keeping watch.

Eventually, they made it to the bow area of *Iron Wasp*, where they were marched into an airlock lounge and stood along a wall. The airlock opened and they were sent through in groups of eight.

Inside, it was a passenger shuttle with a variety of types of seating. Or rather, all the seats could be moved up and down, depending on leg length, as Suka Kuri moved hers up as she sat next to him, with Dan and Haydar on his other side.

Straps deployed after a moment, and Uly tried not to flinch as they pulled tight to hold him in place.

He counted noses and everyone was here except for the four in medical.

Hopefully, they were being transported directly to the local infirmary and would be there when Uly and his crew got where they were going.

Wherever that was.

# THIRTY-THREE

DAN HAD WATCHED the Auga move. Normally, that much strength caused muscles to be slow and somewhat awkward, but every one of them had a grace she found impressive. Bio-engineered, as Haydar and Nasrin had said, so Dan supposed that they had aimed for physical perfection there, too.

One-on-one would be tough unarmed, so she immediately began planning how she might escape.

Where they would go would be up to Uly.

She just had to give him the option.

Nasrin was studying her. Dan was used to it by now, so she studied the young woman back.

If Nasrin were Human, Dan would have put her at about twenty for age. Almost adult, but not quite there yet as everything settled in. Dan felt like she had about a decade of hard roads and sometimes less-than-intelligent decisions on the youngster.

"You plan for more violence?" Nasrin asked in a whisper so faint that Dan had to lean in to hear it, which caused more than one tentacle to brush her hair or ear.

Weird feeling. Dry and snake-like, without the rasp of scales.

"What do the Auga do with new species?" she asked.

"Study them, I presume," Nasrin said. "Oh!"

"Yeah," Dan nodded. "Kinda like how the *Danumash* punks were keeping your folks so they could study them."

"You will resist," Nasrin said. It was not a question.

Dan nodded.

"We are already a long ways farther from home than I have ever been," Dan admitted. "Iethert would have been the farthest I'd ever been from home had we landed. If they are taking us into the center of the galaxy, we'll need to find a way home. And to get you home."

"You still believe that will be possible?" the woman asked.

Dan shrugged and thought about it for a second.

"Uly will move heaven and earth to do it," she finally decided, thinking about the many weeks she had spent around the new officer, watching him make decisions and react to emergencies. "Not sure about Suka Kuri or Ethir and his cousins."

"If we are free, there are many options," Nasrin replied. "While you have seen the piracy side of things, and participated, that is much more rare in the wider galaxy. We should be able to arrange passage to places that will get us home eventually."

"You, perhaps," Dan nodded. "There are currently no travel and trade corridors connecting to Human space, are there?"

"There are not," Nasrin shook her head. "At least not as far as I am aware. You will need to buy a ship?"

"Or steal one," Dan chuckled. "We're kind of experts on that topic now. At least my people. We can train the rest of you pretty easily."

She watched the Mazhin woman lean back and consider. The tentacles that had been caressing Dan's skin and hair also withdrew, which was better but also strange.

"I must speak to Haydar and Piruz," Nasrin announced. "It

may be that the Convocation decides to remain in Human company when you do so, but I am not the person to make those decisions."

"Is that Uly?" Dan asked.

She hadn't poked too much at the Mazhin and their social structures. Weird by Human standards, but coherent enough.

"Once a decision has been made within the species," Nasrin nodded. "This may be something that we work out within the smaller group first."

"Well, I've enjoyed your company," Dan admitted. "You've taught us lots and helped us in any number of ways, so my vote would be for you to remain part of the larger crew."

"Thank you," Nasrin smiled. "You have been a most welcome change from the *Danumash*."

Dan watched the woman close her eyes as the shuttle began to ping and rattle as engines and systems came up. Dan did the same, then leaned forward and slipped a hand through the gap in seats to the row in front of her, where she rested it on Uly's shoulder.

He had everything on his shoulders, it seemed, and hadn't complained once. Far stronger and tougher than his skinny frame would lead you to believe.

Stubborn.

He'd see them home.

Or go down fighting. With her at his side.

# THIRTY-FOUR

YET ANOTHER SHIP Uly found himself on. If the Ononguli ship had given the impression of high ceilings and narrow doors, the Auga vessel was almost the opposite, as he was marched at the head of his little convoy through corridors that gave him more of an impression of tunnels.

Low and wide, as befit the Auga themselves. Yanouk and especially Hiko had to hunch to walk, though Suka Kuri was fine as long as she didn't bounce too much when walking.

The lighting in here was dimmer than he was used to. More yellow as well, instead of the pure white of Human vessels. Not as golden as Ononguli. Not bad enough that he couldn't read, but his mind kept wanting to reach for the dimmer switch to dial it up ten percent so he was more comfortable.

They walked.

Empty corridors with few hatches and no crew other than the few Auga leading and the few more trailing. Cattle herd, if that wasn't too rude of a description for his crew, with cowboys moving them along.

Eventually, they entered a wider space. It looked remarkably like the converted bay where he'd first met the Mazhin, right down to the metal bars with gaps closing off individual cells.

This cell block, however, was three decks tall from what he could see. Both sides of the vast room and the bottom of a U, with this top end open with long trestle tables. Presumably, the prisoners would be fed down here and allowed to exercise. Or whatever they might do.

Looking up, Uly guessed the space to be a little under half full. Whatever that meant. If this ship was on anti-piracy patrol, the problem was greater than he'd anticipated.

That, or this ship just kept you locked up until they finished a patrol sweep and turned you over to the warden somewhere. Yes, that felt more likely.

He wondered how long some of these folks had been in here. And if that counted as part of their eventual sentence when they did come before a judge.

The guard at the front of the convoy stopped them in the middle of the room and turned to look at Uly. Above, the room had fallen eerily silent, when he had been expecting catcalls or verbal abuse.

But then, many of those folks had either never seen Humans before, or had come off *Iron Wasp*, and weren't really in a position to be bullies right now.

"Human," the guard snapped. "Should you be separated by species or gender?"

Uly had to translate the words to understand.

"No," he replied after a blip. "Clustered would be nice, but this crew can be mixed however is most efficient for your needs."

Never be an asshole to the guy with a gun pointed at you. Thorley Eldridge had unfortunately never grown up enough to understand that, but Uly remembered his own teenage years.

Chemical and hormonal imbalances that made him definably crazy for at least half a decade.

Assuming he was sane now.

Eldridge would have hopefully grown out of it eventually. Or learned to keep his mouth shut better. Even Uly wasn't going to assume that a *Danumash* scion would suddenly develop an understanding of others.

Racial, class, and cultural superiority was baked into the *Combined Crowns of Danumash* at a DNA level, it seemed.

The guard grunted and pointed.

"Groups of eight, then," he said, turning and starting towards a staircase up.

Uly followed, going up stairs and past cells filled with Ononguli for the most part.

Uly walked into the first opening when the guard gestured because he was first in line. Haydar, Dan, Nasrin, Suka Kuri, Yanouk, Piruz, and Ethir joined him, and the door slid shut on rusty wheels.

Looking around him, Uly suspected that this group wasn't a random assemblage of folks. Not based on who had been with him walking through the Auga ship.

Crew. And these folks, while they might not be ship's officers, were the ones he would rely on to do things and know things.

Eight bunks, in stacked pairs, large enough for even Hiko's enormous frame to be comfortable. To Uly, that spoke of preparation for any species the Auga might encounter and need to capture.

Hopefully, the food would be safe and nutritious as well.

What was it that the commander of the Auga had said? The records of *Iron Wasp* would need to be processed and understood, after the crew and prisoners had been processed.

Hopefully, that included both the medical needs of Doctor

Atwater as well as the care and feeding of Humans who were new in this sector.

The walls in these cells were transparent, but Uly assumed tough enough that an angry Emro with a bunk couldn't so much as scratch it. This was designed and built as a prison. He had no reason to assume they'd half-assed the job.

Uly watched through the clear walls as all of his people got settled, with Beranger, Travers, and Wyndham each in a different cell. That had to be on purpose, but he could ask Dan about it later. Similarly, the Mazhin had spread out and mixed with the Human crew, mostly mechanics like Sadeq and Bahadur with Marlowe and Blakeslee. Vahid and Omid were in the next cell over with Huff and Kolya.

Again, organized into teams, each of which had a general mix of skills, instead of all the mechanics in one room and sailors in another and each species group isolated.

He had a crew. Now, Uly just had to figure out what to do with it.

He turned the other direction once the last of his people was accounted for. The cell on his left had five Ononguli. None that he knew, but Uly assumed that they were sailors from *Iron Wasp*, stuffed eight to a cell until their jailers ran out with an odd number.

The five scowled back at him. Beyond, Uly could see several more that he had walked past. Again, none he knew, but the number of filled cells gave him a perspective on the crew. Hundreds, and he presumed more still on the ship repairing it for the authorities to take into custody.

The battle hadn't been one-sided, to hear Marlowe and Sadeq do play-by-play as if it were a sporting event. At the same time, *Iron Wasp* had been getting the sharp end of the stick for once, pounded time and again until something had broken aft, and the ship had given up.

Uly was glad that Conductor Sobol had chosen surrender over death, however personal his reasons.

Dying today prevented escaping tomorrow.

He turned back to his cell. And his Command Council, if he was feeling exceptionally ambitious and arrogant.

Dan was his Second-in-Command. Haydar and Suka Kuri both brought their own kinds of expertise from distinct, alien perspectives. Piruz might yet prove to be a horse thief, given the way he'd been able to locate or help Kolya and Marlowe refashion parts to keep *King Hewitt II* sailing. Ethir and his cousins had been laborers traveling to a new contract, never losing the smiles from their faces. Nasrin and Yanouk were dancers, artists, conversationalists, and beautiful women, so he was feeling exceptionally blessed to have them around, if only to look at.

Better than Marlowe's grizzled face, anyway.

Uly gestured his team closer and sat on a handy bottom bunk.

"Do we know what might happen next?" he asked, looking around at his experts.

All eyes turned to Haydar, but that was to be expected. He had a big brain hidden behind those mobile tentacles.

"I noted the name of the ship as we came aboard," he said, nodding to everyone. "Audit Vessel 01794572158."

"Audit?" Uly asked.

"In *Danumash*, they would perhaps be classified as a gendarme cruiser," Piruz spoke up. Horse thief, and all that it implied in both languages. "Much larger than an Interceptor like *Iron Wasp*. Conductor Sobol had no chance at all in battle if this Audit Vessel was what kicked him out of warp. And with surprise, as they were taken so quickly."

"The police have taken them and us into custody?" Uly asked.

"Indeed, Captain," Haydar replied. "We will likely be considered as evidence of a crime, if you will, once we give testimony."

"Evidence of a crime?" Uly asked, mostly to confirm.

Haydar had a particularly wicked gleam in his eyes.

"*Danumash* would be in the same boat," he chuckled. "Save that all of those sailors but one had chosen to become part of your crew before *Iron Wasp* intruded. Otherwise, folks like Huff and Wyndham might have been taken and jailed in a different part of the ship with the officers of *Iron Wasp*. Instead, they are here with you, with the symbolism that implies."

"Thank you," Uly said. "I didn't understand the story you were telling the Auga commander when he came for us. You were protecting the Human sailors?"

"They have earned our trust, Captain," Piruz interjected. "I would not have believed it two months ago, but the deaths of men like Winter and especially Botterill have shown us just how much of it was driven by the officers and nobles, rather than the servants and peons that make up most of the *Seven Kingdoms*."

Uly nodded gratefully, aware that Haydar and the others had rescued him from a trap he'd never even seen opening beneath his feet.

"You said the officers of *Iron Wasp* are in a different part of the ship?" Uly perked up, circling back.

"That is correct, Captain," Haydar replied. "Officers are removed to prevent them from organizing the crew into troublemakers."

"And I'm here, along with Huff and Wyndham, because we're evidence, rather than suspects?" Uly asked, looking at everyone.

Shrugs rippled across wide green shoulders, narrow pale ones, and blue ones.

"Someone let those two know to keep their mouths shut,"

Uly said, turning pointedly to look at his three Mazhin cohorts. "Quietly."

The nods he got back confirmed his idea that they could somehow communicate silently with their tentacles. It wasn't any sort of mental ability, but he suspected that it had to do with scents, considering how carefully they had rearranged all laundry operations on *King Hewitt II*.

As long as it got done.

"And what can we do at this point?" Uly asked.

Shrugs greeted him. They were prisoners still, having only changed who the jailers were. For his Mazhin friends, that was the third time, but they seemed to be accepting it phlegmatically.

He refused to accept it at all.

But there was nothing he could do.

Today.

# THIRTY-FIVE

HAYDAR HAD COME to an even greater appreciation of Captain Ulysses Fortier. None of the Mazhin had told the man the range of senses that came with tentacles, but he had apparently figured out far more than any *Danumash* officer or doctor ever had.

Of course, none of them had actually listened to his kind. Or looked at them as anything but aliens to be poked and prodded initially, then sent to work designing new systems for the *Combined Crowns* later.

Uly had paid attention quietly. Absorbed things that challenged his understanding of the universe, then changed who he was to adapt to it. In that, he was one of exceedingly few such creatures, of any species, that Haydar had ever had the luck to know.

Uly had needed to change and grow as circumstances changed.

So he had.

And continued to do so.

Nasrin and Piruz shared their scent, their thoughts, of the Human as the group sat quietly in a cell and allowed time to pass. The crew still had Marlowe's card deck, plus the six projectable reader tablets, which had ended up spread out across the four cells allotted to them, with Blair Mitchell and Leith Masters having been brought down at one point to check in with their fellows, but being kept closer to the primary medical facility otherwise.

Apparently, Doctor Spence had decided to remain a prisoner in the hospital rather than return to face his former charges, silly as that might be. Or perhaps he merely wished to remain close to Doctor Atwater as she slowly recovered and began physical therapy that would tell the Auga a wealth of useful things about Humans.

For now, the other cells were mostly quiet. The Ononguli crews had been fed and then marched back to their various cells. The *Batyr* crew, which was how Haydar thought of the mixed force, had gone down as a block and been fed.

It had the feeling of evening.

Nasrin caught his eye and drew his attention now.

She had been classified by those fools in *Danumash* as a *Social* slave, at a time when he was a *Technical* and Piruz a *Mechanical*.

How little they had understood, assuming her to be some sort of prostitute to provide sexual release and gratification to the various males.

Haydar was simply happy that none of the Humans had been willing to lower themselves, as they saw it, to fornicate with an alien. At least on that short of a trip.

Had the *Danumash* voyage gone longer, that might have changed.

He caught a glimpse of Uly, seated quietly in the back corner closest to the Ononguli side and deep in thought.

How badly things might have otherwise turned out, but for the luck of that particular draw.

They were all in a much better place now, however poorly it seemed.

Nasrin asked a question, gesturing with her tentacles to the wider arena of the prison section of the ship.

*All of them?* he asked her back.

She nodded.

Haydar assented. Some good might come of it.

*Only in the doing could the knowledge be found.*

Nasrin rose with the grace of her kind and her youth, reminding Haydar of joints that hurt in the morning and days he needed to be careful lifting heavy things lest he stress a muscle and hurt his back.

He watched her move to the barred doors of the cell.

Uly had locked in on her movement and openly stared. Dan watched. Suka Kuri and Yanouk had been murmuring but stopped. Ethir was confused. Piruz grinned as widely as his face would allow without cracking.

Outside, the noise was men and a few women, mostly Ononguli but a few other species stuck here and there. Talking. Arguing. Squabbling, perhaps, given tempers and constraint.

Then Nasrin opened her mouth and began to sing.

She had a voice like a songbird, high and piercing, cutting across all the other noise and causing one person after another to fall silent and listen.

Her song carried across the bay alone, but then she reached the end of the first verse and both Omid and Suka Kuri joined her for the chorus. The second verse heard all the male Mazhin voices join in, including his, though Haydar knew he sang with more enthusiasm than skill.

Still, it added to the rumble underneath as the deeper male voices seemed to lift Nasrin on their shoulders, ringing off the many flat surfaces in here and yet not turning muddy in the process.

Looking through the clear walls into other cells, the Ononguli had been hypnotized. Mesmerized by her song, falling silent and still, with many of them pressed up against their own cell doors to better hear.

It was a song of love and loss. Not one of Haydar's favorites, as it tended to strike him as more of a dirge, but it was always a hit with sailors—of whatever species—as it spoke of time away from home and friends never to return.

Nasrin finished the first song, drew a deep breath, and moved on to a second. Again, Omid and Suka Kuri came in quickly, with the men joining later. Interestingly, Haydar could hear echoes from the Ononguli cells as many knew this song and began to quietly sing along, almost under their breath, but multiplied by the hundreds of men and women in here.

Suka Kuri sang alone after that, a song Haydar had never heard before, speaking of the joy of creation. Exactly how the Moss School of Emro saw the universe. Then Omid sang an aching solo. Her voice was a lower alto than Nasrin's. It didn't carry as purely but dug deeper into the bones of your chest as you listened.

Haydar kept watch, but the Auga who were their jailers didn't interrupt. Didn't demand that the prisoners keep silent.

Likely, they saw this concert as the exact opposite of a prison riot, as Nasrin and the other women held all the other prisoners in the palms of their hands, calming them before bed.

The Auga were listening, however. After the sixth song trailed off to nothingness, they dropped the lights in the cell block to a darkness sufficient for most people to sleep.

Concert over, but no comments. No applause, either, just a silence that stretched.

Haydar wondered how many men and women Nasrin had sung to sleep with her voice.

He turned to see Uly shiver once as if awakening from a dream. As he might have been.

The Captain turned to look at Haydar and simply mouth the word *Wow* before settling back into the dimness of his corner to think again, but Uly had a smile on his face now.

It was good.

# PRISON BARGE

# THIRTY-SIX

ULY HAD GROWN USED to the smells of Mazhin, Emro, and Thogin. Human as well. Even Ononguli, though they tended to have less of a smell. There had still been an amazing number of them in the cell block.

Now, they had all been transferred again. Marched in groups of one hundred, so Uly had ended up in a larger cell with roughly forty Ononguli sailors. He'd initially been worried about that, but then he heard his new cell mates bragging to the others about being with *The Songbird*.

That was how they thought of Nasrin. She had sung for them many nights, often putting the entire cell block to sleep, along with Omid and Suka Kuri.

It was weird.

Bathing had become a weekly affair, which nobody appreciated, as folks got stinky in that time. Apparently, Auga had almost no sense of smell.

At least tempers weren't as sharp as they could be, in a cell with five distinct species mixed in. It helped that Uly's group had mixed in with the tail end of *Iron Wasp*'s crew. Mostly mechanics and engineers, rather than the combat troops who had been the first marched out of the ship and were at the other end of the cell block.

One of them walked close now, acting like Uly was an officer in charge, even though he'd been nothing but their prisoner a month ago. And their prey before that.

"What's up, Mykola?" Uly asked.

He was leaning against the bars to the cell. Unlike others, who were using that to watch their fellows or chat with the next cell, Uly was studying the design of the ship. Haydar had called it a prison barge. Something of a holding pen for everyone brought in by the Audit Vessels.

"Sir, do you know what's supposed to happen next?" Mykola asked.

Among his kind, he was a bit taller and heavier, but lacked the muscles of the combat troops who lifted weights regularly. Mykola Pasternak enjoyed good food and worked machines with his hands.

Uly nodded towards Haydar, chuckling internally that the man had been elevated by the Ononguli to something of a sage and oracle.

Just like Uly had become their commanding officer somehow.

Uly wasn't sure what that said.

"I do not, Mykola," Uly replied.

The Ononguli man had asked for specifics. Uly could speculate, but that led to discussions about which and how many of Mykola and his fellows were likely to end up jailed for decades, life, or merely executed for their crimes.

The Auga didn't stigmatize many crimes. Those that made the list carried harsh penalties.

Mykola hung his head and nodded.

"Me and the boys are sorry we captured you, sir," he continued. "Part of the job, and Lady Nasrin has been amazing to hear and even meet. Wanted you to know that before they hauled us all off again."

"Thank you, Mykola," Uly said. "Keep your head up, though. You've all been professional sailors, so it might be that they just enlist you somewhere else, where your talents with machinery can be put to use. It will be the officers like Conductor Sobol and Bakhtiyar Kobolle that have to take responsibility."

"And Ruvim Boyko, sir?" Mykola asked in a careful voice.

"I intend to swear out a complaint specifically against that one, sailor," Uly growled, letting some of his anger at things surface. "He killed a prisoner under his authority. Doesn't matter that Eldridge started it. Boyko could have simply walked away. I will see him hung for that."

"Hung, sir?"

"Place a rope around his neck, Mykola," Uly said. "Tied in a loop and pulled tight enough to catch him. Depending on the punishment, some jurisdictions will drop him from a height and let his weight break his neck instantly. Others would slowly lift him off the ground on a winch to strangle. I prefer something quick and painless, but he deserves no less for what he did."

Ononguli had hair like Humans and many other species. Thick on the head and sparse elsewhere. Boldly red skin, but Mykola had gone pale now. Almost down to where Kolya got when he blushed.

"What about the rest of us?" the Ononguli man whispered.

"You're just sailors, Mykola," Uly reassured him. "Even your Conductor. Boyko is my only foe."

Mykola took that as a dismissal and nodded once before retreating to a section of the cell where his kind had clustered. As with the Emro and Thogin, the edges between the two groups were starting to blur, but that would take time.

Uly assumed that this prison barge was just a temporary

thing, while pirates and smugglers were *processed*, to use the Auga word.

Not even Haydar had any clue as to what that meant.

Uly nodded to the universe and moved to where Dan was seated now. She'd turned into head of security around here, on top of everything else, but a word from her was usually sufficient to shut down any argument, long before it came to blows.

Interestingly, even Ononguli fights had been stopped that way.

He had to remind himself that most of the men and three Ononguli women with him were simple sailors. All of their officers and most of the senior enlisted, plus every single one of the bullies, had been separated out somewhere.

There had been more than a few arguments and brawls in other cells as a result of putting all the troublemakers together. Uly didn't mind it happening elsewhere.

He slid in next to Dan, not quite touching thighs but close enough to feel her heat. He needed some, for reasons he couldn't name. The galaxy felt cold today. That, or thinking about Boyko had left him spiked with adrenaline.

"What's our status?" he asked quietly.

Across the way, a group of his sailors were watching some musical vid with a small group of Ononguli. Again, starting to mix in but not there yet.

"The two crews have high morale," she replied in a murmur. "Mostly, that's you."

"Me?"

"Good example of the right kind of officer." She grinned when he looked over. "Most of them are probably used to folks like that punk Dupuis who you replaced. I keep coming back to how he would have handled all this and we'd have been dead several times over."

Uly nodded. She'd told him about the man. Sounded like a

rat to Uly, but he'd not worked with him back on *Marshall Castillon*.

"Thoughts on the prison itself?"

"None," she said. "Haydar and Piruz thought that maybe our ship triggered a larger alert here when they dropped off so many prisoners, so the locals had to bring in help. That we're in a holding pattern until they get enough judges and courtrooms for everything."

"Processing," Uly said. "But nobody knows what that means."

"Correct," she said. "How are you doing, Uly?"

"Holding the heavens on my shoulders," he joked.

He meant it as a joke, anyway. It came across more serious. She certainly sobered.

"Anything I can do?" Dan asked.

"Everything you have been," Uly replied. "I've got an amazing command team here. Even the Ononguli have started to think of us as officers. Don't know what that gets us, but something. I keep watching and waiting for some moment when somebody might let their guard down long enough for us to do something. Anything."

"Do we even know where we are?" Dan asked.

Uly turned to Piruz, not surprised to find the man looking back. Many of the people in the cell were watching him. Uly nodded the man closer.

"Thoughts on galactic coordinates?" Uly asked.

The *Horse Thief* tilted his head right and left.

"According to some of the others, *Iron Wasp* was cutting down a flank," Piruz replied. "Trying to stay right on the line between Imperial Sectors Nine and Fifteen."

"Is that important?" Dan pressed now.

Piruz nodded.

"Every Sector is mostly independent," he said. "All systems

are largely self-reliant and draw orders only from their own Sector Capital. Communications between Sectors is slow, official, and bureaucratically sclerotic when it does occur."

"Basically running down a border between two?" Uly asked.

"Assuming that the two sides aren't openly hostile, they shouldn't patrol those zones too closely," Piruz nodded. "Either they are angry at one another right now, or *Iron Wasp* was just unlucky enough to run into a patrol vessel that did feel like ranging all the way out to that edge, instead of just staying closer to home."

"Would that mean we were somewhere on that line?" Uly confirmed. "Nine and Fifteen? Then what? Who has possession of us right now?"

It was interesting that Piruz went blank. Hadn't thought to ask that question of his contacts. His tentacles seized up for a moment, then redoubled their usual swirl.

Uly turned to Haydar fast enough to catch the ghost of a grin on that man's face before it vanished.

What was the old saying about old age and treachery overcoming youth and skill?

They did share a second smile as Haydar rose and stepped close, ending up on Dan's far side when he sat.

"Indications on this vessel, when we marched to our cells, are that this prison barge belongs to Imperial Sector Fifteen," Haydar told them.

"Does that imply anything good or bad?" Uly asked, looking between the two Mazhin men.

"Possibly good," Piruz smiled. "Nine is run better, according to all the old stories. Fifteen is…I suppose sloppy might be a good word to describe things, from what I've heard. Presumably we were on the Fifteen side of the line, unless our captors crossed over."

"If they are poorly run, would they employ a captain willing to antagonize their neighbors?" Dan asked. "I'd be pissed if somebody crossed a line and arrested somebody in my jurisdiction without permission."

Nobody had an answer for that. Presumably, those answers existed somewhere, but beyond their current scope.

There wasn't much they could do, locked in a cell on a prison barge with a decidedly mixed crew of sailors.

Except watch.

And wait.

# THIRTY-SEVEN

DAN HAD HAPPENED to be awake when it occurred, so she'd had the best view from the bars, even as others had piled in to watch. Uly and several Mazhin had been able to get spots next to her, with all the Thogin short enough to slip under and the Emro seeing above heads and horns.

A mass of soldiers had appeared. Auga, but others she didn't know.

"The ones with feathers, beaks, and wings are Zuath," Haydar said for their benefit. "Emro and Thogin you know. The ones that look like fishmen are Khet."

Dan studied them all. The Emro were presumably Sabre School. Warriors trained up from a young age, even as others became artists of the Moss School.

The Zuath were a name she'd heard, but not seen. Heads like chickens, with a crest and feathers. Hexapods, with tool-using arms as well as wings. Reverse-hinged legs like a chicken as well.

Cockatrice, however, not farmyard fowl. This group looked dangerous. And well-armed.

The matching uniforms they wore was a stark contrast to the Ononguli pirates. Gold with red trim. Pants and tunics in those colors. Black boots with the sheen of polished leather. Carbine-sized small arms held professionally with their hands, though they looked utterly dainty in the hands of an Emro soldier. And enormous in Thogin hands.

Cell Block One got emptied with professional care. Individuals ordered out by name loudly by an Auga who looked like an officer, with a running count out loud as that person emerged. One hundred specifically and exactly, lined up in two rows and then marched out of the larger space surrounded by armed guards on high alert.

Not fooling around.

Once they were gone, it was clear that the next group would have to wait. Dan tapped Waltin Gysby on the shoulder to get his attention. He looked up expectantly.

"You set up a watch rotation for the next group," she said.

He was hands down the smartest of the cousins, with Ethir the oldest, Ralphye the tallest, and Hobse the laziest. Hobse was frequently motivated into action by his cousins with swats on the head and kicks to the arse, to the point that it almost looked like a comedy routine when they did it.

Dan hadn't asked how much of it was for show.

Waltin nodded and drew his cousins in, then gestured a few Human sailors and even a handful of Ononguli close. Weird, but if he trusted them, she could rely on his sense. Uly would need more help than merely the Humans when he made his move. Whatever it would be.

She retired to where Uly had gathered his command group.

"It begins," Haydar announced. "Whatever processing they needed to prepare, such work is complete, and they are in motion."

Dan didn't like the sound of that, but she was just a goon here. And Uly's Second-in-Command. The muscle side of the operation, though she did have the cousins working and recruiting.

Shit, was she turning into an officer and nobody had told her?

"I have a theory," Uly offered. "Nothing to back it up, but I want you folks to poke holes in it if you can."

He waited until everyone had nodded. Her, Haydar, Piruz. Suka Kuri and Nasrin had stepped close. Ethir got his orders from Waltin and joined.

How soon until some Ononguli sailor was part of this?

"If I had a courtroom set up here," Uly began. "With everything in place, I wouldn't pull one hundred sailors at a time, just to sit in the gallery and watch. Option one, they are doing exactly that. How likely?"

He paused.

"Unlikely, Captain," Piruz offered when nobody else would talk. "Pain in the ass to keep them secured."

"Agreed," Uly nodded. "Option two, they've already been judged and are being hauled off for punishment. Except that the only punishment that would require all one hundred of them is likely mass execution. Again, how likely?"

"Given that the names included none of the officers of *Iron Wasp*, also unlikely," Haydar spoke. "That ship has a smaller command crew than *Danumash* or *Batyr* as I understand them. Smaller than a Mazhin equivalent by roughly thirty percent, and we run lean that way as well. All of those men and women were sailors. Most of them were combat troops intended to capture a ship that resisted."

"Good," Uly said. "Option three, they have a shuttle docked nearby with one hundred seats in the passenger space. Plus, however many guards you need for that contingent, which might have been twenty plus that officer. They are taking the first group over to wherever they are going to hold them while they start processing them individually. From prison to the transient quarters of the local jail so they are handy when the judge needs the next one. Thoughts?"

"That sounds the most like Auga, Captain," Ethir spoke up. "Speaking purely from personal experience, I've been through a similar process, though not in this Sector."

Dan grinned along with everybody else. The cousins were migrant workers, but they'd been arrested for vagrancy, petty theft, vandalism, and a variety of vice charges at different points along the line. All misdemeanors, but routine.

The constant hustle when you were smaller than everybody else and trying to make ends meet in an unforgiving galaxy.

Nothing at all like *Batyr*, but the Industrial Protectors Party had long since made it clear that the purpose of the Party was to eliminate the tendencies of all governing structures to eventually be captured by people with money. Almost verbatim.

Other goals included open meritocracy, eliminating secrecy, ending inherited wealth by taxing the shit out of it at death, and also taxing the shit out of it while you were alive, so that nobody went hungry or cold.

Might not be the best place to live in splendor, but *Batyr* also wasn't a bad place for the vast majority who were poor.

Auga was more like *Danumash*, from the stories that circulated. Ononguli, conversely, almost reminded her of ancient tales of horse-born nomad raiders, going where they wanted with their herds, and occasionally attacking cities that refused to trade honorably.

Honor to an Ononguli was among the most important things, but it was more often wrapped in the tribe than the individual or even the family.

Looking around, she supposed that the crew of *Iron Wasp* had been all of a single tribe, if she understood the cultural translations.

Ethir cleared his throat as the mirth died down.

"They'll haul this group of eighty-some last, because they loaded us last," the Thogin leader said. "Efficiency and organization. Bureaucracy carved into stone tablets and displayed in the market square, where changes have to be carved into new tablets. Slowly grinding, like an old, tired mule pulling a mill stone."

"Will they process all one hundred before coming for the next group?" Uly asked.

"Maybe eighty-some and then they'll come back for more," Ethir replied. "The bunks when we get there will be empty, but still warm. Depending on where we get sentenced to, we might not see any of the Ononguli again. Don't know since Humans are an unknown species this close to center. The Mazhin at least exist in their records, however rare you folk are."

Dan perked up at that. She'd been given to understand that Mazhin ships were known in Auga and other places. Was that a mistake?

Nasrin caught her sudden attention and blushed. She turned to the other two and some message flowed back and forth, borne on the olfactory winds.

Nasrin nodded to Dan, an implicit promise of—at least more —truth later.

"Excellent," Uly replied to Ethir, possibly missing the secondary conversation flowing by. "I have heard little from the Auga or even the Ononguli that suggests to me that we will be in any better shape after *processing* than Haydar and the others were at *Danumash*, and I would rather be free than a subject in a medical experiment somewhere."

"Are we planning a prison break, sir?" Piruz asked bluntly.

"Yes," Uly said. "I have no idea what form it takes. Or how we'll pull it off. If, however, they are about to put us all on a shuttle, that means we are isolated from their overall control to some extent. Out of the cells that have been our limits since *Iron Wasp* appeared. Possibly in a position to control our own fate again. It has been longer for the Mazhin, obviously, but I cannot imagine you wish to be *processed* any more than I do."

"Damned straight," Piruz replied.

Ethir agreed and Suka Kuri used a profanity so colorful that she blushed after it came out of her mouth. Little old lady living legends weren't supposed to swear like sailors, so perhaps it was Dan's fault for having so many such sailors around the old woman to teach her such colorfulness.

Uly turned to Dan now.

"I presume the need for violence, at least at some level," he said. "They are armed and seemed sharp about it. But this was also the first group. We'll be the last, so I can hope that they'll be tired and ready for it to be over. Maybe looking forward to getting home in time for dinner. Something. I need you planning how we might take control of a shuttle transporting us from here to wherever. You take charge of resources, but I'd prefer not to use any of the Ononguli yet. Not suggesting spies or traitors, but I don't know which way they'll jump, other than the option to escape justice right now ought to entice them to help, once it starts. Questions?"

"Do we assume bad results of remaining in Auga hands?" Dan asked.

"They could have put us in one of the other empty cells down the line, rather than filling in the last cell of the Ononguli crew with the previous prisoners," Uly replied in a hard, cold voice. "That they didn't means that they don't see us as unfortunates swept up in something, but presume we were pirates from some-where else. Not entirely wrong, that last point, as *Marshall*

*Castillon* was engaging in privateering, which is just piracy with a prettier face. We might be criminals in their eyes because our laws and culture don't translate. Or haven't been translated yet. I do not trust their justice."

Dan nodded. Every bit of that logic was sound and echoed thoughts in her own head.

"Should we just go all in on the piracy angle?" she pressed.

Uly considered it, then nodded.

"I'd rather send them an apology later for the jail-break," he said. "From the safety of somewhere far enough away that the letter takes three years to get there. Assume we're just as guilty as the rest of the folks in here, regardless of our intentions and actions along the way. By now, somebody has read all the logs of *Iron Wasp*. That one Auga man in charge heard Haydar's story. It didn't change their minds, so nothing might."

"People will get hurt," Dan stated clearly.

They were verging over into territory where officers gave orders like that. Even if she wasn't an officer anywhere but in Uly's eyes.

Looking around, however, those surrounding her had elevated her.

"Yes," Uly nodded. "But they will have guns pointed at us, so they cannot claim later to be innocent. Only to have lost a monopoly on force. Break that, Dan. You figure it out, then bring in everybody you need."

He rose and walked to the far end of the cell at that, taking up a bunk on the empty edge of the Ononguli part of the larger space. Those sailors reacted with a bit of surprise but calmed down when he stretched out and appeared to take a nap.

She was in charge. He'd given her parameters and expected her to execute organized violence in his name. In a way, it was just like the old days, but Uly Fortier was far better to work with than Michel Dupuis on his nicest day.

Dan looked around at the various options and capabilities within the sound of her voice, even as the others waited for her to speak.

She turned to Suka Kuri with a smile.

"I'm going to need your help," Dan said.

# THIRTY-EIGHT

HAYDAR HAD HEARD the plan in quiet whispers, in case either the Auga were monitoring the cell, or one of the Ononguli decided to try to buy a lighter sentence by turncoating at the end.

The audacity was simply breathtaking. And he'd traveled space and fought in more than one battle in his crazy youth. Before he'd turned into a responsible adult and elder.

Or whatever he was these days.

All of the other cells in this chamber had been emptied. Eight of them, with only the ninth remaining. Dan and Ethir had developed a feel for the *processing* speed, being prepared when the previous two occurred and having everyone settled in and organized.

The police team returned for the last time, noisily walking across the empty chamber, boots clacking on metal decks and setting up teeth-jarring harmonics in the stairs.

Haydar was at the door next to Nasrin, keeping watch with Mazhin senses because Dan understood that it went beyond what Humans or Emro could do.

The guards formed up outside the cell, but close enough for

Haydar to taste their scent. Tired, as Uly had expected. Over-worked, based on already moving eight hundred prisoners over the last three days. Well-nourished, but not bright and alive in the way you got when you had a meal composed of various colors of meat, sauce, vegetables, and drink.

This group gave off a uniform scent of brownness. Heavy gravy over old meat to mask the poor quality of the dinner. Rolls with no real butter, using industrially cracked chemicals instead. Vegetables stored frozen for too long, then cooked until mushy, with all the vitamins broken down over time.

*Blah*.

Dan had set up an entire vocabulary for him and Nasrin to use. Brown had been the choice they had settled on after the previous cell was emptied.

"Dull brown," Nasrin said aloud, looking over the group and agreeing with his conclusions.

"Prisoners, step back!" the guard in charge ordered. As he had each time before.

Haydar and Nasrin moved away from the bars and went to a bunk near Uly, close enough to send scents to Piruz next to the Captain if they needed to. Others also cleared space, staying out of the way.

The Ononguli crew were less lackadaisical than they might have been, but Haydar had heard enough whispers to understand that they knew something was up. Just not what. Or how.

Hopefully, they could keep the secret for long enough if they had figured anything out.

"Vitali Havrylyuk, step out of the cell," the head guard called.

Zuath again rather than Auga. The Auga officer had only accompanied the first group, then sent his minions instead. Dan had taken that into account as she adapted her plan.

One of the Ononguli moved out and turned to form the first of two lines.

"Nils Shevchenko, step out of the cell," the Zuath called next.

Another Ononguli sailor, one Haydar had a slight knowledge of from previous interactions.

All the Ononguli were removed first, followed by the four Thogin cousins, then the three Emro.

Then it was time for the Mazhin, individually called forward with him first.

The Humans were called last. All but the four medical staff, who were elsewhere and only rarely seen. Presumably, they would be brought over to be processed, but Uly had ordered Dan to proceed with her plan without them if necessary.

The needs of the many often outweighed the needs of the few, when hard decisions were required.

"Proceed!" the Zuath in charge ordered as the cell emptied finally, and the sailors at the front began to walk. Everyone had milled about under the guard's guns, rather than maintaining any sort of military formation, but the pirates had never worn uniforms, and the Mazhin and Humans had chosen to act just as slack and disorganized.

As a result, the species were mixed up again as everyone started walking. None of the guards had complained, as long as folks walked in two rough lines. Haydar and the others had watched, but there had been no sudden sharpness of emotion as folks moved about.

Dan had the groupings she preferred, after speaking with various folks and understanding strengths and weaknesses.

All Haydar had to do was watch and warn if something changed in a bad way.

The prison barge was huge. He had counted the number of steps to get to the cell block that first time. It took more to get to where they were going, possibly at the other end from where they had boarded. Or at least entirely new corridors and sections of the vessel.

"Prisoners, halt!" came the order.

Prisoners. Not separating the two or three or even five species into more refined groupings, though presumably that was what it meant to be *processed*.

Haydar found himself hoping that he might go to his grave without understanding that verb in an Auga idiom. If he was lucky today and future days.

Two guards opened a hatch and walked through.

"Prisoners, proceed!"

The Ononguli sailors up front went through in double file. Haydar was at the head of the group after the Ononguli, so he went through in the middle and found himself in a shuttle similar to the one that had removed everybody from *Iron Wasp* previously.

Short and wide, as fit an Auga design aesthetic. Three seats, an aisle, four seats, a second aisle, and three on the far side of ten rows.

Ononguli sailors had gone in, but hadn't been organized about how they sat. Or perhaps had gone ahead and filled in the middle seats of the middle section, and stacked themselves rather well against all edges, leaving space where everyone else had aisle seats available.

Almost the exact opposite of what you would expect from a group of random sailors thrust into this sort of situation and told to sit.

It gave Haydar hope.

He took a spot in the front row right where he discovered Blair Mitchell sitting and both could watch and listen. There was a walkway in front of him rather than an immediate bulkhead, so people could cross without tripping over feet. Haydar was shocked to find the nurse here, though saddened that the other three were not in sight or smell range.

All of the seats had shoulder room, though legroom was a bit more cramped for some. Short Auga design, though most of the seats had been lifted for taller folk.

Blair started to say something, but Haydar shook his head and nodded backwards. Blair glanced, saw something, and shut his mouth instead.

The safety harness deployed as before and locked both of them to their seats. As it did with all the other prisoners.

The guards moved to jumpseats at the front and back like stewards on a commercial flight. Haydar doubted that the in-flight meal would be all that great. And the drink cart would not be deployed at all.

Haydar had to fight the urge to look back when Lead Michaels called out.

"Hey, that actually worked!"

Hopefully, it didn't mean anything to the guards, as it came amidst other chatter, but Haydar had been listening specifically for those words. Or the alternative.

That meant that Michaels had just disabled at least part of the security system holding prisoners to their seats.

Now, the fun part would occur.

# THIRTY-NINE

ULY WAS SITTING in the last row on the left section, in the middle next to Suka Kuri on the bulkhead and Dan on the aisle. Dan's plan, with him along to reap the benefits.

"Hey, that actually worked!" Marlowe called from the middle section of the sixth row.

As far from the guards watching as he could get.

Uly went to wiggle the harness holding him to the seat, but Suka Kuri grinned and snapped the latch quietly in one hand.

Emro strength. Even an old woman was far stronger than a Human. And presumably an Auga or most of their other prisoners.

Suka Kuri reached across Uly and broke the latches holding Dan in place as the shuttle began to noisily back away from the prison barge and shift around, tossing people against their harnesses, all of which were ready to be unlocked by Michaels as soon as Dan gave the order.

Automation was a grand thing, until someone could use it against you. In the planning stages, Haydar and Roshan had reminded Dan and Uly that the design work they had been doing for *Danumash*, once upon a time, had been in electronic systems.

Control hardware and software. Machine language stuff. That was why so many of the others were so good at repairing things. They were used to building them once Roshan and Haydar handed them new design blueprints.

Throw in a middle-aged anarchist who had been demoted twice for arguing with officers, a Horse Thief, and a songbird, and Dan had told him she felt like she had the opportunity for a jail-break.

Uly had ordered the mission to proceed. And Blair Mitchell was with them if it worked.

One of these days, he would find a way to return for Leith Masters, Farley Spence, and Jasmine Atwater. Somehow.

Today, he had to get away. Everything after that would be taken care of in its own time.

The shuttle had broken away from the prison barge, but they had no idea how long the next flight might be. Presumably less than the several hours that being unable to take potty breaks might entail.

They didn't have long.

As the flight smoothed back out from the roughness of departure, Nasrin began to sing. Omid and Suka Kuri took it up, then many of the other sailors as well, including Ononguli as it was a song they knew.

Song filled the compartment. Normally, Uly would expect folks to relax about now, but all this was part of Dan's plan to distract.

He looked over a shoulder and noted four guards in the compartment, two at the front and two at the rear. Why would you need more if the prisoners had been behaving prior to this and were locked to their seats for the flight?

Had Marlowe failed, three teams each had an Emro close by.

Yanouk was beyond the stages of student now but had never fought to hurt someone with her bare hands. Still, like Suka Kuri and Hiko, she had the strength to break things casually.

Nasrin finished her first song and began a second one. It had a louder chorus, so Uly wouldn't have heard the latches unlock if he hadn't been specifically paying attention for it. Marlowe had succeeded in unlocking all the prisoners.

Dan moved.

Time was measured in seconds now, because some Ononguli sailor would raise a ruckus about being able to stand up if he wanted to. Sailors tended to be rowdy types, because quiet, bookish ones didn't usually set out to see the galaxy.

Uly was up immediately after Dan, moving in her wake as a protector on her flank. Elsewhere, Nasrin, Wyndham, Beranger, Travers, and several others also exploded into motion, each charging an assigned guard with instructions to use maximum violence.

Dan had drawn an Emro guard by the luck of seat placement. That one was still latched down and had his head turned to look quizzically to his right, where Nasrin and the others were moving.

The man appeared confused, more than concerned, but that changed when he noticed Dan coming right at him.

Then his eyes got huge.

Uly surveyed things and shifted around to Dan's left. She rushed right at the guard and punched him in the throat, one of the few soft spots on the species according to Suka Kuri.

The man began to choke. Uly reached in and ripped the carbine out of his hands before he managed to do anything with it, then turned to the rest of the room, ready to shoot.

Amazingly, all of the Ononguli sailors were still seated. Still singing, in spite of Nasrin having fallen silent. Omid and Suka Kuri had carried it.

All four guards were down, disarmed, and defused. One Emro, two Zuath, and one Khet.

Uly handed the weapon to Dan and started jogging forward. Phase Two would occur at the front of the space, through a door up onto a flight deck that Uly needed to own right now.

Marlowe was already in motion, along with Sadeq. They got there first and were studying the security panel.

"Do the guards have a key or badge?" Uly asked, looking at Wyndham.

"Not that I've been able to find, sir," the Midshipman replied.

Uly turned back to the two troublemakers.

"Get it open," he ordered.

Where Michaels had gotten the tools, nobody had asked. Like the readers that had appeared, because the prisoners from *Iron Wasp* hadn't been stripped and searched. Marlowe and Sadeq did something and the panel opened, revealing innards completely beyond Uly's training.

He didn't need to know everything. He had good people. They needed to know what he wanted done, then Uly could get out of the way and let them make it happen.

The door slipped open. Dan was through before he could move, hip-checking him out of her way. Wyndham followed, both armed while Uly just needed to be in a position to understand the tactical needs of the situation.

And the strategic.

Short corridor. Cockpit with two seats, but only one was occupied right now.

Dan moved right up next to the Zuath woman piloting and pointed the gun into her face. The woman's beak fell open in surprise and her head crest stood up perfectly straight instead of being kind of flopped over as normal.

"Do not speak," Dan said simply as Uly got there. "No

sudden movements. Nod if you understand and would like to survive this. I have other pilots who could fly this ship."

Uly didn't know if that was true, but the dead calm way she said it to the woman convinced the Zuath to nod choppily.

Haydar appeared next, having trailed them into the forward space. He started typing on the co-pilot's console, then turned back to Uly with his tentacles standing almost perfectly straight out like he'd touched a live wire or something.

"I believe the vernacular equivalent would be to call this area an impound yard?" Haydar said.

"What do you have?" Uly asked.

"Any number of other ships around us," Haydar replied. "All appear to be flightworthy, but are currently parked in stable orbits. Interestingly, *Iron Wasp* is one of them."

Uly turned to the woman pilot.

"Is that true?" he asked sharply. "The pirate Interceptor *Iron Wasp*?"

"Your ship, right?" the woman asked.

"No, but close enough," Uly replied. "We were prisoners of the Ononguli before we were prisoners of the Auga. Is that *Iron Wasp*?"

"It is," she nodded. "Evidence of crimes committed."

"Then what would happen to it?" Uly demanded.

"After all the trials?" she asked in a confused tone. Uly nodded. "It would be flown to either a yard to be sold or perhaps broken up, depending on the value."

"Flightworthy right now?" Uly asked her.

"Probably," the Zuath woman nodded. "Hasn't been here long enough to have been put into cold storage like some of them. Might not be here long since you were the last group to go before the Tribunal."

Uly considered his options. Running away had always been number one, but he'd been assuming a small ship they might hijack. Something the size of *King Hewitt II* with his smaller crew, however expanded by three Emro and four Thogin.

*Iron Wasp* was a warship. An Interceptor, to use Imperial parlance, though he would have called it a heavy frigate back home. Less than a light cruiser, but more than enough to get him home.

And what could *Batyr* do with access to Ononguli technology? Turn the war with *Danumash* sideways? Conquer the *Combined Crowns* and liberate their peasants and peons from the aristocracy that felt an ownership stake in people's lives?

"Haydar, where is this shuttle bound?" Uly turned to the man.

"Main station," Haydar replied. "About ten degrees forward around orbit and somewhat lower."

Uly turned to the pilot.

"Is there a crew aboard *Iron Wasp* keeping it running?" he demanded.

"Likely," she said. "I heard that it suffered a failure in the cooling system that caused them to surrender originally. Easy fix if nobody is shooting at you, but the ship wasn't all that damaged. Folks were expecting to see it sell for a pretty penny."

"You will come about and set course for *Iron Wasp*," Uly instructed the woman. "If you do as I order and don't cause any troubles, I will send you and your guards home with this shuttle when we leave. As Dan said, I have others that can fly us instead. What is your decision?"

"You're going to steal that ship?" she asked, beak fallen open again.

"We're staging a jailbreak, in case you hadn't realized it," Dan pointed out to the woman. "Add this to the crimes when you tally them up later."

Uly grinned at the raw shock on the pilot's face. Possibly the most surprising thing she'd ever seen but having a gun in her face certainly didn't excite her.

"Okay," she said quietly, blinking overly large eyes too rapidly as she tried to process.

"Haydar, shut down all external communications," Uly ordered. "Monitor to see when someone finally realizes what we're up to, but don't reply. Turn off all markers and scanners as well, so we maybe look dead or a rock floating through space. Anything to make people forget us."

"I'd sing, if I thought it might help," Haydar chuckled.

Uly nodded and turned back to the corridor.

"What are you doing?" Dan asked.

"Recruiting a crew," Uly replied.

# FORTY

ULY WALKED out of the flight deck and noted the faces watching earnestly. Amazingly, all the sailors were still seated, other than the ones with guns on guards or keeping watch.

He walked to the middle of the front row and took a deep breath.

"We've captured this shuttle," he announced, waiting for the cheers to die down before he continued.

"Better news, right now, we are turning to approach your old ship, *Iron Wasp*," Uly called.

This time, cries of surprise and confusion. About what he'd expected.

"My intent is to steal the ship and sail away as fast as we can go," he continued. "I have a small crew, so we should be able to do it, at least for a time."

Uly paused as that sank in with all the Ononguli folks. They were pirates but had indeed largely been engineering staff rather than bridge crew or gunners. Or the combat goons that had been part of the first group to be processed three days ago.

"All of you are pirates," Uly reminded them. "We've been captured by the Auga Empire, and you know what they do about pirates better than me, because I'm just a barbarian hick from the hinterlands."

Laughter in spots now as they started to relax. To calm from the confused adrenaline of an escape attempt.

"I would like to know how many of you would prefer to escape with me, rather than remaining behind on this shuttle to be subsequently *processed* by the Auga Empire," Uly called. "How many of you think that prison will rehabilitate you into good, little Imperial citizens? Would you rather be free?"

Roars now, full-throated as these men and women got a second option instead of a lifetime in a small, gray box.

Uly held up both hands to quiet them, but that still took a few moments.

Silence eventually reigned.

"You men and women sort yourselves out into training and responsibilities," Uly ordered them. "We've got five prisoners that need to make it home safely when we flee, so remain in your places for now, but be prepared to run to your stations when we board *Iron Wasp*. I will need a team to get all the bridge systems working, and the rest of you aft working to get engines and generators online so we can run like hell for the wilderness. Marlowe, Kolya, and Sadeq, stand up."

All three did and Uly pointed to them.

"These three are in command of engineering until I say otherwise," Uly ordered. "You will treat them as Chief Engineers, but you will also need to take responsibility to get things warm and moving so we can escape. Go about your usual duties while you listen for orders. I have no idea how quickly they will chase us, or with what, so we're going to run hard, fast, and random. See to your duties, ladies and gentlemen."

Uly turned and headed forward again as folks broke out in cheers behind him.

He was committed now. They all were.

Hopefully, he could pull it off.

# FORTY-ONE

DAN'S PLAN had gotten them this far, but she'd reminded Uly several times that this would be where planning failed. Knowing which ship they might take, assuming that the shuttle they were on wasn't the one they stole.

She listened to the cheering from the main cabin as he walked back in. Uly looked like a commanding officer, but she'd been around long him enough to see the doubt and concern in his eyes. Worry, but for everyone that he was dragging deeper into a mess, rather than about himself.

Dan smiled when he turned her way. That seemed to lift some weight off his shoulders, because his eyes cleared as he smiled back.

The birdwoman pilot was maintaining as calm and normal a flight as she could, with Haydar standing right next to her and watching like a hawk.

"Will *Iron Wasp* challenge us when we get close?" Uly asked.

"I doubt they'll even notice you docking," the pilot replied. "At best, a skeleton crew aft maintaining some of the generators on and life support. Nothing else since it didn't need to fly anywhere."

"Can you dock us all the way forward?" Dan asked. "Bow airlock?"

Every head turned to look at her at the same time, so Dan smiled.

If nobody thought of it, they wouldn't be defending against it.

"Sure," the pilot said. "Why?"

"Don't you worry," Dan said. "All you have to do is get us aboard, then wait while we get everything warm. Once we're ready to flee, you back away and make it home safe. We'd prefer not to kill everyone doing this. We are, however, prepared to, as your Emro guard aft discovered when I knocked him out."

"Emro?" the woman gasped. "You took out Grall?"

"By myself," Dan smiled.

Hell, if nothing else, that story would get around and Humans might get a reputation for toughness that mattered the next time an Ononguli raider strayed too far off course. Or the Empire decided to explore Sector Seventeen more fully.

Zuath eyes were large and round, much like the chickens that came to mind when she looked at one. They could get huge when the beak fell open in shock again.

Dan just nodded serenely, aware that Haydar was holding chuckles inside from the grin on his face where the pilot couldn't see.

Nasrin had taught Dan the Mazhin form of Tai Chi during their combined lessons. Assume the first punch has already been thrown and react defensively, then knock someone down. From there, you can run or keep fighting, but while in control.

She and Uly had knocked this shuttle crew down. Time to run.

Out the front windshield, the long, curved lines of *Iron Wasp* began to resolve itself into a ship. Smooth lines, which just didn't look right to Dan's eye, since it could never land on the surface of a planet. Without atmospheric issues, why streamline?

But looking at it now, she understood. *Iron Wasp* looked like a blade. A sword to be held in one hand while attacking. People seeing that coming at them would be intimidated.

Those that could be.

*King Hewitt II* hadn't had a chance, completely unarmed after the bridge hit punched a hole side to side. The lone Neutron Omnipulsar had been destroyed, not that it could have done much against *Iron Wasp*.

Even below and locked up in a prison barracks, Marlowe and Sadeq had been impressed with how well-armed and tough this ship was.

"Thirty seconds to dock," the pilot announced in a professional voice.

"Lock us in then shut everything down when you are docked," Dan replied. "You'll go aft with the other four prisoners until we're ready to depart. Less chance of any misunderstandings that way."

The pilot shuddered, so she understood exactly what Dan was implying.

*Iron Wasp* had turned from a ship into a wall. The shuttle slowed to a walk, then a crawl, then tar on a warm day. The airlock dock aligned on the pilot's screen then locked in with a bright beep and a soft bump.

"Shutting engines down now," the pilot said, falling back on her training and checklists since she had nothing else upon which to operate.

Dan nodded, then got the woman up and aft.

Uly was already there, with Beranger and Travers. Wyndham looked like he would be in charge of the prisoners, which made sense. He'd never killed anyone.

Dan marched her prisoner over and Wyndham took charge of her. All five were in the last row, and Dan heard the click as Marlowe reset the locks holding the woman to the seat.

She turned to Uly and smiled grimly.

"We're going to have to run the whole length of the ship if we want to surprise folks aft," he reminded her.

"You will be up on the bridge with Huff, Roscoe, Blakeslee, and Haydar," Dan countered in a tone that brooked no argument. She was in command of this part. "The rest of the crew should have spent more time doing PT while we were locked up. Nasrin and Yanouk will be able to keep up. Even Marlowe's old legs should be good. It will give your pirates a new appreciation of how their lives are going to change when they start acting like sailors."

She'd said that loud enough that others could hear her. Dan turned and smiled evilly at the engineers just now catching on that running for their lives hadn't been a euphemism.

Worse, three alien women were intent on making them look bad in the process.

She looked around and found Marlowe at the airlock.

"Open it up," she ordered.

# FORTY-TWO

ULY HAD LET the first group, the big one, go through first. They had two of the guns with them. And several killers. Wyndham had the third weapon, and Uly had taken the final one for himself.

A ship's bridge was no place for careless beam fire. If something got destroyed, he wanted to be able to blame nobody but himself.

One of the Ononguli sailors had volunteered to lead him, a man named Yuriy Kovalchuk who claimed to be qualified to sit bridge watches. Right now, Uly just needed someone who could get him there quickly enough that he could take control of things.

This being a pirate ship, Uly assumed that Conductor Sobol had overrides on his bridge that let him control damned near everything. Mutiny in a formal navy was a hanging offense. For pirates, he presumed it really just turned into a change of bosses.

Sobol hadn't struck Uly as a trusting kind of guy.

Yuriy led, with Uly hot on his heels, and the rest of the team strung out behind him as they pounded up staircases from the lowest deck to the highest.

They hit a landing and Kovalchuk paused. Huff and Roscoe were first to catch up, blowing from the run.

"Through this hatch you turn left and go about ten meters, sir," Kovalchuk said gasping. "Bridge hatch is on the end of the corridor forward, with Conductor's main office just on the other side of this wall right here."

"We are not expecting anyone," Uly reminded his team as they gathered. "That being said, we have no way to know what will be there, so follow my lead and be ready to take cover or tackle anyone. I'll shoot if necessary, but again, these are just crew doing a job for a paycheck. They didn't sign up to be in my war, other than being the police on duty when all this happened."

Kovalchuk still looked a little in awe at that, but Uly supposed that the man thought like a pirate first and a sailor second. The Ononguli regularly reminded Uly of nomads from the endless steppe on some primitive world, if you picked them up and gave them starships to replace horses.

Uly wondered if he'd added their tribe to his crew. And what the implications of that might be in the future.

They took one last moment to catch their breaths, then Uly stepped into the corridor, looking to his right to confirm that it was empty. And clear as far as he could see. Someone had left every hatch frame open going aft, against all sailing logic.

You wanted those hatches closed in case of breach or fire, keeping each section isolated as much as possible.

He chalked it up to being in the repair yard. Or the impound lot, as Haydar had called this place.

Clear, he turned the other way and started walking, carbine in both hands ready to shoot or be used like a club. Roscoe and Huff were close, with Blakeslee and Kovalchuk trailing. Others were still coming, but Uly needed to move, and move quickly.

The hatch looked exactly like the one that had trapped Uly in the prison barracks for so long, but it opened when he got close, unlike that one.

Inside, the bridge was dim but appeared empty as he swept it left to right with eyes and carbine.

Uly stepped in and realized that it was oval shaped, with the inner portion down one step from an outer ring walkway. One station that was obviously for the Conductor, centered and facing forward towards a large display screen on the wall. Two other stations with their backs to the Conductor, also facing forward. More than a dozen more around both wings facing out.

Uly moved to the center and down a step, standing next to Sobol's chair but not sitting.

Not yet.

"Let's go," he snapped at the others as they slid into stations and started bringing them live.

Nothing appeared locked, so they were able to move quickly.

"Sir, should I bring the room lights up some?" Kovalchuk asked.

"Yes," Uly said. "Normal levels. And the heat as well. It's a little chilly in here."

"I've got life support," Kovalchuk announced in a calm, professional voice. Like he had done this before.

"Engineering here," Huff called. "Starting to dial up power slowly and bring the engine reactors up."

"Blakeslee?" Uly asked.

"Passive sensors only, sir," Blakeslee replied. "Station is asking the shuttle to respond. And why they docked with the prisoner's ship. I'm not sensing any alarm in their voices, at least not yet. No telling how soon they wake up."

"This might be the first time they've ever had something like this happen," Uly reminded everyone. "The other groups went peacefully and got processed. The station might not know what to do when they lose control of the situation. Blakeslee, are there any other ships anywhere nearby that might be big enough to be a threat?"

"Checking that now, sir," the man said. "The *Auga* left everything here on passive, so I have a complete scan of nearby space going back weeks. Couple of big ships, but nobody within ninety degrees of us at this moment."

"Roscoe, work with Blakeslee and plot a course for warp," Uly said. "And make it random in speed and directional changes. I don't care where we end up, as long as we don't hit anything while we're running. No straight lines, please. We can sort that all out later."

The crew laughed. Straight lines were what let people trace you and run you down.

Like had happened to *Iron Wasp*. And *King Hewitt II*. Twice.

They waited for a while as the great ship slowly woke from her nap, like a dragon in some fantasy novel.

"Comm, I have Engineering online," Kovalchuk called. "Chastain."

"I'll take it here," Uly said, finally moving to sit in Sobol's place. He keyed the line live and saw her face appear in a tiny screen. A weight vanished off his shoulders. "How did it go?"

# FORTY-THREE

DAN WENT FIRST through the airlock, following a friendly Ononguli sailor named Mykola Pasternak. She didn't trust any of them, at least not yet, but he had volunteered, and moved at a good pace. Not enough to outrun her, but she could hear fewer and fewer people close behind her. Beranger and Travers, because they knew what she was like and had kept up their training. Nasrin and Yanouk, the taller woman's longer legs making up for a slower pace.

Behind that, a long line of men and women, with Piruz and Sadeq closest and all the rest of the Mazhin mixed in with Ononguli and Human. And Thogin and Emro.

Utterly weird, but she'd watched every step of the way as Uly had worked his charm and skill to win people over.

Including her.

"That's wrong," Pasternak gasped as he ran.

"What's that?" Dan asked, stretching her stride a little to come up beside him.

"All the hatches are open," he said between breaths and

steps. "Should be closed, even in dock. Dumb if you have a leak."

"They weren't planning to keep the ship," Dan reminded him.

"Yeah," Pasternak agreed, "Still stupid habit to get into. Even for those Auga punks."

Dan just grinned and held even with the man. Ononguli considered themselves tougher and meaner than anybody else in the galaxy, with a barbarian's disdain for civilized folk when you caught them muttering.

They did make lovely starships, though.

"That's engineering there," Pasternak pointed as they ran. "Main airlock should always be closed at both ends in case you have an explosion. Shit could take out the whole ship configured like this."

Again, living in dock. Dan guessed that waiting for the airlocks to cycle took too long, so someone had started cutting corners by leaving them empty. Save themselves three whole minutes each way.

Not someone trained to warships, obviously. Everything was done that way for a reason. Usually involving safety of the ship and crew.

Cut corners bleed you. She'd been taught that early on. Pay attention to the rules and regs, then assume that they were put in for a reason.

Usually in response to lives lost.

Today, however, it would get her there and hopefully on top of whoever was minding the store before they could stop her.

Assuming that the stampede of boots behind her didn't cause them to panic.

Dan didn't slow down as Pasternak did, blowing right by the man. But then, she and Beranger had guns and he didn't.

She exploded out of the mouth of the engineering airlock into a three-decks-tall open barn of a space, filled with giant, metallic trolls squatting here and there.

There was a station where three people could stand while facing aft to have the generators in front of them. A Khet, a Zuath, and a Thogin on a stepladder were working, but it had the appearance of standing around having coffee while the machines did the heavy lifting.

All three turned back to the sound of her entrance. Of her mob.

Mouths fell open when they realized that there were guns pointed at them.

"Don't do anything stupid," Dan called with a smile as she kept jogging towards them, the tip of a deadly spear. "I'd like to take you all prisoner, put you on the shuttle that brought us here, and send you home when this is all done. How's that for a deal?"

The Thogin was in charge, based on the number of stripes on his gold and red uniform's sleeve. Looked older than Ethir, but Ethir was only Dan's age, relative to lifespan. This one felt like a lifer Engineering Lead, back on *Marshall Castillon*. Marlowe's cousin, in a way, without the serial demotions.

"Who the hell are you?" the Thogin asked.

The other two already had their hands in the air. Everybody turned her way.

"Pirates." Dan laughed as she got close enough to speak instead of yelling. "This is now my ship, and my crew will detain you. Unless you want to get frisky in the process, and I have to shoot you."

Yanouk had obviously walked up behind her, because the Thogin Lead leaned back to look up at the tall woman.

"No problems here," the man said. "Pirates?"

"Call it a jail-break," Nasrin said from Dan's immediate left. "The hospitality was lacking, so we decided to take our business elsewhere."

Jaw-dropping shock on the three.

"How many others are aboard?" Dan demanded sharply.

"Six besides us," the Thogin Lead replied, hands finally up like the other two.

"Where are they now?" Dan pressed.

"Up a deck in their quarters, probably," he said. "Or the crew lounge."

"Beranger, take custody of the prisoners," Dan ordered. "Marlowe, Kolya, Sadeq, do your magic. Everyone else, hop to! Travers, you're with me."

She turned to the Thogin man.

"Let's go find them and keep the rest out of trouble, shall we?" she asked.

Dan motioned him and the other two to one side to get them out of the way. Yanouk and Nasrin joined her, as did Travers. The Ononguli crew flowed immediately to work, with Human and Mazhin only a step behind them as people figured out what needed doing.

And got to it.

Jail-break.

# FORTY-FOUR

DAN LED. Beranger had the Khet and Zuath prisoners at the rear of the column, while Dan kept their boss up with him. He didn't smile as much as Ethir or the others did but had that same attitude a short guy got around tall women.

She smiled as Yanouk shadowed the fellow. Might even be doing that on purpose.

Out of Engineering, they turned and went through a hatch and up a flight of stairs. Dan stopped the Chief here.

"A reminder," she said. "Everyone can be comfy prisoners sent home on the shuttle in a while. Or they can be dead. It really depends on you. What's the next step?"

He scowled at her, grimaced, gritted his teeth, possibly considered rolling his eyes. If they weren't on opposite sides of the law, she might have liked the guy enough to offer him a job.

Today, however…

"Through here," he gestured. "Cabins and lounge for the machinist staff on the right. Half should be asleep right now, and the other half goofing off, knowing them. Ignore any smoke alarms unless you can actually see open flames, because third crew are dorks who get stupid when they get bored. Yes?"

"Yes," Dan agreed with a commanding smile. She was in charge. She could afford it. "You wait here with Beranger and a few of my folks while the rest of us round up your crew."

She nodded and the big group split into two, with Nasrin and Yanouk staying with her and Travers. Good enough.

Dan opened the hatch and looked left. Empty corridor clear to the bow maybe. Open hatch with lights and music on her right, so she moved that way. All other hatches appeared closed.

She turned to Nasrin and pointed to a spot.

"You wait right there in case someone comes out behind us," Dan ordered.

Nasrin was at least as dangerous unarmed as Dan was. At least. Beranger had the other gun, so that left Dan to shoot anyone. Hopefully, intimidation would be sufficient.

She stepped to the hatch and pointed her gun at the room.

Three Thogin males. Boys. Dumbasses, as one of them was bent over, and the second appeared to be in the process of lighting farts. The third was watching a vid with headphones on, bopping along to music.

Dan shook her head and cleared her throat.

The two looked up like mice suddenly discovering a cat. Or juveniles hearing the apartment door open when Mom got home.

Long, silent pause.

"Shit," the one with a lighter in his hand said distinctly.

"Up against the wall, face in, hands up," Dan ordered. "I've taken the rest of your crew prisoner. Don't make me shoot your sorry asses at this late stage, okay?"

The first two moved. The third one looked up at those two, then turned owlishly to look at her. His eyes got HUGE, then his mouth fell open.

Dan crooked a finger for him to stand, then pointed at the others.

Hilariously, the man kept hold of the player and still had his headphones in but managed to touch his nose to the wall.

Dan moved out of the way as Travers and the others got them frisked, then moved all six prisoners to couches and chairs.

The boss Thogin turned to the other three and sighed.

"I will deny this later if asked," he began. "But I'm glad she didn't have to shoot any of you stupid mooks."

He looked Dan dead in the eye.

"Cousins, ya know?" he asked.

Having spent time with Ethir and his, she nodded. Thogin family relationships seemed more like an ongoing standup improv scenario than anything but seemed to work.

"Beranger, these are yours." She turned to the Chief. "Which cabins for the rest?"

"Starboard forward from here," he nodded, settling in.

Dan nodded and exited, again taking about half the team with her.

The first hatch opened to a Zuath male sleeping in the nude atop the covers. It was not a pretty sight. Even with feathers.

She stepped close enough to tap his foot, noting the chicken-like scales from the calf downward. He stirred, opened his eyes with a dreamy smile, like she was an angel descending to bless him with a wet dream.

Dan slapped his foot harder the second time. He flinched. Sat up. Woke up to the gun.

Hands went up.

Dan stepped back and gestured him to follow.

He did. Still nude. Still…aroused, but that was deflating quickly.

Which was just fine with her.

Yanouk put an enormous hand on his shoulder and directed the man towards the lounge while Dan moved down a hatch.

Khet this time. Sleeping with a damp rag over his forehead, presumably for humidity. The species was amphibian, with both lungs and gills, and needed to immerse in water regularly for hydration.

He stirred when the light from the corridor spilled on him.

This one was wearing a hooded onesie that zipped up the front. In neon green.

"Too early," he muttered as he sat up, catching the rag and turning to look at her.

Then his face got comical.

*Seriously? You've never once had a successful jail-break around here?*

His mouth opened and closed, again and again. Nothing came out.

"You're my prisoner," Dan informed him. "This way."

Nasrin took him and led the fellow aft.

Third hatch.

Dan took a breath and hoped that this one would be boringly normal. Especially after the last two.

She opened it and looked in.

Emro. Female. Yanouk's size, with Hiko's muscles. Heavy sleeper, from the snores. Dan moved into the cabin and found a spot she could withdraw to shooting if it became necessary.

Even Engineering Emro would be twice as strong as her.

She reached out and tapped a foot. Nothing.

Tapped it harder. Got mumbles in the woman's sleep.

Dan slapped the bottom of her foot with an open palm. Painful but not damaging.

The woman sat straight upright.

"I'm awake!" she yelled.

"Good, now behave yourself or I'll shoot you," Dan offered politely.

The woman looked over and blinked several times.

"Oh."

"Stand up and walk out into the corridor," Dan ordered her. "The rest of the crew are my prisoners. You join them and then we send you home when we leave. Am I clear?"

"Prisoners?"

"That's right," Dan nodded.

More blinks.

"What species are you?" she asked curiously.

"Human," Dan said, then growled. "Move. We'll talk more when you get rounded up with the others."

That got through. The woman rose, wearing a T-shirt and sleeping shorts. She walked with fantastic grace to the hatch, then paused.

"Oh!" she said. "Lots of you."

"This way," Travers said from outside.

Dan followed. She got back to the lounge and counted noses. Everyone accounted for.

Dan relaxed and took a deep breath.

Nine prisoners. Wide mix of species. Eight male and a female.

As long as they behaved, she had enough people and guns to control them. And enough guns to end them if not. Dan let that scowl wash over the group. They reacted like engineers, all but the Emro woman.

"Shortly, the plan is to steal this ship," she said simply. "The Captain, Conductor, whatever, will put you on the shuttle that brought us here before we leave. Right now, you stay put while I talk to him, then we'll move on."

She studied the oldest Thogin. The boss. He nodded, presumably taking responsibility for everyone.

Dan could have cleared the ship with live fire had she wanted. The look in the Thogin's eyes recognized that.

Dan nodded and headed back down to Engineering.

Koyla was in the middle, with Marlowe on his left and Sadeq nowhere to be found. Presumably fixing something. Or telling someone how to fix it.

"We good?" she asked as she got close.

"Better than good," Kolya grinned at her. "They apparently took the time to fix whatever broke before, then do a full maintenance cycle on everything here. We'll sail out of here like we just got out of a six-month drydock when the captain gives the word."

Dan nodded. Good.

Too many things had gone wrong. And done so in ways that most of it had been out of their control immediately.

Felt good to be able to take charge again. Action.

That passive shit was for the birds.

She found a comm and dialed up the bridge.

"How did it go?" Uly asked when he came on.

"No casualties," Dan replied. "Nine prisoners under guard right now. Kolya is happy with power systems. I assume bridge is good?"

"We're ready to go as soon as the shuttle backs away," Uly said. "Go ahead and bring your prisoners forward and we'll get that off the list next."

Dan nodded.

"On my way," she said, cutting the line.

It would be nice to win one for a change.

# FORTY-FIVE

ULY WAITED by the airlock as Dan appeared with a motley mob following her. He'd already checked in on Wyndham, but the Midshipman was handling things with a verve and authority that hadn't been there three months ago.

Before the youngster had accidentally joined the *Batyr* Navy.

If nothing else, Uly would be proud of the future officer Dan was turning Wyndham into. Proud to know he'd been there.

*Danumash* might not appreciate it, but they'd all burn that bridge later.

For now, he studied the group walking out of the main corridor.

Mix of species, with two of them in sleeping clothes.

"Who's in charge of you lot?" Uly asked as they came to rest.

An older Thogin male stepped forward.

"That would be me," he said.

Uly nodded to the man.

"I am Ulysses Fortier of the *Batyr* Navy," he replied. "Thank you for maintaining this ship as well as you have, as I'm about to steal it. Your next assignment is to get home safely, which is all I'm trying to do at this point as well. Questions?"

"Are you lot really pirates?" he asked.

"The Ononguli were," Uly said. "I suppose you could say some of the Humans were privateers, which is a little more formal, but amounts to essentially the same. I'm not here to start a war, Chief. I want to get my people home. All of them, which amounts to a lot of homes now, so I don't have any time to waste."

He nodded to Dan, and she got the group moving. An Emro woman at the back of the group, wearing a tight T-shirt and tighter shorts paused, as if wanting to say something.

Indecisive.

She was staring right at him with some question on her face, so he nodded, and she stepped out of line, with both Nasrin and Yanouk flanking her. And Dan pointing a gun at her back, while Beranger had taken the rest into the shuttle.

She stopped a polite distance away but was still a huge woman. Maybe two hundred and thirty centimeters tall. One hundred and fifty kilograms of mass that looked like it had been carved from jade.

"Yes?" he asked.

She turned to look for Dan.

"She said your species was Human," the woman said. "That you're pirates from the far ends of Sector Seventeen."

"Close enough," Uly replied. "Should that matter?"

The woman hesitated, still indecisive. Biting her lip even, while not making eye contact.

Uly waited, still ready to simply fall to the ground if she moved suddenly. Yanouk looked thin and wispy standing next to the woman, which wasn't something Uly ever thought he'd say. Muscles on muscles.

"I'm Sabre School," the woman finally announced. "I wanted

to be a warrior, but the Auga refused and made me serve in engineering. Said I was too smart to be Sabre and should have been Moss."

Uly saw the empathy on Yanouk's face. Emro culture venerated those two Schools, though not everyone joined them. Most Emro were merely people, living lives as best they could. To be good enough for the one and forced into the other must be an especially painful torture.

He turned to Suka Kuri, seated in a corner where she was hard to see, and nodded the woman to step closer.

He'd trust the opinion of a living legend.

"Your name?" Uly asked.

"Anari Supasei, sir."

Suka Kuri stepped close and Uly moved a half-step back. Three Emro women took up a lot of space and almost made him feel like a child standing next to them.

Suka Kuri seemed to be asking an entire series of questions from the tone of her voice, but the jargon was so esoteric that Uly hardly followed any of it. Almost a private language. The original tongue of the Emro, rather than Standard that everyone shared? At one point. Yanouk got involved as well, making a case one way or the other from the emotions.

Uly glanced over at Dan and got the sort of shrug he felt like offering the universe.

Finally, the conversation faded. Suka Kuri turned to Uly and smiled.

"The Auga are utter fools," the old woman pronounced with great authority.

Uly asked a question with his eyes.

"Anari is absolutely Sabre School," Suka Kuri nodded. "Her intelligence simply marks her as one that might rise to mastery given time."

"Round peg, square hole?" Uly asked.

It took all three women a moment to process that idiom, then Suka Kuri leaned back and howled with laughter.

"Indeed, Captain," she finally said when she got control again. "And the Auga have a hammer they were convinced would fit this woman into the slot of their choosing."

"Then what are we doing with her?" Uly asked.

Living Legend. He would absolutely defer to her wisdom. Sabre School were warriors trained from birth. If she really meant to join his crew, she'd be third behind Dan and Nasrin on the security side of things.

Looking at Yanouk beside her, he decided that Anari would also be far down the line of even the most interesting women aboard, to say nothing of the rest of the crew.

"She has volunteered to stay with the ship when you depart, Captain," Suka Kuri said. "Has taken appropriate oaths of honor to become a member of your crew, serving with the rest as an equal."

"And you trust her," he asked, including both Suka Kuri and Yanouk in his question.

"I do," Suka Kuri said.

Yanouk also nodded.

Uly turned to the tall woman and studied her intently. Muscles. Solid.

Jade green, but looking closer, someone had carved her out of marble that happened to be green. Black hair. Dark eyes.

Nervous, but proud, standing there in skin-tight everything that reminded everyone she was a woman.

"I am convinced that you might be making a mistake, sailor," he said. "But if that is your wish, and these women support you, welcome aboard."

She smiled a mile wide and for a moment Uly thought she was about to grab him in a hug, but she caught herself before anyone tackled her.

He turned to Nasrin.

"I'll let you and Yanouk get her sorted out," he said. "Dan, let's get the rest home."

# FORTY-SIX

HAYDAR WAS on the bridge of *Iron Wasp*, studying things in the computer somewhat at random. Sterling Huff was in charge while Uly was below, and Drew Roscoe was working with Delbert Blakeslee to plot the escape course they would take.

Uly, Dan, and a variety of others burst through the rear hatch at something of a jog, but there didn't seem to be an emergency.

"Scanners, where's that shuttle?" Uly called, even before he slipped into the Conductor's station.

The others followed him down to the lower level, but while he sat, they all remained leaned against the railing that circled the room. Watching. Haydar came up with an odd number when he counted. One too many Emro. Big woman. Sabre School from the look of her.

Nervous, which was probably good, but flanked by Suka Kuri and Yanouk.

"Backing away now, sir," Blakeslee replied. "Thrusters only."

"Roscoe, get us in motion," Uly ordered.

"Engineering, forward drive going live," Roscoe called out. "Stand by for warp-bubble."

It had been many years since Haydar sat on the bridge of a warship. He'd retired from that life long before being captured by *Danumash* raiders and forced to keep being a laboratory scientist. Ulysses Fortier had brought it all back, but in a good way.

Haydar looked at his boards now, echoing the passive sensor feeds from Blakeslee. When the Auga had parked the ship here, they'd left the passive sensors on, absorbing information, so Haydar had weeks of data about ships in the vicinity with which to manipulate.

Like any good data nerd, he'd been wallowing in the information presented, though unsure exactly what he could do with it.

With two notable exceptions.

"Captain," Haydar said now, causing a great many heads to turn his direction. "I'm highlighting the two vessels that Blakeslee noted earlier. One is pointed exactly the wrong direction to quickly chase us, but the other could follow. Neither are currently at alert, but that will change shortly, as the station has begun to panic."

"The one that could chase us," Uly said. "How big is it?"

"Striker class, Captain," Haydar replied. "At the light end, but still far heavier than this vessel."

"Understood," Uly said. "Roscoe, let's get crazy."

"Coming up!" Roscoe said eagerly.

Haydar watched the alerts being sent out as the station finally figured out what was going on. To some degree. Ships would start to respond, but only slowly because this was not a busy sector capital world. More like the county prison out in the sticks, if he had the Human idiom correct.

At least the *Danumash* one. *Batyr* looked at it differently, with a much more communal and social approach to culture and governing. Individualism, yes, but geared towards the greater good.

That stood in stark contrast to the classist *Fuck You* approach of *Danumash* to such things, where money and power overruled everything, including sense and sensibility, it seemed. Where familial connections got the incompetent into positions of dangerous power.

*Batyr* was smaller, but much better run. At least as far as Haydar was concerned.

All Haydar's sensor feeds went blank as the warp-bubble formed, and *Iron Wasp* was contained in her tiny, private universe.

Haydar leaned back and powered things down.

Until this moment, he hadn't allowed himself the freedom to believe it would ever be possible.

But Uly had done it.

Had pulled off something that might never have happened before. Though if it had, the Auga would never talk of such a thing.

But, according to his Human friends, the Auga in charge would have done many things differently along the way if they were working from the lessons learned from previous escapes.

Uly Fortier had broken out of an Auga prison barge, stolen a warship, and was currently escaping.

Haydar felt a smile rise up from his very soul.

# FORTY-SEVEN

ULY HAD GATHERED what he thought of as his command group in a nearby conference room. Dan as Second-in-Command. Sterling Huff as Acting Lieutenant. Drew Roscoe as formal Sailing Master.

Haydar, Nasrin, and Piruz representing the Mazhin crew. Suka Kuri and Yanouk speaking for the Emro, with Hiko and Anari aft helping in engineering. Kolya and Marlowe, splitting the duties of Chief Engineer with Sadeq, who was aft running things as the ship fled on a pre-programmed course. Ethir Ewen speaking for the Thogin.

Uly didn't have any Ononguli sailors to speak for the rest of the crew but assumed that a few would emerge from the larger mass once they relaxed about actually getting away. And abandoning their mates to whatever fate the Auga Empire would subject them to.

Uly had a small glass of brandy in front of him, taken originally from the stocks of *King Hewitt II* and left aboard *Iron Wasp* because the Ononguli hardly drank, and the Auga didn't consume alcoholic beverages in any great amount. The Humans around the table were drinking with him, as were the Mazhin. The others had found things for themselves, with a particularly pungent tea smell emanating from Yanouk's mug nearby.

Uly looked around.

"We appear to have done it," he said, one hand raised to forestall the celebrations. "For now. They'll come after us, but since Roscoe is sailing a random, corkscrewing pattern with many changes of direction, it will be much more difficult for them to trace us, at least until they somehow manage to put an entire fleet of small ships on our trail. Even that will fail eventually unless they get lucky. How do we stay free?"

He looked around and got puzzled and confused looks back. But then, with the exception of Haydar, he didn't really have any officers handy. They generally had a different way of thinking from the enlisted folks and civilians around him. A whole set of training over and above knowing how to fly and fight and fix a ship.

And Haydar refused to confirm anything. Still, he wasn't lost in some of the conversations a civilian would have been.

Uly turned to the man.

Haydar cleared his throat and smiled weakly.

"Actually, having Roscoe fly the ship right now is probably the safest thing," he replied.

"How so?" Uly queried.

"I've marked a few important worlds to avoid in his charts," Haydar said. "Sector and departmental capitals that are likely to be heavily patrolled and able to lend resources to chase us. Past that, he has no idea which worlds are which, and so his sailing course looks like utter madness to an outsider trying to plot an intercept."

Uly turned to Roscoe and caught the man's embarrassed nod.

"As long as it works," Uly reminded him.

"Aye, sir," Roscoe replied with a nervous grin.

Civilian sailing master in training. Hylda Hobbs had done an amazing job training him, too. Uly was just sad that he never got to meet what was obviously an impressive woman from the way the *King Hewitt II* side of the crew all spoke so well of her.

These being the same folks that pretended to spit on the deck when discussing Captain Winter or Knight Botterill.

"Do we know how quickly the warp trail will fade in real space?" Uly asked, turning to his paired machinists.

"We're tuned tightly, sir," Kolya replied, as he tended to do unless someone asked Marlowe a direct question. "That makes it better. Couple of hours, at most. We're leaving less of a trail to begin with, so they'll have to work their asses off to even chase this lone, gray wolf down."

Uly liked the imagery, but it didn't sit right with him.

"Sir?" Kolya asked, catching his frown.

"Lone gray wolf. Wolves are pack animals, Kolya," Uly replied. "We're on our own out here. We need a better term. A better name for the ship."

"You do not intend to keep the name *Iron Wasp*?" Haydar asked, somewhat surprised.

"*Iron Wasp* is a pirate ship, Haydar," Uly grinned. "Or was, before it was captured by the Auga Empire, with the Conductor and most of his crew thrown into whatever prison is appropriate for them. No, we'll need a new name. Gray Wolf has style but sets the wrong tone for what we need to do."

"Cats are solitary," Dan spoke up.

"And lazy ambush predators for the most part," Uly replied. "Loud at other times. I imagine that we'll have to prey on a few folks, just because we'll need supplies, and I have no idea what we'll do for money or contacts otherwise. We need to be smart. Crafty. We need to think sneaky."

He smiled as an image came to mind.

"You've got something?" Dan asked.

"A fox," Uly nodded her.

He paused to bring up the console at the table and start typing, but then remembered that he was on an Ononguli ship, and they wouldn't have the right database.

"I'll need to look it up to show everyone, but there's a particular breed of fox on many Human worlds," he said, giving up typing and reaching deep into memory. "Canid, so related to dogs and wolves, but smaller. Sneakier. Smarter, too, if I recall correctly. Lives in the desert so they can go a long time without food and water. If I recall, they have been domesticated in the past, but generally are wild."

"The Corsac Fox, Captain?" Marlowe, of all people, asked.

"Yes, that's it," Uly snapped his fingers. "Corsac. Thank you, Marlowe."

He held up his brandy glass in a toast to the table.

"Ladies and gentlemen, I propose we shall rename this ship the *Corsac Fox*. We'll need to run far and wide and hide from far more dangerous foes, because my primary mission has not changed."

"What's that, Captain?" Suka Kuri asked.

"To see you all home," Uly replied.

The others held out their glasses as well. And smiled.

"The *Corsac Fox*," they said in unison.

# CORSAC FOX

# FORTY-EIGHT

ULY HAD SPENT four days sleeping, eating, and living on the bridge of the newly renamed *Corsac Fox* while the ship tore madly through space inside the cozy cocoon of their warp-bubble. The others had done much the same.

Engineering was in much better shape, with so many machinists among the seventy-odd people who had joined him in the jail-break. They'd managed to set up proper watch rotations and start assigning ranks and duties to folks, including training. Other Ononguli had taken over jobs in wardrooms and cleaning out bunks from folks left behind.

Uly had ordered that everything be boxed up and labeled for the absent crew members, though he wasn't sure he'd ever see any of those people again. Still, it put his new crew in a good frame of mind to treat their old comrades with some measure of respect. It would still take a while to organize and clean a ship this size.

Humans, Mazhin, and Ononguli were all roughly the same size and shape, so they had vast stocks of clothing that could be used, though nothing at all like uniforms right now. Instead, whatever the previous Bursar had bought cheapest and then sold on to pirates. Quin Butcher was in charge of that for now. Eldridge had been Assistant Quartermaster on *King Hewitt II*, so Uly would have to find someone for that chore.

All those chores. A ship this size normally assumed at least thirty officers handling various tasks. Were it a proper warship, perhaps sixty, with a crew of between three and four hundred, though Uly didn't need an entire troop of combat soldiers for boarding enemy vessels and stealing everything.

Today.

He reserved the right to change his mind later.

Instead, he looked around and noted Roscoe hard at work on navigational programming. Huff, Blakeslee, and Kovalchuk were off duty right now, hopefully sleeping in one of the nearby bunks, because there'd been no time to organize the whole ship.

Just evict the former occupants and run like hell.

Roscoe leaned back and stretched. Uly understood that feeling. He rose and walked across the lower center to one side, where he wasn't talking any louder than a murmur.

"So where are we?" Uly asked.

Roscoe almost levitated out of his seat as he yelped in surprise, then turned a sheepish face to Uly.

"Good news, bad news, sir," he replied. "We were kinda in the middle of Imperial Sector Fifteen when we started. So far from home that it doesn't show on most maps until I zoom back enough to show a quarter-slice of the galaxy."

"Where are we now?" Uly asked, leaning against the rail itself and using that to stretch stiff muscles.

He really needed a shower but had been skipping a lot of things as he tried to be everywhere and do everything. The ship itself was in fantastic shape, so he presumed that the Empire had been in the process of getting ready to sell it. It was the crew that was stretched even thinner than him.

They could fix it and fly it. That was about it.

Roscoe fiddled with his projection and several hollow red boxes appeared in the air.

"This is Fifteen, sir," he began. "We were in jail at Vynchen, and are staying well away from Cyne, the Sector Capital. That and a few systems with major naval bases according to Haydar has me mostly going farther away from *Batyr* with every hour we sail."

"Every hour we sail is that much more freedom," Uly reminded him. "Especially if they expect us to try to return to the Human portions of Sector Seventeen."

"Would they expect that?" Roscoe seemed confused, which was good as far as Uly was concerned.

"We're not from around here." Uly chuckled. "Either we're trying to get home, or they'll have no clue whatsoever about our future course."

"Kinda true now, sir," Roscoe grimaced. "We're several hundred light-years straight-line from where we started, but maybe ten times that actual sailing distance, with all the switch-backs, curves, and crazy I've programmed."

"Consider this your Master's Certification then, Roscoe," Uly said simply. "Nobody else could have gotten us this far. Nobody."

That brightened him up immediately.

"Thank you, Captain," he said.

Uly nodded.

"Keep it to soft spots and uninhabited zones as much as possible," Uly ordered. "We won't need to stop for food for a while, so we can sort all that out later when we get close."

"Aye, aye, sir," Roscoe replied with a smile.

Uly returned to his chair, then looked back as the main hatch opened and Huff walked in.

Staggered in, maybe. Uly remembered being fifteen and

wanting to sleep all the time as his body kept growing. Huff was already a centimeter taller than he had been when Uly met the young man, to the point his cuffs and pants were too short.

He had a mug of Human coffee in one hand that he sipped before a yawn stretched across his face.

"Ready to relieve you, Captain," Huff said.

"I am relieved," Uly replied. "Roscoe's planning more sailing. You should work with him and Haydar to plot some cultural maps we can use."

"Cultural, sir?" Sterling asked, possibly not quite awake yet.

"We're privateers, Sterling," Uly said. "Pirates, however fancy a name you want to hang on it. Escaped Imperial prisoners, and all that implies. I know that we cannot make it all the way home from here without stopping for supplies, so we need to figure out places where we might either barter for things, or take them, however unfortunate that might be."

"Should we be recruiting a bigger crew?" Sterling asked.

"Let's settle this one first," Uly said. "There aren't likely to be any Humans in the places we're headed for now. Nor Mazhin, if I understand Haydar and Piruz. Everyone we meet will be aliens, at least to us. Emro, Thogin, Zuath, Khet. Something. Again, cultural maps so we can figure out where to go and who to talk to."

"Aye, sir," Huff said.

Uly watched as Huff moved to the Conductor's chair and sat, while Uly moved to the hatch. It opened and Dan was standing there.

"You look terrible," she announced, like it was a surprise to anyone.

"Exhausted," Uly said.

She surprised him by turning and hooking his elbow with hers.

"Understood," she said. "Now, we're going to put some food

in you, then give you something from the medical supplies so you can sleep."

"I need to be ready for any emergency," he said automatically, but she shushed him.

"The ship can't fight if someone knocks us out of the bubble," she reminded him. "If something breaks aft, we have machinists to fix it. You do not have to do everything."

He shut up at that point. She was entirely right.

Instead, Uly let her drag him farther aft than the office he'd crashed in for several off-periods. A hatch opened and she pulled him into a larger cabin.

"What's this?" he asked.

"Sobol's," she replied. "I had it cleared of anything personal for now so you can take it over as yours. I'm directly across from you in the cabin that belonged to a guy named Kobolle. First Officer. Fits, since I'm your Second-in-Command these days."

Uly nodded and studied the space. Desk in one corner for working. Sofa and chair in another corner for relaxing and entertaining. Small kitchenette, even. Through an open hatchway, he could see a second room that looked like sleeping quarters, with a private bath off that.

God, a shower sounded so good right now.

Dan led him to the chair and put him in it.

"Uniforms," Uly looked at her as she took a spot on the couch.

"What about them?" she asked.

"You and I are in maroon for *Batyr*," he said. "Huff and Roscoe are in the black and gray of *Danumash*. Haydar and the Mazhin wear the brown that *Danumash* required of their slaves. Anari wears the gold and red of the Empire. Everyone else is in whatever colors and styles they could buy."

"And?" she asked.

Uly could feel the exhaustion catching up with him but forced it back so he could focus on the woman across from him.

"I was thinking about it while I was talking with Roscoe earlier," he said, trying to find the words through the grim haze that seemed intent on claiming him. "We're not a crew yet. The pirates might never have been. We need uniforms as a way to bind everybody into a larger whole. A unit. Almost a family, if I can be so bold and rude, because that's what we are. Or will need to become if we intend to survive this."

"Should we put everyone in maroon?" Dan asked. "I've not checked our stocks with Butcher to know what he has. Maybe we could turn the machinists loose on making dye that would work?"

"Maybe," Uly replied. "At the same time, it doesn't have to be maroon. They aren't enlisting in the *Batyr* Navy. This is just us until I can get various folks home, with the assumption that you and I will be the last."

"With you to the end, Uly," she said quietly.

"Thank you." He nodded sagely. "I think you need to put Wyndham in charge of Security entirely for now, while you formally take over as First Officer."

She started to object but he shushed her now, returning the favor.

"You'll learn," he grinned. "Same as I'm doing. I'll find a way to blackmail Haydar and Piruz as well, turning them into officers. I need you to think about who else we should promote as Lieutenants along with Wyndham and Huff."

"Are you certain?" she asked after a long pause.

"Absolutely not," Uly laughed. "I'm making up every bit of this as I go. That seems to be the secret."

"What is?" she pressed.

"Look like you have a plan," Uly replied, finding some seriousness. "React quickly and with authority, even if you are wrong. And then learn how to admit you were wrong and learn from it."

He paused as she absorbed that.

"You know what?" he asked. "I'm thinking maybe a nap now and food later might be a good idea. I hadn't realized how little I had left in the battery until I sat down."

She rose and smiled.

"I'll come back for you in a while," Dan said.

At least that's what Uly thought she said as darkness claimed him.

# FORTY-NINE

DAN PUT a blanket over Uly and left him in the chair for a nap. He'd always been skinny, but had lost even more weight, until he almost looked like an animated skeleton with skin stretched thin over it.

Outside, she considered the things he'd said. Knowing Uly, he wouldn't forget them when he woke. Instead, his unconscious mind would have been churning on them and come up with plans. That was what made him so much more effective than that punk Dupuis, or the rest of the officers she'd known.

Smart. And always thinking forward rather than brooding, which described too many people she knew.

She added several more items to her mental list and then headed aft to the wardroom. She would have said officer's wardroom, but the crew wasn't big enough to separate the two groups. Plus, Uly was the only real officer here, with everyone else pretending.

Like her.

Vahid was in his kitchen. Big. Industrial. Spotlessly clean.

Space for a crew of ten to be cooking and prepping all at once, but he was alone for now.

Still cycling through volunteers to find ones he wanted to train as cooks.

"Change of plans," she announced as he looked up from his pots. "Uly's asleep in his new quarters."

"Good," Vahid nodded.

Immediately, he turned a few things down and rotated other things around.

"How long?" he asked.

"I should probably wake him in no more than two hours," Dan said. "Or someone should."

"Want him eating here or there?" Vahid asked.

Dan considered it. What was it Uly had said about looking like you had a plan, then learning to admit you were wrong later and learn?

"There," she decided. "Fix something I can deliver and he can eat quietly. And I need to put weight back on him, so something with energy."

Vahid smiled and lifted a lid from a medium-sized pot on the cooktop. The sudden smell of chicken broth caused her mouth to water.

"It's a Human dish I learned from the assholes," he said, referring to *The Seven Kingdoms*. "Chicken and noodle soup. Ancient, according to them. Easy enough to make. Planning to add this to his rotation, swapping out coffee routinely so he gets nutrients and salt."

"Excellent idea," Dan agreed.

She thought for a moment, then moved to the wall comm and dialed buttons.

"Bridge. Huff."

"Lieutenant, Uly's asleep in his quarters, so don't wake him," she said. "I'm headed aft to talk machining. Route any questions to me there."

"Understood, sir," Huff replied.

Dan cut the line and caught Vahid's nod that she was in charge.

Because she was, however strange that felt.

*Danumash* had treated Vahid and the others like valuable pets when they'd been slaves. Dumb but capable within limits of feeding other Mazhin slaves and keeping them alive in Vahid's case. They had no clues as to the true depths of his art.

Similarly, the others had been machinists and scientists, not counting Nasrin and Omid, who were kept around for *other* duties.

Dan turned back to talk to the chef, though she wasn't entirely sure why.

Maybe because they shared something in the way she'd been treated after leaving her home on Aurtan? Dark-skinned folks were the majority on that world, but visages got much lighter as you moved deeper into *Batyr*. And especially closer to the *Danumash* frontier.

"Sir?" Vahid asked as she stood there in thought.

"Color, Vahid," she mused.

"Any one in particular?" he asked, somewhat at a loss.

"Humans come in a wide range of skin tones," Dan tried to explain, searching for the words that wanted to break through. "Do Mazhin? All of you that I know are fairly pale pink with blue tints underneath. The Emro seem to be fairly uniformly greenish. The Ononguli come in a distinct red. Only Humans run such a range."

"Agreed," Vahid said. "There is some spectrum among my kind, but nothing like yours. Does it matter that much in *Batyr*? *Danumash* always preferred the lightest tones whenever possible."

"*Batyr* is not as loud about it, but there is still something of a caste distinction in certain places, based entirely on skin."

"And where do they rate someone as dark brown as you?" Vahid asked.

"Badly," Dan nodded. "At least on less sophisticated planets. Mostly whispers, whereas in *Danumash* they would have been shouts."

"Good thing you've got Captain Uly, then," Vahid said.

That caught her off guard. Then it made perfect sense.

Uly didn't consider the color of her skin. Or how remote her homeworld was from Gralbo, the *Batyr* capital where he'd been born.

He saw all the various species around him as people. As a crew he was trying to forge into something of a found family, at least until everyone could get home.

*Did she even have a home?*

Dan felt her entire psyche stagger under the weight of that question.

"You okay?" Vahid asked, paying sharp attention to her from the way his tentacles awoke.

"Mental breakthrough," Dan offered, aware that he was reading her at a much deeper level than even most Humans could achieve. "I might take some of that chicken broth to sip on, if it's ready."

He smiled at the deflection and grabbed a mug and a ladle, filling it with such deliciousness that Dan found her mouth watering more, before he even handed it to her.

She nodded and headed down and aft to talk to the machinists.

Did she have a home?

Dan was floored that she didn't have an immediate answer to that question.

She'd been born on Aurtan. Been stationed out of Berizzan while serving on *Marshall Castillon*.

When had she decided that she wasn't ever returning to her old vessel?

Crew nodded and smiled at her as she walked by, but Dan's response was mostly automatic, and nobody stopped her for anything important.

She wasn't going back to *Marshall Castillon*. Or Lieutenant Dupuis and his snide superiority. And *mostly* quiet racism.

At least he'd never attempted to force her into any sort of sexual relationship. Thank whatever gods existed that rules and regs would have gotten him tossed out of the service for being involved with an enlisted crew member under his command.

Willing or not.

Because she might have been angry enough to go down with him in that case, just to make sure he was booted out of the service for it.

All of *Marshall Castillon*'s crew came to mind now. Not counting Beranger and Travers, the other security goons she'd left behind were also the kind to side-eye her dark skin and kinky hair. Kolya didn't care, but he was about as much of an engineering nerd as you could get.

Dan was pretty sure there were entire days when the man forgot to speak. Or chose to remain in perfect silence with his mechanical thoughts.

Had Captain Savatier specifically gotten rid of crew he didn't like? Gone beyond Uly and saw a way to remove her from his ship?

A lot of things suddenly fell into place at that thought. Subtle, but unmistakable.

*Danumash*, at least, was still worse.

Eldridge had spoken his mind on Day One and been busted in rank for it. Huff and Wyndham had, if nothing else, learned to shut their mouths, but Dan also didn't think that either of them had that sort of deeply ingrained virulence in them, beyond the reflexive racism of their class.

Being a prisoner of various alien species had finished what she'd started in opening their minds, just as Marlowe Michaels had made a point of browbeating his three into proper mindsets.

But did she even have a home?

Dan walked into the Engineering space and noted Sadeq standing at the console. Several of his tentacles immediately rotated back to track her, but that might have been the chicken soup that was more than half gone.

She walked up next to the man and studied his face.

Man. Alien, certainly. Tentacles instead of hair. Blue underneath instead of pink. Pale instead of dark.

But just another crew member under her command.

Huh. Her command. Uly was asleep, so she was in command of this warship.

"I don't suppose you brought two?" Sadeq asked as he grinned.

"Nope," Dan said with a grin, finishing the last sip. "The *Spatula* has more forward when you come off duty. Or if you needed to send someone forward to get some."

"If I did that, they'd drink it all, unless I sent them for two." He chuckled. "Vahid's chicken soup is divine. Humans don't have the taste receptors for certain things so he modifies it to also serve Mazhin needs."

"Huh," Dan replied. "Really?"

"Indeed," Sadeq nodded. "The *Danumash* never ate our food, but on *King Hewitt II*, as we were being transported, some of the crew would sample things. Same as when we were back at whatever facility they had us working in before *Batyr* got too close and they had to move us. Unfortunate decision on their part. Excellent for us."

"So where will you and all your cousins go when we find your kind?" Dan asked.

Sadeq turned to look at her with surprise. Then consideration.

"If you could find the Mazhin out there, some of us might want to spend a week or three catching up," he finally replied.

"But?" Dan asked.

"We have our own Convocation now," he said, gesturing with both hands to the room around him.

"I'm still not certain I understand," Dan replied.

"The Humans of *Danumash* forced a bunch of prisoners from various clans and planets to work together," Sadeq explained. "To do so, we formed our own group. Our own tribe. Our own Convocation. When you and Uly rescued us from that servitude, we shifted that around and included the Humans, with Uly taking over as Speaker for Haydar, who never really wanted it in the first place."

"Why did he take it, then?" Dan asked.

She'd skirted around these issues many times, but never gotten deep into what it all meant. Today, she wasn't sure why Sadeq was being so much more open than in the past.

Or had he asked that same question, and found that he didn't have a home, either?

"We like to venerate age," Sadeq replied with a grin. "There's a strong survivorship bias there, because you have to be lucky and good to not screw your life up before you know any better. Uly's got it in spades, in spite of youth. We wanted to tap his luck."

"Hitched yourselves to his star?" Dan asked, starting to understand.

"Have you seen what that man's pulled off?" Sadeq laughed, arms outstretched. "And we're still going. Absolutely, the Mazhin venerate luck. How else do you survive?"

"And the others?" Dan asked.

"Captain Fortier has extended his crew, his clan, far beyond the limits of Human and Mazhin," Sadeq shrugged. "He's the Speaker. We're just along for the ride at this point."

"And the Mazhin don't worry?" Dan asked. "Do you even care?"

"Luck, boss," Sadeq reminded her. "Everyone here brought some amount of luck with them, to be in the right places, the right cells, at the time. Look at all the folks in the other cells on that prison barge. None of them are free today. That's the Captain's luck playing out before your eyes."

"You are officially weird, Sadeq," Dan said, failing to keep a straight face.

"You've spent too much time around Haydar." Vahid laughed warmly. "He's a bit of an old, wet hen at times. Piruz can explain it better if you want those sorts of details."

Dan nodded and considered. *Corsac Fox* was becoming a home. A family. Lucky folk, as he'd said. Those smart enough to step up when presented with the opportunity, including Suka Kuri and her students, or Anari. Even Kovalchuk.

"Okay, who should we look at for officers among the machinists?" she asked, pivoting the conversation to more serious points. "Uly wants me to start identifying candidates."

"You've got the three of us running the shop as equals right now," Sadeq nodded. "We're all good at the hands-on side of things, but never have any of us been in charge of things. Roshan's the smartest, hands down, but not the most social creature you will ever meet. Haydar is close, but neither of them are really used to being in charge and making decisions. Do we need to make decisions immediately?"

"We do not," Dan decided for him. "But soon. If that involves making all of you lieutenants for the time being and not having any Adjutant or Commander over you except me, that will work for now. At some point, decisions about promotions and maintenance cycles will need someone to sign off. You three figure out how to do that and get back to me. Questions?"

"Where are we headed next?" he asked out of the blue.

"No clue," Dan shook her head. "Was going to ask Uly, but I put him to bed for now, and Vahid made soup for when he wakes up. What will you need first?"

"Ship's in amazing shape." Sadeq gestured again to the equipment around them. "We can draw fuel for the reactors from any gas giant with the right atmosphere. Crew will be an issue if you want to do anything but sail. Not enough people to manage generators and guns at the same time."

"That was the impression I had as well," Dan said. "Do any of the Mazhin know Sector Fifteen?"

He just roared with laughter.

"We're been out with you barbarians in Seventeen for too long, boss," Sadeq finally managed, speaking through his giggles. "And before that over in Twenty-Three, most of us. You probably have a better idea than I do. I just fix machines."

Dan nodded.

"Keep me posted then," she said, turning to leave.

Dan headed forward along the main corridor, pausing at each frame for the hatch to slide open, laughing to herself at how long it took. Better to keep the pirates at bay with them closed.

Lots of enlisted folks had been swept up in Uly's net, but no officers. Experienced sailors and the Midshipmen, which was a term for a youngster considered an Officer and Gentleman in training, but Huff and Wyndham were still kids in all the meaningful ways.

She'd served for ten years, but never been in charge of anything except snot-nosed punks fresh out of training.

That needed to change. She needed to step up and lift some of the weight from Uly's shoulders. And help him find folks to promote to help run things.

Outsiders need not apply though, she decided. This ship was turning into a found family, a family business, maybe.

They needed allies, but not more than that.

Not yet, anyway.

She nodded and found herself looking forward to the challenge.

# FIFTY

HAYDAR STUDIED the group that Uly had assembled today and nodded. Uly, Dan, himself, Ethir, and Suka Kuri.

About as broad and weird a representative sample as you could get. And that was just the crew.

At some point, they needed an Ononguli representative, just for balance if nothing else.

The group was in Uly's new quarters, which had a table just big enough for everyone to sit or stand near and pace.

Uly looked better than he had. It had been a hard week on the run from the Auga prison barge, but something had changed. Several things, actually.

According to Vahid and Sadeq, Dan had found herself, whatever it was she had lost, and was turning into a First Officer. Haydar had lived in terror that Uly would demand he step into that role.

Threats to the other Mazhin to keep their mouths shut about Haydar's youth had apparently been sufficient. At least to date.

He was a scientist, not a pirate. Okay, maybe a piratical scientist, but still.

Uly rapped his knuckles on the table, the other hand holding a mug of Vahid's chicken soup from *Danumash* stores stolen several times now.

They would need to find chickens to raise at some point. Or a planet with chicken farms.

Or the equivalent.

"We do not have a problem today," Uly began, immediately moving everyone to a different state of alertness in a most subtle way. He sounded like a commanding officer. "But we need to start looking forward."

Nods around the table.

Suka Kuri was on the couch, claiming that she would break any of the fragile chairs. Sitting in one, Haydar doubted that. She just wanted a pad under her butt, because these were an extruded polymer shaped to an Ononguli's backside. Not the most comfortable for anyone else.

He considered dashing over to the lounge chair before anybody else took it.

"What's ahead of us?" Ethir asked.

"Physically, more Imperial space," Uly nodded. "It's the social and emotional aspect that we need to address."

"Oh?" Ethir pressed, while the others paid attention and let the tiny man talk.

Ethir Ewen might be the least educated member of this group, at least by formal training, but Haydar had long since been delighted to discover that he could give Piruz a run for the money when it came to fast-talking. The tiny man was a born hustler.

"The Ononguli portions of the crew are pirates," Uly said. "Technically, so are the *Batyr* portions of the Human crew, though we served under proper military discipline along with the *King Hewitt II* crew. The remainder are mostly folks swept up in something larger and given really no choice but to go along."

"Speak for yourself," Suka Kuri replied. "I might not have enjoyed portions of my incarcerations, but I'm quite content with the current situation."

"Hear, hear," Ethir agreed. "You think it was random luck that caused us to join your group on *Iron Wasp* the first time? Or to stay quiet when you were planning to break out of prison?"

"We're likely to have to return to piracy," Uly said. "Privateering is not on the table."

"Why not?" Ethir asked. "Are you not still operating under your original orders to capture the *Danumash* vessel *King Hewitt II* and salvage the cargo?"

Uly studied him for a long moment.

"Technically, you could interpret it that way," he said in a sideways kind of voice.

"Technically correct is the best kind, boss." Ethir laughed. The others joined in. "And what do those orders entail, anyway? Never had a chance to ask before."

"I took possession of *King Hewitt II* after a lucky shot had destroyed the bridge and killed all the *Danumash* officers aboard," Uly explained. "From there, I was supposed to navigate it to a friendly port, though I am not certain how Captain Savatier thought that would happen."

"Meaning?" Suka Kuri spoke up.

"He means that our old Captain was probably setting Uly up for failure," Dan replied. "To get killed. If nothing else, getting rid of him because they didn't trust him."

"Why would they not trust you?" Suka Kuri asked.

"His father is a senior Party official of *Batyr*," Dan explained as Haydar watched. "Extremely senior. They probably saw him as a spy from home, set to discover something they were doing or report on them and get everyone in trouble with Senior Command."

"So he abandoned you?" Ethir asked. "What a putz."

Haydar had to agree, but he'd also heard stories from the others: Kolya, Beranger, and Travers. That conclusion made the most sense. And this Savatier had probably been expecting Uly Fortier to die in the process. Or at least be gone for six months or a year before he managed what might have been an impossible task.

Not the mark of a good captain, of that much Haydar was certain.

"At this point, you do have a cargo," Haydar joined the conversation. "Myself and the others. You were supposed to get us somewhere. I presume a *Batyr* port?"

"Again, technically yes," Uly said, tilting his head. "That might mean that you became prisoners of the *Batyr* government and the Industrial Protectors Party, until they learned everything you could possibly tell them that they didn't already know. Personally, I don't see how it would be that much of a change from where you were the day before I rescued you."

"Agreed," Haydar said. "Another name for bondage, most likely. However, that just reinforces the original point."

"How so?" Uly asked, but Dan saw it. She perked right up and grinned.

"If you are a pirate, you aren't subject to those original orders, Uly." Haydar smiled. "You are instead a pirate, doing piratical things. At some point, you could find ways to divest yourself of this crew you have assembled, and return to *Batyr* space with one hell of a story, but that is not an immediate task, is it?"

"Abso-freaking-lutely!" Ethir replied. "I think we owe a few people a bit of grief for all the shit they've caused us over that half-year. Empire and Ononguli alike. How do we pay them back, save by stealing their shit? Or blowing it up?"

Haydar was a bit taken back by the vehemence of the little man, but he supposed that being perhaps the smallest intelligent species in the wider region might cause one to live with a chip on the shoulder. The Ononguli crew had it from being captured so far from home. Dan had it from the racism among her own kind, both *Danumash* and elements of *Batyr*, according to Vahid and others.

Haydar decided to go a little out on a limb.

"Uly, what do you think we should do?" he asked, putting the emphasis back where it should be.

The man in charge.

"This is an Ononguli ship," he said slowly, obviously assembling his case as he went. "Taken from them and the Empire. We have enough crew to sail for a while, but not really fight a major battle with anybody our size. If we intend to pirate, we'll have to hit someone significantly weaker. That rubs me the wrong way entirely. I joined the Navy to protect people."

"Uhm…" Ethir hemmed, drawing all eyes over to him.

"You know something," Suka Kuri spoke accusingly. Smiling, but she sounded like a mom who had just walked into the kitchen and found you stealing cookies.

Not that Haydar had ANY experience with that sort of thing.

"Maybe," Ethir said, managing to draw the word out to four syllables in the process.

"Spill," **MOM** ordered.

"Weaker might be a state of opinion," Ethir said. "How about unguarded as a better euphemism?"

"Oh?" Uly asked, looking all perceptive and interested now.

Ethir shrugged and tilted his head back and forth.

"So…let's just say that this wasn't the first time my cousins and I have been incarcerated by Imperial authorities?" Ethir began, only to be drowned out by laughter.

They'd heard several stories. Mostly from Waltin, whom Haydar recognized as the smartest cousin. Ethir was in charge because he was the sneakiest.

"And anyways, I can think of a few places that might not be all that well guarded," Ethir said. "Especially since we happen to have a warship capable of blowing shit up when we get somewhere."

"Such as, you juvenile delinquent?" **MOM** asked.

At least she was smiling now. Haydar had almost gotten up to put imaginary cookies back at the tone of her voice.

"Anybody here know of a planet called Zhoralong?" he asked, looking around hopefully.

"No," Uly said. "I work on the presumption that *most of us* have never been in Imperial Sector Fifteen."

More chuckles at his emphasis.

The cousins had definitely traveled a wider path than Haydar had in his misdemeanor youth. Never felonies. Probably.

"Right." Ethir nodded. "Zhoralong. Kinda a district jail. Also something of a district storage yard and supply warehouse. Middle of nowhere, which is why they did it, as most of those planets are Zuath or Thogin, with the occasional Ugotha who got lost. Everybody pooled their taxes to build up facilities on Zhoralong because it was central to about a dozen systems with maybe half a billion combined population across all of them."

"Why so small?" Dan asked. "Most planets expand rapidly once you establish them."

"Several mining colonies." Ethir shrugged. "Couple of farm worlds, one of which is mostly ocean and exports frozen fish by the megaton. Zhoralong is halfway civilized, comparatively, but that ain't saying much."

"Defenses?" Haydar asked now, flashing back to things he didn't discuss in polite company.

"Jail station has a few things to mostly keep girlfriends from trying to break their honey out," Ethir said. "If it was all on the surface of a planet, I'd say three-meter-tall cyclone fence topped with razor wire and a few lights. No guard towers or attack dogs running around. Space just means warehouse cluster with a bunch of old ships of various sizes in shutdown mode. Plus emergency stuff for planetary catastrophes. Won't be great, but we oughtta be able to pick up months of food packs that Vahid could stretch into something interesting."

"What about prisoners?" Uly asked.

"What about 'em?" Ethir countered.

"As has been noted, we're short on crew," Uly said. "If we staged another jail-break, could we turn it into a recruiting drive?"

Ethir shrugged at that.

"Most of them are probably serving short stints for drunk and disorderly," he said. "Or maybe petty theft. Thogin aren't big on assault and battery, unless we can gang up on someone, as you know."

More laughter. The cousins worked as almost a single being with eight hands when they had to. Haydar could see them swarming a drunk in a bar and tackling the poor sod.

"But?" Dan asked.

"Maybe?" Ethir offered. "I was thinking supplies and shit, not crew. We got lucky before, so I don't want to speak for these folks. Might all be losers when we get there."

"How many ships in the motor pool?" Uly asked, causing the room to sober quickly.

"Lots, last time I was there," Ethir said. "Big and small. Military and civilian. Emergency response and such, ya know? Freighters filled with stuff to deliver to an emergency, plus command-and-control vehicles. Couple of people movers so you can deliver crews as well. The sort of shit you confiscate and reconfigure so you have it handy, instead of having to rely on whoever's in port when a mine collapses or a plague hits a world. Auga are big on being prepared for that sort of thing. They were just never expecting Humans."

The chuckles returned. Nobody expected the Humans. Or rather, Haydar corrected himself, Uly and Dan. Captain Winter and the others killed on *King Hewitt II* would have probably gotten themselves killed along with Eldridge, unable to shut up around aliens.

Or they'd have gotten snitty with the Auga and been thrown in prison for a stretch. Possibly to serve a labor sentence somewhere on a farming colony or in a mine.

Making themselves more useful than just taking up space in a box for years. That was reserved for the ones not going to be around long, like Zhoralong apparently, or the ones too dangerous to leave running around where they might escape. Or kill other prisoners because there was something wrong in their heads.

All eyes turned to Uly. He nodded to the room.

"Ethir, you work with Roscoe to see what we might have in the astrogation computers," Uly ordered. "And update it so we have a better understanding. I'm not certain that rescuing more prisoners would be net positive, if they turn out to be more trouble than they're worth, and I won't impress sailors just to have warm bodies. Wouldn't do any good, long term, if they don't want to be here. On the other hand, stealing supplies and gear from the Empire has its charm. Questions?"

There were none, so Uly nodded. Haydar found his feet and considered his options.

He wanted to go back to his lab and invent shit. Roshan was getting a serious lead on him at this point, and that would never do.

On the other hand, the Mazhin needed to be present in the room at times like this, when policy was being made that affected all of them. The others had made him do it because he'd been the oldest before.

They'd also made him act as Speaker against his will, but nobody had complained once about Uly taking the job.

Maybe, just maybe, the kids needed to finally step up and let Haydar go back to being a pirate scientist instead.

As he made his way out of the hatch, he started thinking about how he would rank the various folks on his team.

# FIFTY-ONE

ULY DIDN'T WANT to say he had recovered, but he did feel as though he'd gotten back to maybe the days aboard *King Hewitt II*, when everyone had started to pull together and act like they wanted to survive.

Dying stranded in deep space had to be the worst possible way to go, if you were without engines and power, and waiting for the life support to finally die. You eventually went to sleep in the cold and never woke up.

He had those nightmares still. Not as many as previous months, except for the one that had just roused him from the bottom of the well of sleep with a scream still echoing around his new sleeping quarters.

Fortunately, nothing in here smelled of Ononguli. Not like the rest of the ship frequently did.

Omid had put her foot down and thrown out the crew members who had been assigned to laundry and cleaning, rearranging everything until she was satisfied before letting any of them get involved again. That had also involved wiping down the walls and surfaces with water in his cabin and creating new patterns of laundry.

Uly didn't have the olfactory senses to understand what she'd done, but he could appreciate that this ship didn't smell like any other warship he'd ever served on.

Mazhin tentacles. The need to paint with smells as well as colors when decorating a room.

Or doing laundry.

Uly checked the clock on the wall. Middle of his night, though ships never slept, and it wasn't like there was a star handy to establish a circadian rhythm. Folks pulled a four-hour shift towards the beginning of their day, with a four-hour break in the middle, then a second four hours at the end. That created overlap with other folks in this stretched-thin crew, so you had time to do things, and be awake to take care of feeding yourself and such.

Middle of the night. His night. Middle of the day for others. Blakeslee might be in charge of the bridge right now, as long as nothing had gone wrong.

Uly considered rolling back over and trying to sleep. Probably a waste of time at this point, as he was too wound on that spike of adrenaline to accomplish anything. Instead, he got dressed and decided to walk.

His old Captain on *Vanguard Lesauvage* had often been found in the middle of the night walking the corridors of the ship. At the time, Uly hadn't understood why.

He did now.

All those things beyond your control that manifested in your dreams as nightmares.

The ship was running on normal lighting as he emerged from his cabin. It was somebody's noon. Blakeslee and others, if he had the roster correct in his head.

So he walked.

Somebody was paying attention to him, though, because Dan

appeared from around a corner and fell in beside him. Except that she was walking with purpose and had to slow back down for him to catch up.

Uly was ambling. At best.

"Is everything okay?" she asked as he came even with her.

"Couldn't sleep," he replied. "Decided to walk."

"Oh," she said, crestfallen.

Probably expecting an emergency.

Uly wondered if she'd been off-duty and maybe asleep as well until roused by someone's panic at seeing him when he should be asleep. Except that she had the rotation after his, so she should be late in her day and getting ready for bed. Maybe.

"I don't understand," she finally said as they walked a few more steps.

Uly nodded. They were close to the kitchen, so he led her that way. Some tea without caffeine might be good about now.

She followed without comment. That was one of the things he liked most about Dan Chastain. If she didn't have anything to say, she didn't just blather to fill the room with noise. Kind of like him.

They moved to the line for hot water and nodded at crew members taking care of folks on duty. Chatter around them, but his presence seemed to suppress their exuberance, so he got his tea sachet and mug of hot water and nodded Dan to follow.

Out into the corridor, he found an office that wasn't being used right now and put her behind the desk while he sat on the outside.

Still, she watched without comment.

"Thank you," he said as he got his tea to steeping properly.

"For?" she asked.

He gestured to the ship around them. And the crew. And the universe.

"I couldn't have done any of this without your help," he

reminded her. "I've been giving orders and moving, but that only works if people agree with me. Support me."

"You're in charge, Uly," she replied.

"Only because people think I should be in charge," he countered. "The Mazhin saw me in charge and agreed, so they made me their Speaker. I'm still not sure what that means, but as a captain, it's good enough for now. Suka Kuri and Ethir listen and don't challenge that I'm in charge. Most of that comes because you accept me."

"You're the officer here," she replied. "I'm only an E-8 Enlisted, Uly. Kolya's only an E-7. You're the one that decided, even before we boarded *King Hewitt II*, that I should be your Second-in-Command."

"And you're doing a fantastic job of it." Uly nodded. "I can plan for the future because you're currently handling all the administrative work that you usually have lower officers for on a *Batyr* ship. I don't have a cast of Cornets, Ensigns, Lieutenants, and Senior Lieutenants to dump work on. You're doing most of it, along with other enlisted folks serving well beyond your ranks. Or civilians who have chosen to put themselves under what is functionally military authority. Or whatever I have when we all turn into pirates. So, thank you. I could not do this without you."

"Oh," she said, dark eyes understanding now. "You're welcome, Uly. Every step of this has been you, planning and executing. Even when we were prisoners, you kept things organized when others might have fallen apart. When the Ononguli got taken by the Empire, you had a plan. And it didn't work out, but it didn't need to. And later, you figured out how we could escape. Then how to steal this ship and flee. You're the heart and soul of this."

"Thank you," he replied.

"So why are you awake in the middle of your night?" she asked.

"Nightmares," he replied.

"Is that common?" she asked.

He shrugged.

"They were bad once I came aboard *Marshall Castillon*," he said. "They've gotten worse over the last few months. I mark it down to stress more than anything. So many things I can't fix. Or that might go wrong and doom us all."

"Should we abandon this raid and try to sail someplace where we could get home without everybody?" she asked.

"I'm not sure most of them would want to leave," he said. "Unless you and I stole something small and only grabbed the Humans. That might be rather insulting to the rest, since they've all committed to this. No, I'm more afraid of what happens if we go the other way."

"Other way?" She seemed confused now.

"As Haydar pointed out, the Mazhin are likely to turn back into prisoners if we haul them to Gralbo, or any *Batyr* world," Uly nodded. "Since they have appointed me to *Speak* for them, that means that as long as they choose to stay around, I can't go home. If pressed, I would guess that the same holds for Suka Kuri and her students. Or Ethir and the cousins.'"

"Can't go home?" she asked slowly.

There was something in her eyes, but Uly didn't honestly know the woman well enough to tell what it was.

"Can't go home," he agreed instead. "So technically, I have to go Unlawful Absent to protect my friends. Considering how Captain Savatier treated me, as well as you, I wonder if I should just walk away from a Navy career in my mind, as well as in reality. Go pirate full-throated, as contrary as that is to my nature and my training. Stop being an Ensign in the *Batyr* Navy and never go home."

"What would you do?" she pressed quietly.

"I have no plan," he admitted.

Uly felt that he could do that with her. She was his Second-in-Command, and if something happened to him, she would be in charge. Or Haydar would have to take over again, as little as that appealed to the man.

She seemed to collapse a bit at that.

"I do have some ideas," he offered, watching her perk up again.

"Oh?"

"We need to hit a place like Zhoralong for supplies and such," he said. "And then find similar places we can attack, as long as we can stay ahead of the law. Your expertise with aliens and shadowy ports will come into play there."

"I'm hardly the expert," Dan replied.

"Then deputize Ethir and whoever else as lieutenants, Second-in-Command," he grinned at her. "I'd like to get as far away from the Auga Empire as I can. Then we'll need to set up a base of some sort."

"Planetary or mobile?" she asked.

"Mobile for now," Uly decided. "If we can steal a freighter loaded with long-term food supplies and emergency equipment, there's no reason not to haul it off and park it somewhere. And we can move it around later as we need. People are going to be the big problem right now, so eventually we'll need to find a place where we can recruit crew and rely on folks to protect us. I imagine that the Auga will be pissed enough to send big ships looking for us, once news gets out about who we are."

"Steal another ship?" Dan had a complicated look on her face. Disbelief. Avarice. Rage. All rolled into one.

"Something big and easy to fly," he nodded. "*King Hewitt II* was a shipper-sized transport before Sobol apparently blew it up. Something larger would be nice. Maybe all the way up to a

Dropship-sized monster that could barely still land on a planetary surface. Great place to hide something, as we could shut down all the transmitters at that point. Needle in a haystack to locate it."

"And we're never going home?" she probed, circling back.

"At this moment, Dan, I have a lot of reasons not to," he said. "And hardly any in favor. What do you want out of all this? I've kind of assumed your wants and needs too many times, when I should have asked, so let me make up for that now. Where do you want to be in a year or five?"

"Not aboard *Marshall Castillon*," she said definitively. "Not back where I have to deal with the sorts of quiet racism I get anywhere outside of Aurtan. Especially not anywhere near *Danumash*."

"Then let's stay out of Imperial Sector Seventeen," he grinned. "I've recently come to discover a whole bunch of other places we might go. Empires and star nations all over the place, filled with interesting new aliens to talk to. None of that needs to be anywhere near the tiny Human districts."

She smiled, so he counted that as a win. There were hardly any Humans aboard, and she had the extra disadvantage of being the only female one at present, with Jasmine Atwater still a prisoner of the Auga somewhere, along with Spence and Masters.

On the flip side, the crew had female Ononguli, Emro, and Mazhin, so she might have folks to talk to when the men didn't understand. He routinely didn't understand women. Having a sister who was so much younger as his only sibling hadn't helped, because he'd been off doing his own thing by the time she really started turning into a person. As a result, they'd never really fought like Dan and her two sisters, to hear those stories.

"Then what?" she asked.

"I suppose that eventually we'll have to turn into our own pirate nation or something," Uly said. "Assuming that there aren't any already out there for us to find."

His tea was steeped now, so he pulled out the sachet and started to drink. She did the same and they fell into a companionable silence filled with smiles.

Sure, he was making it all up as he went, but he had help. Friends, even. Folks committed to seeing this through.

He nodded to himself and to his First Officer, and wondered what it would be like to live as a pirate.

# FIFTY-TWO

ULY HAD a full bridge crew today. Everyone had rotated their sleep patterns to be awake and ready to run for a day or three of just catnapping.

And he had his Lamellar vest. Someone had stuffed it into a personnel locker after taking it from him when *Iron Wasp* captured them. The crew had found it when cleaning and sorting. He wore it today along with the same Exoripper pistol and Shadowwhip sword that Dan had handed him before they left to storm *King Hewitt II*. Little marks of home, but they were also exotic in the eyes of everybody else, which made him stand out.

Pirate Captain, or something.

Dan was seated at a dark station, turned around and watching. Like him, ready for combat, but she only had a jacket of isomorph over her suit. Useful if someone had an energy weapon, but not that great against swords or projectiles.

All of the weapons from *King Hewitt II* had been stored in a box on *Iron Wasp*. Then left there because the Auga Empire hadn't gotten around to emptying the ship for sale.

He almost felt like he was at home.

*Corsac Fox* was sitting at the edge of the Zhoralong system. Out in the darkness where they were invisible. That had let folks all get a good night's rest and a hearty meal before the adventure began.

And it had given Blakeslee and Haydar several hours of passive observational data about the system itself. They were too far away to see anything with a telescope from here, but every ship in space pinged an identification transponder, often with relative coordinates to the big station in low orbit.

Quiet. As Ethir had called it, the middle of nowhere, with not much traffic coming or going. Not a lot of ships in orbit either. Bunches of pings from ships parked and shut down for long-term storage, mostly about a quarter of an orbit trailing the main station that Ethir identified as the jail.

From personal experience.

Uly grinned at the man, sitting next to Dan and all set to engage. He wasn't trained for this sort of thing but had the most experience with the system itself. It made him a useful scout.

His crew were at high alert and in high spirits everywhere he'd looked.

Uly turned to Sterling Huff, sitting across from him.

"You ready?" Uly asked.

The youngster gulped once and nodded. Not that Uly was offended. He was going to be in charge of *Corsac Fox* with Blakeslee and Butcher as his only real bridge crew, while Uly took Roscoe and Kovalchuk on the raid.

Uly had considered swapping those roles, but he didn't think that Huff was ready for something this big. Better this time if the young man had the guns. Again, barely enough crew do things, but today everyone seemed to have risen above themselves.

Next time, hopefully it would be old hat, though Uly didn't suppose he ever wanted to fall into a mindset where just sailing up and taking anything he wanted became habit. Too easy to slide fully over to evil at that point.

As it was, he justified most of this in his head by the fact that the Auga Empire hadn't rescued him when he was a prisoner, and had instead thrown him in with the other pirates.

*As ye reap, so shall ye sow...*

Uly took one last look around at the faces surrounding him. Human, Thogin, Emro, Mazhin, Ononguli. All looked back with expectation. Possibly hunger.

They'd been victims, many of them, for a long time and of a rotating cast of villains.

Today, they got to strike back. That seemed to have lit a fire in many souls.

Uly opened the general intercom and drew a breath to the bottom of his feet.

"All hands, this is Captain Fortier," he announced. "Shortly, we are going to strike a blow for our freedom. For ourselves and our place in this galaxy. Most of you have been on the wrong side of Imperial law, so today you can bring that as well. We are going to hit hard and decisively, then run like hell for the hills, laughing as they try to catch us. Because they will fail. We will be free, and we will build on this for future raids. Future missions. So, thank you for believing in me and your crew mates. We'll need one hard push, and then we can relax. Sailing master, take us into warp."

# FIFTY-THREE

DAN SHIVERED WHEN ULY SPOKE, watching the man transcend to a new level. Confident and tough. Ready for battle, even when that involved taking on an empire with thousands of planets and population numbers that were starkly incomprehensible.

"Warp bubble engaged," Drew Roscoe announced. "Seven minutes to target."

"Huff, you have command," Uly ordered. "Remember that you can shoot back, but don't start anything unless it becomes necessary. If they suddenly bring up serious firepower, we'll abort and run like hell on the route Roscoe has mapped. Everyone else, hang tough and think of today as the beginning of our war."

Dan rose when Uly did. Ethir slid off his chair and fell in, as did Roscoe.

She led. As of now, she was in command of the assault team. Uly was along because nobody knew what to expect, and he wanted to be there to make decisions that Huff wasn't prepared for.

Yet.

Like Wyndham, he was coming around. Like Wyndham, she wasn't quite old enough to be the youngster's mother, but she had nieces and nephews not much younger from her older sister Jocelyn.

They flew down the stairs not because they were in a hurry, but because she had excess energy and needed to bleed it off big. On her left thigh, her Mark VI Heavy Exoripper was a comforting weight she'd missed, as was the Icemace currently collapsed in a pocket on her right side.

Dan didn't want to think of them as security blankets, but she also didn't want to lie about missing them.

She was back. *Marshall Castillon* was there in her head, and some dumbass *Danumash* ship had just been forced out of warp and been pounded hard enough that she could board it. Or was being pounded and Captain wanted them taken by a fast strike team.

Dan smiled as she hit the bottom deck and exited. Uly was right on her tail, with the others strung out up the stairs. Wyndham was in the boarding lounge, already suited up and wearing a Battershield tunic over that to stop knives and crossbow bolts. And possibly fragments, if someone blew up a shrapnel device designed to puncture suits. Even armored ones.

Beranger and Travers were lined up in the corner, next to the cousins and Piruz.

Nasrin Monfared was the one Dan wasn't expecting. Especially suited up and ready to go in something that she'd taken from Ononguli stores. Still, helmet space for horns meant that she had volume to fit tentacles when she put the helmet itself on. For now, it hung at her hip.

"What do you think you're doing?" Dan asked.

"Going with you," the woman said simply. "I'm trained for close combat. Not many others are. Plus, I have some technical background. Not as much as Piruz, but he can't punch anybody worth a damn."

Dan nodded at that. Piruz was fast talking, but he was a horse thief. *A lover not a fighter*, to use the Human vernacular, though Dan had never once considered that the Mazhin was male.

Not her type. Not one bit.

Still, Dan recognized the grim set of Nasrin's jaw and tentacles. And felt Uly step up beside her, so she turned to the captain. This was one of those situations where he could overrule her. Dan was torn on whether or not he should.

"It will be dangerous," Uly began, but Nasrin cut him off with a laugh. True mirth.

Dan grinned. They'd all watched Nasrin dance. Dan had the depth of training and understanding of close combat forms to know just how deadly all that was when she sped it up to fighting speeds.

"Okay, fair point," Uly conceded. "What do you know about piracy?"

"Nothing," Nasrin replied evenly. "I'm here to hurt people Dan needs hit."

That, she could do well. And the Mazhin woman might outweigh Uly, though Vahid had done a good job of putting a few kilograms back on the man. Not enough, but he no longer looked like death warmed over.

Most days.

Dan supposed she did as well, but losing a few kilograms to stress had her back down to her mass when she'd enlisted a decade ago, so she didn't mind.

Uly grimaced, but his heart wasn't in it.

"Your idea or Piruz's?" he asked.

"Haydar's, actually," Nasrin replied. "Yanouk would have been here too, but we couldn't find a suit big enough, although I suppose Anari would have demanded precedence there, being

Sabre Emro. You'll need to steal or buy two armored suits for them at some point."

Dan had considered that, but not brought it up to Uly. He already had enough things on his mind, but she had a mental note to look in stores of the ship they stole. All that emergency gear meant that there might be suits for Emro. Maybe even armored enough for use in combat, if they were emergency rescue things you might wear in disaster areas.

She smiled at Uly when he looked at her.

"Your operation," he said simply, ceding everything back to her authority.

Just like that.

It was still breathtaking that a light-skinned officer looked at her and saw competence first. Before skin color or gender. Acknowledged it and that was that.

Dan turned to Nasrin. Studied the woman. Noted the jut of the chin and the way her tentacles hung like angry spikes around her head, challenging the room.

"Wyndham, she needs a pistol," Dan announced, turning to her newly promoted Security Officer.

He was growing into the job well.

Nobody had liked Rigby Botterill, so the title Knight had been officially retired, along with that asshole's penchant for randomly ordering everyone to do sets of pushups to keep them fit and on their toes.

Good riddance.

Nasrin started to object, but Dan waved her off.

"I don't care if you never draw it," she said. "You need to look threatening. And you might need to cover someone we take prisoner. Easier to point a gun at them than to beat them uncon-scious and tie them up. Trust me on that one."

"Okay," Nasrin nodded.

At least her tentacles relaxed, shifting back into a roiling ball of snakes.

Dan looked around. Nobody else had a sword, but those were more the mark of an officer than anything, though she knew that Uly had trained with the weapon, from the records she'd seen in the before time, as well as talking to the man.

"All hands, this is Acting Lieutenant Huff," came the announcement. "Stand by to drop out of warp in thirty seconds."

Dan turned and entered the airlock, the others falling in and arranging themselves.

It was time.

# FIFTY-FOUR

STERLING HAD BEEN an Astronomer's Mate, once upon a time. Fifth Midshipman by seniority, behind Bertrand, Elihan, Thorley, and Irving.

Today, he was the only survivor, besides Solomon who didn't count because he was an Armsman, not a sailor. Not that Sterling would tease his friend too much about that.

They were all stepping into shoes too big to fit right these days, hoping that they could fake it well enough for Captain Fortier.

He looked over at Blakeslee, and they shared a nervous nod. Drew and the captain had programmed everything ahead of time, with Mr. Ramezani bringing his Mazhin expertise.

Sterling looked over at the Mazhin scientist who had come forward when Captain had gone below. That had put Sterling in charge. He figured he needed all the help he could get, so he'd asked Haydar Ramezani for that assistance.

Too many lives on the line.

Sterling studied his screens. Ten seconds until the bubble

popped and they were naked in front of the whole school. He wondered if anybody else had that dream or if it was just him.

He swallowed and took a breath. Right now, he didn't need his voice cracking on him.

Gotta sound like a Lieutenant.

"All hands, we have emerged," he called as there were suddenly stars around them again. "Sensors, give me a read-out, but do not execute a scan."

Following the script helped. Captain Fortier had written it with Roscoe's help. Words to say. Buttons to push. Things to do in a set order that would make you act like an officer should.

Sterling was grateful for the process, as he'd never been in charge of any ship until Captain Fortier arrived.

Certainly never one with guns.

"Forward Battery, this is the bridge," Sterling said, going down that checklist. "Your tubes are unlocked, but fire control is on the bridge. Stand by to reload and repair, but we are not moving directly to combat."

He hoped. Nothing on Blakeslee's scans had indicated any warships around here. Search and Rescue vessels and tugs, but not guns.

He'd happily slip in, stand around looking menacing, then slip out again quietly.

"Nav, I have our target," Blakeslee announced, also following a script. But that script was in his head. Delbert Blakeslee was five years older than Sterling and at least as smart. And better qualified, though not an officer, even in training.

Just a sailor.

Sterling Huff was in charge of a warship today, God help us all.

Sterling dialed in the readouts and engaged the thrusters, swinging the ass end of the ship around some as they started forward.

Ahead, a monstrous snowflake of metal hung in space, with ships like holiday ornaments hanging from many of the branches. Most of them were small. Couriers and small Shippers, when Captain wanted something at the big end.

And trusted Sterling to find it for him.

"Sensors, I need a short range, directed ping," Sterling said next. "Stack the results by mass, largest to smallest."

Down the checklist. Doing all the things Captain Fortier had thought to write for him, so much more than Sterling had ever gotten when he'd been a Middie in the *Danumash* Navy.

Today, he was a pirate. Serving under a pirate.

He watched Haydar Ramezani take Blakeslee's results and do something to them. Some sort of data science magic that Mr. Ramezani was known for, a dark art that sailors rarely learned.

Which was exactly why Sterling had asked him to come forward after the Captain had left. Fortier had once explained his own process. Find smart people and put them into the right role, then stand back and let them work.

Sterling could learn that. Do that. Watch it happen as two of those tentacles turned towards him like eyes.

Sterling had always been fascinated by the Mazhin, but *Danumash* had been strict about how the...slaves...were to be treated. He was happy that none of them held him accountable for the stupid things others had done to them before.

He was certain he'd said and done stupid things around them himself, but First Officer had come down on everybody exactly once, then expected them to behave better.

Sterling was trying.

"You'll want number three, I think," Mr. Ramezani said as he transmitted a list over to Sterling's screen.

Why that one? At least a third smaller than number one, which was a mega-freighter. Oh, that one was too big to land on a planetary surface. And mostly empty. Number Two likely would have been Sterling's first choice. It was configured as a hospital ship and ready to transport personnel both directions.

Why Number Three?

Then he saw it. Loaded to the gills with emergency supplies. Far more than Number Two, and much of that volume appeared to be military equipment.

Huh?

His confusion must have been obvious when he looked up, because Mr. Ramezani was smiling.

"Imagine a prison revolt," the Mazhin scientist said. "Or a rebellion on some planet, where you needed to land troops with Number Two, and then arm and equip them from number three. We don't have people, but we'll get them. Useful if we have gear for them when they arrived, yes?"

"Yes," Sterling said. "Thank you."

Mr. Ramezani smiled and nodded. His tentacles seemed to smile, too, if that wasn't too weird of a thought.

Sterling adjusted his flight path a little. Down and to port before coming to rest, so he was where the First Officer needed to be if she and her team were going to steal it.

"Blakeslee, anybody notice us yet?" he asked.

"Nobody awake, sir," the man replied with a grin in his voice. "Automated systems picked us up and are querying. I'm lying to them about being a transport load of meal packs for delivery. We'll see how long it takes them to actually wake up, but Mr. Ewin doesn't have a high opinion of traffic control in this system."

Sterling nodded. Captain Fortier had explained how their escape from the prison barge might have been the first time such a thing had ever successfully happened to the Auga Empire. And this raid might be as well, considering that most pirates would probably want to steal warships or take hostages they could ransom later.

Not stealing emergency supplies from a disaster response ship out of a system motor pool.

"Security Team, we are coming alongside your target," Sterling announced as he vectored the thrusters and the gyros. Astronomer's Mate. Pretty damned good at sailing a ship, as well as navigating it, though Roscoe was actually qualified to be a sailing master back home, according to the Captain.

Still, Sterling was the one who had the most important job.

Right until the two bosses left the ship.

And maybe then, too.

# FIFTY-FIVE

ULY HAD HIS HELMET ON, and a display at fifty percent transparency as he got Blakeslee's list of ships. And Huff had made the exact right decision on targets. Uly was practically salivating at the prospect of all the stuff he could steal from it.

Ships were expensive things to operate. Crews required regular feeding and supplies. Uniforms, entertainment, whatever. Parts broke down from hard use or simply sitting in a solar wind's charged environment.

He was standing behind Dan and Beranger, feeling like he was about to storm *King Hewitt II* again. Behind him, more troopers, plus a couple of Ononguli machinists who were qualified to help get engines and generators up to power for flight in a hurry.

It was apparently a pirate specialty, once Uly had asked. He was happy to have experts. Many of them, once the topic had been raised quietly.

A whole crew training as pirates, which was only vaguely similar to sailors.

"Security Team, we are coming alongside your target," came the call over the comm.

Wyndham had sealed them up previously and evacuated the airlock. The far hatch was open, and Uly could see part of a ship directly across from them. He cleared his display to ninety percent transparency and flexed his shoulders, even as Dan did the same.

He watched her prepare, going through a quick stretching pattern that Uly found a bit distracting. But then, she was an attractive woman in fantastic physical shape. He'd not paid that close of attention to that side of things up until now, since he was an officer. Plus, she was under his command.

About as against the rules as you could get back home. He wasn't back home. In fact, Uly was a pirate, so he could pause and appreciate her as a woman, instead of as a competent and deadly Second-in-Command that he could trust with planning and executing a raid like this.

She did that well, too. She did most things at least well, if not amazing.

He nodded when she glanced back.

"Security Team, stand by to move," she said.

Automatically, Uly checked around him for green lights on other folks' helmets. As they were doing to him. You paid attention, so that someone didn't suddenly black out when their suit failed and gave no warning.

They might still, but there were external lights that would hopefully warn you ahead of time. In time to do something, at least.

Dan moved. Uly followed.

The suits had short-range thruster packs. Not as good as the backpacks they'd used to board *King Hewitt II*, but adequate today. The Ononguli hadn't kept those, or the Auga had taken them. Nobody was sure, and his Ononguli crew didn't remember seeing them.

Then they were in open space, floating across.

Uly hadn't appreciated how big this facility was when looking at it on his screens. Enormous. A hexagonal bullseye in space, with several dozen ships attached. Shut down and waiting.

And Sterling Huff had found him the perfect one to steal.

Uly followed Dan in, trailing a dozen others behind.

The hop was short. *Corsac Fox* had come to rest just about as close as you could get without risking contact. Excellent flying, but he'd expected that from Huff. The lad was going to turn into a fine officer one of these days. All he lacked at present was seasoning and experience, and that was happening as they watched.

Dan maneuvered the group to an airlock on the side of the freighter, landing feet first on her magnets, then adjusting as internal gravity was just enough to define a down.

Uly used his thrusters to stop out a few meters, so that his inner ear didn't have to adjust yet. As with many things Security did, that was an acquired skill. He hadn't.

Others got in there and went to work while Uly looked around at the rest of the facility. Could he sneak back a second time later and steal another ship this way? Or would the Empire wise up?

Better, could they? Others had spoken of the intensely bureaucratic system. Almost sclerotic in nature, where changes took months or even years of discussing and argument before they were even put into policies, let alone acted upon. Where each Sector was almost its own sub-empire, fiefdoms not speaking with others unless necessary and ruthlessly defending their own borders, cultures, and paradigm.

Could he slip back in here when he'd had time to recruit more crew, and steal several ships at once? Even Uly wasn't brazen enough to assume he could hit a place like Zhoralong twice without a big warship being permanently moored here to stop a third raid from happening.

He'd have to come back and scout at some point. Might be even ruder than today.

"Team One, airlock is opening now," Dan announced, drawing Uly back to the present.

A hatch slid and folks entered. Uly went last and used the bars on either side to stabilize himself as down suddenly appeared and demanded to know what he was doing up there.

Only about fifteen percent of normal gravity. Enough to make things fall. And him stumble had he not had the bars to hold on to.

Big airlock. Five meters wide. Twelve long. Personnel door, but he could see where this entire end could retract into a wall, turning this into a corridor. Enough space for a ground transport to be driven right up and presumably inside if you were on the ground, or a small shuttle to either dock outside or a smaller one to actually land inside. Maybe a thrustered flatbed with cargo nets.

Lights were on, but only enough to show the interior. Everything screamed *long-term-storage*, so they had to move quickly to get it all powered up. Nothing in orbit had been big enough to challenge *Corsac Fox*, so everyone over there would keep their distance. However, the authorities would also yell for help, and Uly had no idea how close an Auga warship might be to answer.

Dan shut the airlock once Uly was through.

"Wyndham, we're closed here," she announced as air began to fill the space.

"Opening inner doors," Solomon Wyndham replied crisply once the lights on the far wall went green.

Uly headed that way. Not that he needed to be first to board, but he was the only officer here, so if something weird came up, he might need to be there to make a decision. Simply storming an enemy ship, however empty, was something everyone else on this team had done more times than him.

Wyndham had triggered the wider door, so the full wall slid sideways and vanished into the bulkhead. Cargo space beyond.

Good design. All the cargo could be accessed quickly, rather than isolating it into individual holds requiring a lot of work and swearing to get out.

And the bay in front of him was packed full.

"Shit, that's beautiful," Uly murmured as Dan came up next to him. He started reading labels.

Written Auga was different from written Standard, so he wasn't entirely sure what he was looking at. However, pallets that were roughly three meters square were stacked into the distance in front of him, with a six-wheeled forklift on his immediate left.

He glanced over and caught Dan's grin through her faceplate.

Uly gestured for her and Wyndham to precede him. Nobody knew if there was a skeleton crew on the ship. No way to even guess ahead of time, since they hadn't known which ship they were hitting.

Both drew their pistols now. Uly refrained. He needed to think like an officer here, rather than another gunner. Dan already had enough firepower with her today to start a war.

To win a war.

"Sirs, turn left here to head aft," one of the Ononguli sailors spoke up. "Main Bridge should be straight up from there, with a tiny maneuvering bridge forward when you're trying to dock without a tugboat. Reasonably standard Auga design."

"You lead," Dan ordered the fellow.

Uly nodded. Find smart people. Let them show off their expertise and learn from it.

Two Ononguli moved to the fore and set off at a pretty good

pace, almost loping in the low gravity as the Humans and others trailed off behind them.

The ship was big, but only had a length a bit over twice the beam. Wide and flat, like a horseshoe crab or a leatherback turtle at sea. Three more enormous cargo holds all the way side to side, with huge garage doors separating them, and they came to an internal airlock.

"This lets the rest of the ship be in shirt sleeves while teams unload cargo in space," the sailor in the lead said as he gestured. "Through there we might find people. And might not."

"Wyndham and Beranger, you are now Team Two," Dan said. "You go with him and keep the machinists safe. Team One will continue up to the bridge."

Uly nodded and shifted around to stand behind her, with Roscoe behind him. Travers fell in at the rear, behind Nasrin as the rest split into a second column.

Dan pressed a button and the airlock door opened. Unlike the big ones for moving cargo, this hatch was two meters wide and three tall. Enough to move equipment about, but not pallets until you broke them down.

It was a tight fit, but they got everyone in and then lights came up fully. Almost blinding, but he'd been set for the dimness of the cargo hold, so Uly squinted until he could see again.

"Opening the inner doors," Dan said.

Uly watched a forest of guns point outward, but the corridor was empty.

And well lit. People killed the helmet lights they'd been using up until now.

"Sir, this is it," the sailor said, gesturing to a stairwell going up and down.

The vertical column was open, which rubbed Uly the wrong way. But then, he came from warships, where you expected damage to breach you to space. Vacuum alarms.

Death. Every stairwell was isolated, and could be separated by decks as well.

This was open floor to sky. He shook his head, then caught the same motion from the others. Also offended at Auga naval architecture?

"Team Two down," Dan ordered. "Team One up. Travers and Monfared with me. Fortier back."

Uly wanted to complain, but she was right. And he'd put her in charge. Instead, he watched Gennady Travers and Nasrin move up into her shadow, while he and Roscoe trailed.

Safer, he supposed, but he hadn't joined the Navy to be safe. That was for the rear echelons who lived cozy lives and never went aboard warships.

Three flights of switchbacked stairs and they came to the top deck. End of the stairwell. Dan and Travers covered the door while Nasrin opened it. Nothing beyond but corridor.

And a helpful sign indicating the bridge was to the left as they exited.

Travers turned right and watched the hall. Dan led the rest left. Well lit up here as well. Clean, though Uly could see a few places where oil had leaked or at least stained the deck. Metal decks, walls, and ceilings painted a soft, yellowish saffron that seemed to show off every bit of dirt it had picked up.

Nobody around. And no sign of anybody. That was good. The last thing he needed today was to take prisoners, though he ought to be able to shove them through a hatch onto the station itself.

Dan and Nasrin had reached a hatch, helpfully marked Bridge. They opened it and followed guns in. Uly stood around waiting.

"Okay, it's safe," Dan called.

Uly nodded to Roscoe, and they slipped in.

Whatever he had been expecting, this was not it. Flat deck.

Square room. *Corsac Fox* had stations where bipeds sat comfortably while on duty. There were no seats in here beyond a single one off to one side without any terminals or anything near it.

Instead, every single console was on two thick columns. Uly presumed that they could be elevated, living in a world with Thogin, Auga, Ononguli, and Emro potentially working side by side.

He walked to what looked like the main console, where the only seat would be a few meters behind him, over his right shoulder. Presumably a Conductor or someone in charge, comfortable while all the crew stood for hours on end.

The Auga Empire gave off that sort of stench to a professional sailor.

Roscoe was with him. Dual console about three meters wide. Inclined about twenty degrees. Buttons, dials, gauges, and local displays, plus a flat wall in front of them where a screen could show things.

They'd studied a lot of designs while preparing for this, so Roscoe found the ON switches quickly. Then reset everything up from Auga level to Human height.

Uly studied the results, toggling quickly through screens and menu items. Thankfully, everything was written Standard, with only a few Auga words in a different character set.

"Engineering, this is the bridge," he said when he found the right controls. "What is your status?"

"Powering systems up from sleep now," the Ononguli sailor replied sharply. "Estimate ten minutes to have it stabilized and ready for departure."

"Keep us posted," Uly said, cutting the line.

Big ship. About as long as *Corsac Fox*, but four times as wide across the beam. Six decks instead of four, but set up for a tiny crew, since most of the volume was for dedicated cargo holds. All the supplies he needed for a long time, so they could hide somewhere and then focus on how they might recruit more pirates.

Uly would ask when he'd turned inside out from the man who had first stepped aboard *Marshall Castillon* after transferring from *Vanguard Lesauvage*, but he had spent a lot of time considering each of those steps.

You boiled a frog slowly, as the saying went. Not all at once, or it will hop right out of the pot.

He'd been boiled slowly as well. Ostracized on *Marshall Castillon* by his supposed junior officer peers. Sent off by Captain Savatier and likely abandoned to his fate. Captured by Conductor Sobol. Captured by the Auga Empire. Thrown into jail with the other pirates rather than being rescued from captivity.

Throw in a jail-break, grand theft starship, and here he was, about to throw in more grand theft starship.

Uly caught Dan standing off to one side and staring. He wondered what acrobatics his face had gone through while he was lost in thought and his hands were on autopilot on the controls.

He shrugged at the woman and gave her a halfhearted smile.

"Huff, this is Fortier," he said instead of trying to explain to her. "What is your status?"

Life support was on, but the air read pretty stale up here, so he wasn't about take his helmet off until everything got refreshed.

"Main Station is beginning to complain," Huff replied crisply. "Blakeslee has them convinced that we're delivering more supplies, so we have two departments arguing about precedence."

"Explain, Mister," Uly said, confused.

At least the line was encrypted. Humans apparently knew far more about signals encryption than the Auga had ever imagined, and then Haydar and Roshan had taught him several new tricks on top of that.

"One department wants us to finish unloading before sailing over there and presenting our papers," Huff chuckled, his voice hardly cracking as he spoke. "The other demands that we get everything properly approved immediately because we're doing forms out of order and that will require other forms to explain variances, as well as hearings and after-action reports."

Uly replayed that in his head twice and it still didn't make any sense.

But then he remembered the old joke. Why did the word bureaucracy end up with so many letters? It had a government contract.

The Auga seemed to take the concept of *forms* to a frightening level. He wondered how they had ever managed to conquer so many systems. Unless they brought that sort of organization to their military as well. Then you might grind someone down given enough time.

Hadn't his Ononguli crew said that they were largely left alone in their home districts, but that every tribe would immediately unify to attack any Imperial incursion into their space?

"Do you have them sufficiently snowed?" Roscoe asked.

"Trying to sound like you, Drew." Blakeslee laughed at the other end. "With a little bit of Blair thrown in when he starts mimicking Doctor Spence. Confusion reigns."

Uly had heard a few of those impersonations. And the level of caricature Blair Mitchell managed when he was on. He could only imagine the effect on Auga Bureaucracy.

Could they bamboozle this entire operation, right up to the point that they stole this ship?

"Keep at it," Uly ordered.

*Hey, if it actually worked…*

He turned to Dan and she was smiling. She mouthed *Are you okay?* at him.

Uly nodded. Stress. And that last step into active piracy.

Up until now, much of what he'd done had been reactive. A victim of circumstances dictated by other players.

But going out and stealing an enemy vessel was different. Cutting it out of moorage and sailing off with it was him taking the offensive. Dictating terms. Establishing *Agency*.

Shaping his destiny finally.

He only had to jettison nearly all of his previous life, and the mindset that went with it, to do this thing.

Hell of a leap.

"Bridge, we're bringing up reactors now," the call came. "Life support is active, but you'll want to stay bottled up for a while yet. We're ready on thrusters, whenever you want to detach from the station and back away."

"Excellent work," Uly replied. "Huff, move to your next position and stand by for us to follow."

He nodded to Roscoe and watched that man's hands fly over the console like a pianist. The entire hull rang as a half-dozen clamps let go in sequence.

Then they brought up thrusters and inched away from the station like molasses on a cold day. *Corsac Fox* was already clear and slowly moving straight up like a submarine surfacing, so Roscoe maneuvered into the opening presented.

A red light started flashing on Uly's console. That would be someone on the Main Station, finally getting around to noticing that something was *wrong*.

He clicked the side of his face plate and opened it so he could talk on their line. The air was flat, with a smell like something had died so long ago that the ghosts had forgotten about it by now. Something organic had spoiled somewhere, Uly presumed.

He clicked the control and heard the comm come live.

"Uhm, hello?" he asked, sounding lost and a little confused.

Anything to keep a bureaucrat off-balance.

"Cargo Vessel 00429490477, what is your status?" an authoritative voice asked. Male. Firm.

Not quite a demand, but that was coming.

Uly decided to go for broke.

"Whoever docked this ship put it in backwards, sir," he replied earnestly, aiming to sound a little miffed at all the work they had to do to fix the initial screwup. Or something. "The near cargo holds are all full, so we need to detach, flip end for end, and then reattach with the empty bays more accessible."

He had no idea if that was how it worked, but it sounded good.

The response was a long pause. Meanwhile, the ship was drifting under power as it got clear enough to run like hell under Roscoe's hands.

"That cannot be correct, Cargo Vessel 00429490477," the man was back. "My records show that the entire vessel is currently full of supplies. There is no space for more."

"What?" Uly demanded. "Are you sure? My records show it only has a half load as of the most recent inspection. Why the hell did you people send us here if we can't unload our cargo?"

Bamboozle. Evade. Confuse.

"I did not order you to that station, Cargo Vessel 00429490477," the man said, frustration starting to boil.

"My orders came from you folks," Uly countered. "Signed by a…hang on…uhm…here it is. Ercanbald Burkhart."

There had been an Auga officer by that name back at Vynchen. Not the worst of them during Uly's captivity, but not the nicest, either.

Uly wondered if the guy was about to be located and interrogated by the authorities. That put a smile on his face, in spite of that nasty taste in the back of his throat from the air in here.

More long pause. Uly studied the controls, but couldn't find a mute switch, so he closed his faceplate instead.

"Roscoe, how are we doing?" he asked.

"Power seems good, sir," Drew replied. "I'd like to get a little farther away before transitioning to powered flight, though."

"Stay on top of it," Uly said. "I'll stall our friends."

"Cargo Vessel 00429490477, you will immediately report to this station and explain yourself," the man returned now. "I have no record of such an officer in this system. Either you cannot read, or you have the wrong planetary system, in which case we will need to uncover your mistake and fill out all the appropriate forms to fix this issue."

Uly considered it for a moment in silence. Not ignoring the man speaking, but maybe muting him to argue with his own crew about who had screwed up. Probably career-ending, from the sound of that berk on the other end of the line.

After a few moments, Drew signaled that he was ready.

Uly smiled.

"Station, we have a problem," he said suddenly, putting as much fear and surprise into his voice as he could manage. "One of my reactors is starting to go supercritical. We're facing an explosive event here. Stand by to scramble all rescue units to assist. Creator SAVE US...AHHHHHHhhhhh........."

Then he cut the line and turned to Drew, flipping his helmet shut again.

"Let's get the hell out of here," he said.

Roscoe slammed a fist down on a control.

# FIFTY-SIX

HAYDAR WATCHED with benevolent joy as Midshipman Huff followed the script that had been handed to him by Uly and the others. The boy hadn't been all that bad when he'd been a jailer. Actually at the better end, opposite Eldridge and a few of the lieutenants who could happily rot in whatever hells the *Combined Crowns of Danumash* might worship.

Huff looked up now and Haydar nodded sagely. That seemed to be his purpose here today. A safety blanket for the young man. If that was all that Haydar needed to contribute, all the better.

Sterling Huff was growing more confident by the minute.

"Okay, I have an alert from the Main Station," Blakeslee announced in a calm voice. "Only eight minutes later than we had originally put down as best response time. Better, somebody also sounded an emergency rescue alert, so I have every boat over there suddenly waking up and starting to blueshift as they come to save us from whatever we did."

"Coming about on plotted course," Huff announced. "Captain, stand by for full power. We will trail in your wake."

"Understood, Huff," Uly replied over the secured line. "Inertia, both physical as well as social, works on our behalf here. They can't any of them move quickly from a dead stop, so we have several minutes, even if there was a warship over there that could engage. Keep your weapons ready to engage, but we should be clear before then."

"Aye, sir," Huff said.

Haydar checked the armaments board. He couldn't change anything, but didn't need to suggest improvements either, as the lad had the 6dm turret lined up to fire back at the station right now. Out of range to engage at this distance, but it would certainly make a big splash if it hit shields.

And cause any manner of panic over there.

Haydar considered suggesting firing a shot, exactly for that effect.

Fear.

For now, however, he continued scanning the results of Blakeslee's scan, noting the various vessels in long-term storage here. Most were no more valuable than their hulls, but even that had value. Nothing armed, but all manner of cargo carriers, though none with as much mass of supplies as this one shifting away from the station.

Still, useful to come back later. Or to sell to an information broker, if nothing else.

*Corsac Fox* likely wasn't the only pirate operating in this Sector. Perhaps the most brazen, though.

Today.

But if you knew what to expect, in terms of defenses and value, that ought to be worth something to folks.

"Mr. Ramezani," Sterling Huff said, causing Haydar to look up from his screens. "Will it be more or less useful in the long-term if we fired a single shot at the station from here? Do we desire a greater panic on their part when they realize we're pirates, or greater confusion when both ships vanish?"

Haydar's smile widened. Smart lad. Willing to ask someone who might possibly have been involved in such shenanigans when he was not much older that Sterling Huff.

Valid question. What would Uly think?

That was the kicker. Humans were both more logical than Mazhin and Auga at times, and completely insane in others.

"Do they have anything that can threaten us at present?" Haydar asked instead, challenging the youth to think.

"They do not," Sterling replied. "The station itself likely has something like 1dm defensive turrets, same as ours, but nothing in our records from Mr. Ewin suggests offensive firepower."

"What would be the response if we came back later?" Haydar pursued.

"If we shoot now, they'll open fire immediately next time they saw us." Sterling nodded crisply. "If we flee, they may think we are far less of a threat, were the Captain to return for a second go at all this stuff. Both have strengths and weaknesses, but I have no idea how the wider Auga Empire would react to the two scenarios."

Haydar was impressed. Sterling had considered both, rather than asking first. He was seeking an expert opinion having recognized that his knowledge was insufficient. He could see why Uly trusted the young man to command the ship in his absence.

"In such a case, what they don't know about us is probably more valuable than knowing," Haydar intoned carefully. "Remember that this vessel is over-armed for the size category, according to Piruz and Marlowe. They will be expecting a pair of 4dm guns, rather than a twin 6dm turret. I think we're better off unknown."

"Understood," Sterling nodded sharply. "There we go. Cargo vessel has transitioned to warp. Blakeslee, any threats along our programmed path?"

"Negative, sir," Blakeslee replied immediately. "Drew has us going up and out."

"Engaging warp bubble," Sterling called, mashing a button on his console.

Haydar smiled.

He was a pirate.

Again.

# FIFTY-SEVEN

DAN WAITED until the ship bubbled up and fled, then grabbed Wyndham, Travers, and Nasrin.

"Uly, lock the hatch behind me," she announced, moving to the door. "Use the cameras before you open it again."

He looked back at her confused for a moment before his visage cleared.

"Good luck and stay safe," he said.

She nodded and stepped through, Heavy Exoripper pointed down the empty hallway.

Nobody had reacted by running to the bridge to stop them or moving down to bother Piruz and the cousins in Engineering. That didn't say that there was nobody aboard.

It was her job to confirm that. Well, technically Wyndham's, but he'd never cleared a hostile warship with live weapons.

Training day.

Dan popped open the faceplate of her helmet and understood why Uly's face had been sour. The air wasn't bad but needed to be fully cycled through the life support generators. And probably needed new filters everywhere as well. The taste was just yucky.

She turned to Nasrin.

"If you can handle the smell, I'd like your tentacles available," Dan said.

Nasrin's eyebrows went up. Or the ridges where Humans had eyebrows.

Mazhin had body hair. Just nothing on their heads, male or female. Not even whiskers.

The woman popped open her face plate, which was so much larger than Dan's because Ononguli needed space for horns. Tentacles peeked out, tasting the air with about the same opinion Dan had.

Yuck.

The same feeling was evident in Nasrin's eyes.

"Ew," Nasrin said.

Dan grinned.

"Yes, but is there anybody aboard?" she asked.

"Gimme a second," Nasrin replied.

Dan joined Wyndham and Travers pointing guns down the hallway, on the off chance somebody had only now woken up to power, lights, heat, and gravity slowly coming up to comfortable levels.

"Nobody has been around here but us for long enough that they've left no trace," Nasrin announced after a few moments.

"Good enough," Dan nodded. "Close yourself up for now, but we'll do it again as we move around. I expect folks have been down on the cargo decks from time to time, if only to swap out foodstuff cans over time. We'll sweep the tower, then move forward. Uly, are you listening?"

"I am," he came on immediately.

"Can you lock every hatch right now and let me know if somebody tries to open one?" she asked.

"Good idea," he said. "Hang on. Okay, that should do it. You want me to unlock them as you go, I presume?"

"You are correct," Dan smiled.

That was something else she liked about the man. He would listen to ideas from a female and give her credit for them, instead of hearing her speak, repeating it, and taking all the credit. Like that asshole Dupuis.

Sweeping the offices and rooms on the top deck was quick. No cabins up here, but the top deck was also pinched in on all sides for whatever reasons.

Next deck was where half the crew supposedly lived, from the signs on the walls. Upper Crew Deck.

Dan figured that the flight crew would live up here, and the machinists would be below, a deck up from cargo, where they could get down to their jobs quickly.

Nobody here, and no signs of habitation as they went room to room. No signs of anything, as a matter of fact. Each cabin had either a single bunk or a double, with one or two empty foot-lockers and armoires for clothing. No art. No clothing. No nothing.

No people. That was good.

Down a deck to recreation and food. Space for folks to relax, read, or watch vids. Dusty enough everywhere to confirm how long it had been since folks had been in here, but she wasn't about to cut corners sweeping. Wyndham needed the experience. As did Nasrin.

"Wyndham, check the pantries for dates," she ordered, just to get him used to that sort of thing.

He did, then emerged a few moments later with a can in hand and the most confused look on his face.

"Uhm?" he said, holding it out.

Dan looked at the bottom, paused, then laughed out loud.

"Whoops," she said. "Hadn't considered Auga dates. Used to doing it this way at home. Nasrin, can you read this?"

Of course, the can wouldn't be printed with *Batyr* or *Danumash* dates she knew. Right?

Nasrin took the can and flipped it over.

"Forty months, roughly," she said after a moment, tentacles waggling back and forth distractedly. "Not entirely new but replaced in the last year or so."

"Okay, so that was the last time we had crew through here, most likely," Dan said. "And all the entertainment might be a little weird, but good for language practice if nothing else. Down some more and we can check in on Piruz and the cousins."

The group laughed along with her and moved to clear the rest of the tower.

# FIFTY-EIGHT

ULY relaxed as the ship was away. Roscoe had plotted the same sort of mad evasion course out of this system that had gotten them away from Vynchen. Inefficient, but extremely difficult to trace, because most people settled for odd zigzags along the way.

He wondered if that was how Auga caught pirates. Let them get lazy and sail in a straight-enough line that maybe a good navigator could figure out where they were headed and go straight. Or be waiting there.

Uly had no immediate course in mind until they got to an uninhabited planetary system nearly fifty light-years from Zhora-long, where they would rendezvous with *Corsac Fox*. Run and hide.

Dan and the others were slowly clearing out the ship, one room at a time. He and Roscoe were alone and locked in on the bridge. Piruz and the Thogin cousins were below.

"So far, nobody aboard," Dan announced. "Evidence suggests that it has been nearly a year as well."

"Good to know," Uly replied.

The ship's inventory should keep his crew fed for at least a year. And stockpiles with parts and metal to make new ones. What would he do with a year?

"Sir?" Roscoe looked over.

"Sorry," Uly said. "Mumbling under my breath. Trying to sort out what we can do with the freedom this ship represents."

"We going home?"

"No," Uly replied. "I'm not sure I can, given things. Not sure I want to, either. If you or the others do, someone will need to tell me, so I can steal you a ship to make that journey."

"I'm enjoying the scenery, sir," Roscoe said, gesturing to the main screen that was currently showing an animation indicating their course and progress. "If I went back to *Danumash*, at best I'm probably thrown into prison for a year for not fighting you and Dan to the death when you first boarded us. Or escaping subsequent."

"Really?" Uly asked, taken aback.

"We're civilians, a lot of us," Roscoe reminded him. "I mean, technically I'm still active duty, but that was six years and out learning the craft from Hylda. Blair's civilian. So are Cleve and Kit. The rest of us pretty much stopped being *Danumash* when *Iron Wasp* captured us. If not long before that."

"If I never return to *Batyr*, what happens to you?" Uly asked, turning to face the man.

"I never return to *Danumash*," Roscoe nodded. "Nobody ever told me that there were this many intelligent species out there doing things. I want to see them all before I go home."

"I might hold you to that," Uly grinned.

Drew Roscoe grinned back.

"I might make you, sir," he nodded back. "I'm not the son of anybody important, so I was never going to rank high in the *Combined Crowns*, no matter what I did. Sterling is the son of a gentleman. Solomon is the fourth son of a duke. They were always going to be officers, if they survived. The others didn't survive, but that's why *Danumash* has so many around."

"What if we have to sneak back later to recruit Humans as crew members?" Uly asked.

He and Roscoe hadn't spoken much. And that mostly on professional topics. This might be one of the first times they'd verged over onto the personal.

At the same time, Uly knew himself to be a private individual, and the *Combined Crowns* prized reticence.

"Probably better if you can recruit from *Batyr*," Roscoe replied. "I mean, *Danumash* is closer right now, but a little too snoopy about us showing up in port somewhere and putting out a help wanted sign."

"*Batyr* would be just as bad," Uly laughed. "If not worse. We might have to slip in and capture some Human ships, then offer the crews the chance to either join us or go home."

"A lot of folks would jump at the chance, sir," Roscoe said earnestly. "Like me, they might have even encountered Mazhin or Thogin. Maybe Emro. None of the others. Everything beyond Mazhin were legends to me, and Haydar and his people were as well until the fleet hired Hylda to transport the team."

Uly nodded and fell silent. Did he really want to never go home? To only slip back into Human space long enough to find more sailors, then head back out into the wider galaxy?

That sounded so much better than returning to duty as an Absent Without Leave Ensign, regardless of the stories he might tell, all of which would be true. Or the power of his father inside the Party to shield him if the fleet got obnoxious about things.

"Food for thought," Uly replied. "How long until we arrive at our destination?"

"Couple of hours at this rate," Roscoe said.

"You fly us for now," Uly decided. "I'm going to sit in the chair and think. Maybe meditate some, so I'm fresh when we get there."

"We expecting problems, sir?" Roscoe asked.

"No," Uly assured him. "Decisions about our future."

# FIFTY-NINE

ULY STUDIED the spot where the stolen ship had arrived. Dan and her team were back from their sweep. Piruz and Ethir had everything running fine below. He could just sit and study the planet nearby.

Habitable, though not inhabited. Human philosophers had posited theories of a long-departed elder race that had come through at some point in the far distant past and seeded any number of planets with life. Not all of it used the same combination of amino acids, but far too many had at least plants and lower animals when Humans first arrived, though no intelligent, tool-using species.

And even then, the Humans were actually fifty or one hundred thousand years behind some of the early leaders like the Auga. The Empire was proof of that.

But life was everywhere. Generally, not poisonous or toxic on most worlds. Possibly venomous in a few places.

This world below them didn't even rate a name in the data banks. Just a long alphanumeric in Auga that indicated life existed and many species could walk on the surface with preparation. Gravity about eighty-five percent what Uly was used to. Air a little thin. Temperature a little high in some places and low in others.

Nobody lived there according to the stolen records. No satellites or radio signals from the ground indicating any change.

He looked up and realized that everyone was watching him. Waiting for him. Uly blushed briefly, then nodded.

"So far, so good," he announced. "Safe and quiet here. Just waiting for *Corsac Fox* to catch up with us, since they remained behind and watched our trail for anybody chasing us from Zhoralong."

"Is this a long-term base we might use?" Dan asked.

Uly tilted his head back and forth.

"Maybe?" he offered. "Too close to a couple of main shipping lanes for my comfort. I'm nervous that a patrol might stumble across our trail coming here some time and jump us. Thought about systems closer to Sector Seventeen, but I assume the Auga will start looking for us there, once they figure out what happened. I'm leaning towards farther away. Someplace maybe closer to Sector Twenty-One and the Ononguli Reaches."

"Why there?" she asked, brow furrowed.

"Closer to home for half our crew," Uly said. "Maybe we can recruit more folks once these get socialized. The Mazhin don't really have worlds as bases like we think of them, and there aren't many Emro worlds around here we can visit quietly."

He started to say something more when most of his board suddenly lit up red with emergencies.

Uly looked down and realized that someone had just come out of their warp bubble right on top of the stolen freighter, but it wasn't *Corsac Fox*.

Rather than waste time cursing, he slammed one hand down to bring the Electroshield Array up and start the Neutron

Omnipulsar charging. Those alarms had been activated when automated systems detected a wavebolt inbound and tracking.

"Roscoe, we're got trouble!" he snapped, bringing the pilot's hands onto controls. "Move us if you can."

"He's too close to get back to warp," Roscoe replied. "But that ship is also small. Maybe we can get enough of a head start?"

"Do it."

Uly concentrated on gunnery. The Omnipulsar was a vertically arranged beam weapon, emerging from the ship's back and drawing a continuous charge from a set of generators aft that were on standby right now. Everything was already cycling up to full power as he brought a targeting hex around on his screen.

"Pirate vessel, you will surrender immediately."

Uly didn't recognize the voice, but they seemed to know him. Someone from Zhoralong that had tracked him somehow? Or guessed right?

He looked closer and realized that the attacking ship was small. No bigger than *King Hewitt II* had been. The Empire called that class *Seekers*, but the one coming after them right now looked like an Ultra-Bomber. The first wavebolt had been a 1dm. Mostly a defensive torpedo, used to engage larger bolts, but perfectly adequate to slam into Uly's Electroshield Array with a wallop.

He targeted it with the Omnipulsar and started damaging the wavebolt as it closed. They didn't move at light speed, so he had a little time. Not much. And only a single Omnipulsar to degrade the effectiveness of the weapon. At the same time, it also wasn't a big ship killer.

"Roscoe?" he asked through gritted teeth, not taking his eyes off the targeting screen as the wavebolt wiggled to evade him.

"Dead stop, max thrust, fighting inertia," the man replied, frustration evident in his tones.

Worst place to be surprised, but there was nothing they could do about it. At least today he had an Omnipulsar to shoot back with. *King Hewitt II* had lacked even that.

And a 1dm bolt didn't have the mass or range. He was able to nearly finish it off before it slammed into the Array. Hardly any damage, and none got through to the hull itself.

"Pirate vessel, that was your only warning. You will surrender or be destroyed."

This time, they seemed serious, like that first one had been nothing more than a warning shot across his bow? A 1dm? Possibly.

A second wavebolt started tracking and Uly felt everything go cold.

That was a 6dm. Ship killer of a scale with cruisers. The sort of thing an overgunned Interceptor like *Corsac Fox* had, when most ships that size limited out at 3dm or 4dm weapons.

The Empire was going to kill his ship, and there was nothing Uly could do about it.

He lined up the Omnipulsar and prepared to go down fighting.

# SIXTY

STERLING WAS ON THE BRIDGE. He hadn't left since before the Captain had departed and put him in command of his first ship ever. Scary, but he had followed the scripts well. And Mr. Ramezani had helped, even if he just sat there most of the time studying his screen.

The man answered questions when Sterling asked. That had done wonders for his confidence.

"Blakeslee, how close are we?" Sterling asked.

He had the estimated flight tracking down on his screen, but they were in their own pocket universe right now, so everything was inertia and estimation.

"We feel a little hot, sir," Blakeslee replied. "That make any sense?"

"It does," Sterling replied. "I had the same impression. Go ahead and bring the Electroshield Array live now. Engineering, we're landing shortly and I want to come in ready for action, in case somebody chased us through warp space. Clear all generators and have gun crews report to their stations."

Marlowe Michaels was in charge aft today, with Piruz

Kossari off with the Captain. Kolya Roux was a quiet type who'd probably rather never talk on the comm and spend his time fixing things.

"In motion," Michaels replied a moment later.

That one didn't argue either, which Sterling had been half expecting. Michaels loved to argue with officers making poor decisions. Sterling marked this moment up as a good one, then.

He'd had a pretty good day, all things considered. Hadn't fucked up anything important. Had made decisions and issued concise orders.

Captain had told him that *now* was usually better than *perfect* when shit went sideways. Pick a course and stick with it, then be ready to change tack when circumstances change.

They dropped out of their bubble and Sterling studied the boards in front of him.

"Fuck."

That seemed to encapsulate everything.

Two signals when he'd been expecting one. Somebody had tracked the Captain somehow, instead of *Corsac Fox*.

He opened the shipwide intercom.

"Kovalchuk, where are you right now?" he called, hearing his voice echo from the speakers.

"Forward guns, sir," the Ononguli replied. "Handling Gun Captain duties since we don't really have any of the experts from the old crew."

And they didn't. Captain Fortier had gotten forty-some machinists and damage control specialists, with most of the combat crew in an earlier batch, along with all of *Iron Wasp*'s marines and officers.

Sterling Huff was in charge of a warship. And about to sail it into combat.

For the first time ever.

"Kovalchuk, take over gunnery," he ordered. "All of it.

Omnipulsars as well as the turret. We have at least one enemy warship chasing the captain, and I'll be too busy flying the ship."

Mr. Ramezani looked up at this moment and signaled.

"I can handle defensive systems," he said simply.

"Go," Sterling said. "Kovalchuk, you own the wavebolts. Drive them off or destroy them. Mr. Ramezani will handle the Omnipulsars."

"On it, sir," Kovalchuk replied.

Sterling cut the line and dialed the thrusters to the top. Overshooting right now was an acceptable outcome, as Captain was lower in orbit and trying to race sideways.

"Blakeslee, what am I fighting?" Sterling yelled.

"Imperial Ultra-Bomber, sir," Blakeslee replied. "They have just fired the first of what might be as many as four 6dm wavebolts, targeting the Captain. Won't know if he has a second pair available until he fires."

"Omnipulsar, engage now," Sterling said. "Put the 1dm bolts into it as well if you can. If not, hit the ship with a 1dm directly to draw his attention up. We can take that kind of fire. Captain cannot."

Sterling saw tentacles acknowledge, but the man never looked up. Weird, but an effective means of communication.

Sterling had studied Imperial warships, mostly because he was a bored, teenaged boy. And an aspiring officer. And aspiring pirate.

Eggshell with a pair of 6dm wavebolts strapped to the outside, rather than fired internally from turrets like *Corsac Fox*. Big torpedoes like you got on cruisers. Or pirates like *Corsac Fox*. Blakeslee suggested that they might have four strapped to the outsides of the hull instead of two, but they were torpedo boats by any definition.

"Kovalchuk, hit him with a single 6dm, explosive warhead," Sterling called.

"Aye, sir," the new Gunner replied. "Explosive loaded. Stand by."

Sterling nodded and turned the ship's bow down and in a little more. Captain was headed to the right, looking down. Ultra-Bomber was straight down, cutting across in hot pursuit. *Corsac Fox* would sail right across his bow if they didn't all swerve off.

*Corsac Fox* had a better Electroshield Array. And more Omnipulsars to shoot with.

"I have a launch!" Blakeslee called. "6dm inbound now. Repeat. 6dm inbound."

"Defensive systems, engage maximum," Sterling said, surprised that his voice didn't crack. "We have more ammunition than he does, so he can't keep this rate of fire up. Give him everything until he surrenders or dies."

A quiet part of his mind noticed Mr. Ramezani looking up with shock in his eyes, before the man nodded and went back to what he was doing. Sterling's hands weren't that sure on the controls, but he supposed that the Mazhin gentleman had a better idea of what he was doing as well.

Sterling was making it all up as he went. He did, however, have a capable warship at his fingertips.

Kovalchuk's bolt was away. The Ultra-Bomber stopped bothering Captain and started trying to stay alive himself. Problem was, the Imperial was too close to both ships to bring up his own warp-bubble to escape.

And Sterling had no intention of letting him go. Not if that punk had already fired on Captain Fortier.

*Corsac Fox* had two Omnipulsar turrets, forward and aft. Both had range and arc of fire to hit that 6dm. Plus the ship had 1dm defensive wavebolts on all four corners. Two of them spoke now, one racing inward to impact the 6dm midway where it detonated in a flash of light.

The second one chased the other wavebolt. Mr. Ramezani

was also killing the one chasing Captain by hitting it with both Omnipulsars, same as that other ship was trying to keep Kovalchuk's bolt from crushing his hull.

Mr. Ramezani's bolt got there first, blowing the 6dm apart a little short of Captain's shields.

Kovalchuk's bolt slammed home on the Ultra-Bomber's Array. Piercing mode might have cut it in half, like had happened to *King Hewitt* that first time. Punched a hole straight through.

Had that *Batyr* bolt been aft, it would have gone through Sterling Huff. It hadn't, so he was here today to save the Captain.

Explosive only. Great big boom spread over a wide surface instead of punching a narrow lance of energy through like a needle made of plasma.

Still, it staggered the vessel. As intended. Sterling saw lights and electrical currents play over the hull as systems failed under the load.

He supposed that he could put a second Six into them right about now, as it looked like they might have suffered some sort of power overload. Nobody likes a 6dm hitting home.

Hell, as close as he was, the Neutron Omnipulsar might be able to damage things. Those were for short range, because they traded damage for coherence, but they could still work against someone not ready.

Or a pair of 1dm defensive wavebolts? He had options. Lots of them.

And no clue which decision would be best.

"Captain Fortier," he called over the open line. "Orders, sir?"

"Stand by and prepare to finish them off if you have to," Captain Fortier replied a moment later.

The Imperial comm frequencies came live, so Sterling brought them on, but left things muted at his end.

"Imperial vessel, you will surrender immediately or be

destroyed," Captain said in a commanding voice. "I will count to three. One."

"We surrender," another voice replied. "Please. Stop shooting."

Sterling nodded. Nothing they could do at this point but die. The only question had been their commitment to the topic.

"Put all your crew in lifesuits and assemble them outside your vessel on the hull," Captain ordered. "If we find anybody inside when we board, all of your lives are forfeit. Am I clear?"

"Understood," the Imperial replied. "Complying now."

The line went dead. Sterling blew out a *H U G E* breath.

"Kovalchuk, keep an explosive 6dm loaded and ready for immediate fire," Sterling said. "Otherwise, stand everybody down and thank you."

He turned to Mr. Ramezani and nodded.

"Thank you specifically, Mr. Ramezani," Sterling said.

"You're welcome, Mr. Huff," the man replied. "You did an excellent job today."

Sterling smiled. He was getting there.

# SIXTY-ONE

ULY FOLLOWED Dan and Travers into the Ultra-Bomber, while Beranger and Nasrin had a team with guns out on the hull watching. Kolya and a couple of his machinists followed.

The ship only had a crew of nine. All Khet when Uly had been expecting a mix.

Or was it more common to not mix crews in Imperial service? Thogin and Emro didn't fit well with medium-sized species, and the Auga were close enough to Human size for that.

Not a question he had ever encountered, so Uly didn't have answers. But he did have experts he could ask later.

Inside, the vessel was fairly simple. Almost plain, lacking decorations anywhere. Bridge at the bow. Crew quarters behind that. Weapons systems to control external torpedoes and a single Omnipulsar, plus a 1dm launcher with a handful of reloads. Engineering. Engines at the back.

Stubby wings outside to hold the wavebolts in launch containers and also give the ship some lift in atmosphere.

They spent all of five minutes making sure nobody was aboard.

"Do we want prisoners?" Dan asked on a private channel only the two of them shared.

"No," Uly replied. "Regular pirates would probably kill them all about now, but I'm not going there."

"Good," she breathed a sigh of relief over the line.

"Dan?" Uly asked.

"Yes?"

"Don't ever let me become that guy," he said.

"Promise," she replied. "So what do we do with them?"

"Disable the ship for now," he said. "Something they can fix, but will take a while to implement, so we have time to run. Time to vanish into the darkness, while they can still get home. I'd like a reputation as a Conductor or Captain that you can safely surrender to. Less chance someone decides to go out in a blaze of glory, ya know?"

"I do," Dan replied. "Switching back now."

"Kolya," Uly said when he was back on the main channel.

"Sir?"

"I need you to do something to the ship so that they can't fire at us when we leave," Uly said. "Also, can't go anywhere for a day or two while they fix whatever it is you did, then can get safely home."

"Middle ground," Kolya replied. "Gotcha."

Uly supposed that was a middle ground. Killing everyone in cold blood, or disabling their ship so they were marooned here, possibly forever, was one end. Letting them go without hindrance was the other.

"Middle ground," Uly agreed. "You and your team get to work while Dan and I go outside and talk to them."

He led her topside and studied the nine figures in suits. If he was reading the external stripes and indicators correctly, there was one officer present. About an ensign or maybe a very junior lieutenant, so Uly's peer, however far removed.

Peer in many ways, though.

Uly walked close and watched the other eight tense. He found the Imperial channel on his comm.

"My plan is to do exactly enough damage to your vessel that we have a one- or two-day head start on you," Uly said. "And to disable your wavebolt launcher and Neutron Omnipulsar entirely, so you are disarmed."

Flinches. Angry rumbles.

"However, after that, you should be able to get back to your base safely," Uly continued before anybody said anything useful. "That's all I'm trying to do for my people, so I understand."

The officer stared openly at Uly, then nodded finally.

"Safe?" he asked in a careful tone.

The voice had an odd reverb. Khet were amphibians, with both lungs and gills. They needed to immerse in water regularly, but Uly wasn't planning on keeping them in their suits long enough for that to be a problem. And they might have devices in there to crank up the humidity.

More questions he'd never imagined asking.

"Safe," Uly agreed. "You don't have anything I want to steal, and I don't need your ship. I will instead leave you here and you'll get back to base soon enough."

"Why?" the man asked carefully. "Why do that?"

His men stirred, but they didn't understand the genesis of the question.

"Because we're all sailors," Uly said. "A long ways from home. It is a risky profession, but it does not have to be lethal. We need to remember that we are not mortal enemies. Merely on opposite sides of the law."

"We would have destroyed you," the officer offered.

"Understood," Uly acknowledged. "But you surrendered, and honored that, so I didn't need to destroy you. I'm hoping you don't give me any reason to before I leave, either."

"No, we'll honor that," the officer said.

Uly believed him. The alternative was killing them all, either quickly or slowly.

What did that solve?

This way, he might at least start earning back some good karma credit later, with whichever Lords of Creation had decided to play such an amazing practical joke on Ulysses Fortier in the first place.

If he was going to become a pirate, at least he could be a polite one.

Hell, it might even matter, one of these days.

If not, at least he could sleep better at night.

A thought caused him to pause.

"How did you find us?" Uly asked the commander.

"This system is part of our regular patrol area," the man replied after a beat to consider things. "No ship should be here, and the transponder identified you as belonging to Zhoralong. You should have no reason to be here. We rightly understood you to be pirates and attacked."

"Understood," Uly said, making a note to fix that, among other things.

He switched channels.

"Kolya, thoughts on breaking things politely?" he asked.

"Taking apart the warp-bubble generator now, sir," the man answered with a laughing lilt to his voice. "Don't have to break anything, since they'll be an entire day just reassembling it then dialing in all the tuning I'm messing up."

"Excellent," Uly said. "Kill his weapons systems so dead that they need a repair yard to fix it."

"Got one of my boys on the case with a hammer, sir," Kolya said gleefully.

It was good.

"How long?" he asked.

"Five more minutes here, sir," Kolya said. "Ten, if you want me hiding parts so they have a snipe hunt first."

"Don't hide anything too badly," Uly ordered. "They still need to get home when this is all done."

"Couple of parts are going into the freezer," the man said. "That ought to be sufficient."

Uly nodded to himself and switched back to the Khet crew.

"My engineer is taking apart your warp-bubble generator," he told them. "Not stealing any parts, so they are still aboard for you to find, but he informs me that it will take you a while to get it all back together. We'll wait a few minutes for him to be done, then I'll be on my way, and you can get to work. Questions?"

"Who are you?" the officer asked. "What species?"

"I'm Human," Uly said. "As are part of my crew. In addition, I have Mazhin, Emro, Thogin, and Ononguli crew members. If you ever tire of being Imperials, maybe you can look us up and become pirates instead."

"And you yourself?" the man asked.

"Captain Ulysses Fortier," Uly said. "Conductor of the *Corsac Fox*. Remember those names when you get home safely."

"I will," the officer nodded.

Uly saw Kolya emerge from the airlock hatch after a spell, waving and heading directly across open space to the ship.

"Gentlemen, we're done here," Uly said. "You stay put for a bit while we depart, then you are on your own and good luck."

He waved Beranger and the others into motion. They backed away while he moved quickly, everyone ending up aboard the two ships.

"Roscoe, do you have a next destination in mind?" Uly asked as the freighter's airlock swallowed him up.

"Plotted and transmitted to Mr. Huff," Drew replied. "Waiting for you to give the order."

Uly switched channels to one that both bridges could hear.

"Mr. Roscoe and Mr. Huff, take us out," he ordered.

<h1 style="text-align:center">SIXTY-TWO</h1>

DAN FOUND Uly in the lounge with a mug of hot chocolate in front of him. And possibly a splash of rum from the smell, though she didn't have senses as sharp as a Mazhin to be certain. He was in a chair, reading something on a tablet.

"Congratulations," she said as she slid onto the nearby couch and smiled at him.

"For?"

"Doing the impossible," she said. "Again."

He nodded but didn't seem committed.

"Might have to make it a habit, if we're going to get through all this," he muttered.

"I'm fine with that," she nodded. "Look how far your luck has carried us."

He grimaced, then seemed to relent.

"Not sure I call it luck that we got abandoned by *Marshall Castillon*," he said. "Or captured by *Iron Wasp*. Or by the Auga Empire."

"Luck and planning found us a way to escape," she reminded him. "And an impound yard filled with ships to steal. And a motor pool filled with more ships to steal. If the Auga showed up in their Ultra-Bomber, Sterling saved the day and we got away again."

He nodded.

"I'd like to not have to rely on luck saving our asses time and again, all things considered," he said.

"So how do we do that?" Dan asked, settling.

One of the stewards minding the kitchen waved at her and held up a mug of something. She nodded. Coffee or tea would be fine. Rum in hot chocolate might be divine, though she would eventually have to find a world with something similar. Or return to Human space to steal more chocolate.

Tomorrow's problem. She turned her attention back to Uly.

He held up the reader in his hands.

"Been studying some of the more remote systems on the farthest edge of Sector Fifteen," Uly said.

"And?"

"And they often have problems with piracy." He grinned at her.

"Not everybody is crazy enough to hit the Auga where it hurts," she offered.

"Indeed," he agreed. "And without all the supplies we stole from them, we'd be in a similar position, attacking mining or farming colonies for supplies. We might be reduced to that at some point."

"But?" she asked, seeing something in his eyes.

"But we're also more heavily armed than a lot of pirates," he replied. "*Corsac Fox* didn't have anything beyond the Neutron Omnipulsars and the four defensive mounts when it came out of the shipyard. Somebody, maybe Sobol, had those added. And went for a 6dm twin mount, which is far beyond what a ship this size should mount."

"So we can kick ass and take names," Dan nodded. "What does that get us?"

"I was seriously considering finding one of those worlds and asking if they wanted to hire us as a private navy," he said, turning so deadly serious that it took her breath away. "Or offering us a privateering contract, in return for a safe harbor and a place to sell all the shit we might steal from someone else along the way."

The audacity of it boggled the mind.

"Would they?" she asked.

Nothing in her career had prepared her for something like that. At the same time, everything up until now had. A decade of privateering for the *Batyr* Navy meant that she understood a lot of those things. And could train others in the day-to-day techniques.

Uly seemed born to play the role of pirate warlord. Look at all the luck he'd had so far.

"I won't know until we offer it," Uly replied. "The cost to them has to be less than the losses from piracy they are facing now. I'm not sure if we can live on that. And if we add crew, our expenses keep going up. Somewhere, we'll need to break even if we want to make this a lifestyle. And we might never go home."

Dan took the mug from the Ononguli steward and smiled at the man. She could smell the rum underneath. She gestured to the ship around them.

"This is home, Uly," she said simply. "I've talked to folks, and none of them want to return to where they were before they met us. Met you. You're stuck with the lot of us, at least as long as you want to keep doing this."

Dan saw the ghost of pain in his eyes, but it was gone again.

Never going home? Maybe. Not everyone would see that as an adventure.

For some, it might be a punishment. Not her.

Dan dreamed.

"Do you think it's a good idea?" he asked.

"I do," she said, flashing back to the crew of that Ultra-Bomber.

They'd gotten to go home afterwards. Dan wasn't sure that would ever be an option for Uly, as long as he had a crew like this. A found family, almost.

"Then I guess you're stuck with me," he said, holding out a hand.

She took it and squeezed.

There were far worse places to be in this universe.

"Do you think it's a good idea?" he asked.

# READ MORE

Be sure to read the rest of the Corsac Fox series!

https://www.knottedroadpress.com/product-category/science-fiction/corsac-fox/

# ABOUT THE AUTHOR

Blaze Ward writes science fiction in the Alexandria Station universe (Jessica Keller, The Science Officer, The Story Road, etc.) as well as several other science fiction universes, such as Star Dragon, the Dominion, and more. He also writes odd bits of high fantasy with swords and orcs. In addition, he is the Editor and Publisher of *Boundary Shock Quarterly Magazine*. You can find out more at his website www.blazeward.com, as well as Facebook, Goodreads, and other places.

Blaze's works are available as ebooks, paper, and audio, and can be found at a variety of online vendors. His newsletter comes out regularly, and you can also follow his blog on his website. He really enjoys interacting with fans, and looks forward to any and all questions—even ones about his books!

**Never miss a release!**
If you'd like to be notified of new releases, sign up for my newsletter.

http://www.blazeward.com/newsletter/

**Buy More!**
Did you know that you can buy directly from the KRP website?

https://www.knottedroadpress.com/shop/

**Connect with Blaze!**

Web: www.blazeward.com
Boundary Shock Quarterly (BSQ):
https://www.boundaryshockquarterly.com/

# ABOUT KNOTTED ROAD PRESS

Knotted Road Press publishes dynamic fiction set in exotic locations and unique non-fiction voices in genres such as autobiography, business, cookbooks, and how-to. Our authors cover a wide range of genres including science fiction, fantasy, mystery, literary, and poetry, appealing to all readers. We offer both DRM-free ebooks and print books for a global readership.

Knotted Road Press
www.KnottedRoadPress.com
www.KnottedRoadPress.com/Shop